# THE DRAGON PRINCE'S BETRAYAL

ELVA BIRCH

# ROYAL DRAGONS OF ALASKA

This book is part of the Royal Dragons of Alaska series. All of my work stands alone, with a satisfying happy ever after for each character pairing, but there is a story arc across books, and this book in particular ties up all of the questions and mysteries. This is the order the series may be most enjoyed:

> The Dragon Prince of Alaska (Book 1)
> The Dragon Prince's Librarian (Book 2)
> The Dragon Prince's Bride (Book 3)
> The Dragon Prince's Secret (Book 4)
> The Dragon Prince's Magic (Book 5)
> The Dragon prince's Betrayal (Book 6)

Read on for a summary of each book that is chock full of spoilers to catch you up!

Subscribe to Elva Birch's mailing list and join her in her Reader's Retreat at Facebook for sneak previews!

# PREVIOUSLY...

*If you've just come here from the previous books, you can skip straight to the first chapter! No time to reread the series before you jump into the final book? This summary has **all** the spoilers!*

### Previously, on The Royal Dragons of Alaska...

Welcome to an alternate Alaska that was part of a coalition of countries called the Small Kingdoms, ruled by secret dragon shifters and bound by a document called the Compact! Publicly, the Compact was a complicated international trade treaty, but actually, it was a magic spell, capable of enforcing the terms of the agreement. All spells in this world eventually faded, so periodically the Compact had to be formally renewed...a critical event scheduled for the early summer.

In <u>The Dragon Prince of Alaska</u>, American accountant Carina uncovered the dirty secrets of Amco bank and was framed for murder. She fled to the kingdom of Alaska in a camper van with her evidence encrypted on a flash drive, where she adopted a stray dog, Shadow, and was caught squatting by a handsome park ranger...who turned out to be the youngest prince of Alaska, and he opened her eyes to a hidden world of shifters, magic, and elemental fae.

Toren never expected to be the one to inherit the crown, but when his dragon insisted that they meet the plucky young woman camping with a dog on royal land, he was astonished to find that she was his mate, magically bound to him by the Compact to establish succession... which means he had to be king instead of his far more suitable oldest brother, Fask! (Their father had been in a mysterious years-long coma, so this put Toren on the fast track for a crown so he can participate in the Renewal.) The road to Carina and Toren's happiness was a bumpy one complicated by the fact that neither of them wanted to rule (though they certainly wanted *each other*), and that several parties were trying to make sure Toren didn't get the crown by killing one or both of them. The plot thickened when Carina's flash drive was stolen from the castle.

One of the attempted murderers was the bastard prince Drayger of Majorca, who claimed he was hired to kill Toren and Carina but had a change of heart, and he brought them the flash drive that he intercepted from a red-haired thief to prove his loyalty as he requested asylum in Alaska. The flash drive was stored safely in the royal vault, but Shadow proved to be a red-headed shifter who had been sent to ensure that the flash drive and any copies were destroyed, as well as Carina herself.

Toren risked being stabbed with the magical dragon-killing dagger that Shadow took from the vault to save his mate, though Carina ended up taking the blow that might have ended his life. Safe at last with Shadow in custody and her evidence in the correct hands, she worried that the mate bond would fade and their love would go with it, but Toren pointed out that the mate bond had already ended, and it never had the power to make them love each other—it only helped them recognize each other and showed them their feelings and possible future, and allowed love to naturally grow between them.

In *The Dragon Prince's Librarian*, Rian, one of the middle brothers, was called to find his own mate, Tania, who was a scholar of the Compact that he had been in communication with via email. Somehow, the librarian had access to an unedited copy of the Compact. This was a major breach of security, and her dissertation was stolen by literal ninjas and erased from the system, along with the copy of the Compact.

Already in failing health and now without a job or academic future, Tania agreed to go with Rian to Alaska, where she became a target for a magical cult that was trying to steal the original pages of the Compact for nefarious purposes.

Though she was not able to figure out why the Compact called two mates, Tania helped identify some of the language in the complex document that might allow them to specify a mate for Fask.

Using the loophole that Rian and Tania found in the Compact, Leinani, princess of Mo'orea (a close Alaskan ally among the Small Kingdoms) and a dragon herself, agreed to come and be bound to Fask and become the queen of Alaska. Unfortunately, she found that she had already been called by the Compact as a third mate for the wrong Alaskan prince, Tray, a jock and the identical twin brother of Rian. *The Dragon Prince's Bride* is an opposites attract, forced proximity test of their loyalties; the two decided to stay apart and let the mate bond dissipate but instead got kidnapped together by Amara and the Cause.

They were trapped together in a shabby hotel room for several months, kept from shifting by necklaces they were forced to wear, as Amara experimented with stealing their dragon power to enhance her magic spells. They were able to listen to her plans thanks to a magical pair of rings that Leinani brought with her that acted as an eavesdropping tool.

Leinani and Tray were imprisoned through Christmas to New Years, and finally escaped with help from Amara's assistant, Mackenzie. They were aided in part by Drayger's half brothers, Talgor and Forsch.

Mackenzie, after helping Tray and Leinani escape from Amara, found herself in the Alaskan palace trying to persuade them to return to Amara's stronghold to rescue the children that the cult leader had enslaved to write spells for her. *The Dragon Prince's Secret* opened with the enraged return of the estranged second brother, Kenth, because his young daughter Dalaya had been kidnapped through a magical portal…and Fask was the only one who knew about her. He immediately knew Mackenzie was his own mate, but she did not return this recognition because she was immune to magic, part of a mysterious gift that allowed her to recognize what a magic spell or artifact would do before it was cast.

A clandestine rescue mission, unauthorized by Fask, freed all of the captured children, including Kenth's daughter, but Kenth was struck by a slow-acting, dragon-specific poison. When they returned to the castle, it was revealed that Dalaya had been tampered with by Amara and had a new kind of power that wasn't restricted to the usual rules of magic and could make things happen by drawing them. Kenth fell into a coma and after three nights at his bedside, Mackenzie despaired of saving him. At the last moment, Dalaya drew a childish spell that cured him.

Mackenzie pointed out that the portal spells that were

used to infiltrate the palace required an anchor spell to be placed, indicating that there must be some traitor in the castle with inside information and access to these sensitive places. She was then allowed to see the Compact itself and realized in astonishment that it was a spell so complex it had achieved sentience and had self-determination. It was also the only thing that kept all magic from falling into chaos and possible destruction of the world, and it was dying. The Renewal, coming in just a few short months, was much more critical than they had ever realized.

When the couple was kidnapped by Amara and Makenzie thought that Kenth had been killed, she discovered that she herself was a dragon (and therefore of royal lineage) and unlocked her own power to ultimately save him, though they lost Amara in that process.

Upon their return to the Alaskan palace, they found that Dalaya had also grown into her potential as a dragon shifter!

Captain Luke revealed that the Compact herself had assured her that the traitor in the Alaska palace was not a dragon, which narrowed the list of suspects somewhat.

Katy was a teacher from Alaska who was hired to oversee the education of all of the children who were freed from Amara while their families were found in <u>The Dragon Prince's Magic</u>. She discovered, to her astonishment, that Raval, the neurodivergent middle brother and magic caster, was her mate. She was all-in with this development, but three days into her job, her entire class was kidnapped by the Cause (which was being so blatant about secret magic, that Small Kingdoms had to do a lot of cover up). She and Raval followed the kids in a vintage magical car that allowed them to rescue all of the children...but which then took them to the tropical island of Mo'orea, far in the past! They remained there/then for several months while the kids and a stowaway puppy grew up and Raval tried to repair the car. When they attempted to return to their own country and time, they ended up even further in the past at the inception of the Small Kingdoms and the introduction of dragons and fae to a world that they were never meant to be a part of.

The children agreed to bond with the dragons and create the Compact to bind magic and establish the Small Kingdoms, and became the first Queens and Kings, as well as the first dragon shifters.

Katy and Raval left the children to their destinies and went forward in the magical car with the puppy, to find that several months had also passed in Alaska in their own time. In that interim, Amara had been apprehended, and the traitor in the palace proved to be Nathaniel, the dog-keeper…and the Renewal is galloping down on all of them.

∽

And now, we go back a short two weeks in time, to directly witness Amara's capture and Nathaniel's exposure from the point of view of the players who were actually there…

## CHAPTER 1

*TWO WEEKS EARLIER*
Any attempt at stealth was abandoned when the first dragon crashed, full-body, into the top floor of the apartment building like a cannonball.

Captain Luke didn't often swear, but she did now, dodging back from the falling wreckage. That would be Kenth, hot-headed and generally indisposed to follow Fask's orders.

"You might as well all go now!" she yelled at the rest of the dragon shifters who were flexing their hands impatiently.

"It worked well enough last time!" Toren shouted, just before he shifted and launched into the air after his brother. Tray, Rian, Mackenzie, Drayger, and Leinani followed him more cautiously. They shifted, climbing, and kicking off the nearby walls until they could clear the narrow space with their wings and swoop in towards the hole that Kenth was tearing in the side of the building.

There was a squeal of brakes and a shout around the corner; it might be night, and dragons might have some natural magical camouflage, but an all-out attack on an apartment building near a town center was not going to pass completely unnoticed, even in a rundown neighborhood of the old city. Somewhere, a car alarm went off.

"So much for trying to do this quietly," Luke groused to Fask, who had remained behind on the ground. "Sure you don't want to join them?"

"You may need my help with the ground advance," Fask said, frowning at the chaos above. The biggest chunks of debris fell into the back alley, but Luke raised a combat shield to deflect a spray of broken glass and plaster, sheltering Fask as she did. She spared a glance back to see that the rest of her guard had taken defensive stances in the covered loading bay and were waiting for her orders.

"Is the perimeter down?" she asked Fask. "We're as ready as we're going to be."

Dragons were more sensitive to magic than humans, or even shifters like Luke, and when Fask nodded decisively, Luke trusted that he knew. She pulled her facemask down, raised a gloved fist, and dropped into a sprint for the loading bay door that had been previously identified as a weak point for invasion.

Two of her men, bearing a battering ram, hit it just as she got there, and she was the first one through the splintered door.

The hallways were dark—they'd cut the electric lines before staging the attack—but Luke's night vision was excellent thanks to her polar bear. Most people underestimated the senses of a bear, believing that their hunting prowess was only due to strength and speed, but her eyesight was better than most humans, day or night, and her nose would put a bloodhound to shame.

It smelled like fanaticism.

After several failed attacks on Amara's strongholds in

search for the missing prince, Raval, Luke recognized that particular scent. It was some mixture of magic and forgotten hygiene, the smell that enchanted devotion seemed to have. Amara's rooms were scented by perfume and fine soaps, but she kept her people in an increasingly oblivious state that precluded caring much for themselves. They only wanted to follow Amara, to listen to her words, to steal magic and power for the Cause. Luke was surprised the cult had survived this long; Amara must be expending incredible amounts of magic to keep them docile and focused on her message in these conditions.

But if the madwoman still had children enthralled to write her spells, that might explain her careless use of precious magic. Luke scowled and hurried them faster down the hallway.

"Let's split up here," Fask said, when they reached a stairwell. "I'll head straight for the top and meet up with the others, you sweep from the bottom for Raval and the kids. I have the advantage of being able to fly out if things go sour."

It made sense, so Luke gave a crisp nod and gestured for her team to follow her down the hallway, searching each room as they went.

Most of the activity would be centered on the top floors, where Amara would have her most loyal subjects and use her strongest spells to protect her from the attacking dragons, but Luke's advance did not go unchallenged.

The cultists, though armed, were hampered by Amara's intellect-dulling control spell, and not as well-trained as Luke's men and women. The royal guard was able to disarm and subdue nearly all of them without injury, using the narrow hallways and darkness to their advantage. Luke used her speed to rush them before they could fire their weapons, kicked out knees, and smashed her custom harpoon spear into the sides of their heads. She fought with the side of it when she could, not the point, but didn't hesitate to defend herself or her people. When she had to use deadly force, she did it swiftly and her regret was as much political as it was ethical; they were royal guards on foreign soil and this was an unsanctioned personal attack. It was the kind of mess that would require all of Fask's considerable diplomatic power to smooth over if they were caught, and the longer the conflict lasted, the more likely that was.

They left a trail of restrained cultists as they swept through the lower levels of the building, climbing to meet the sounds of supernatural conflict that were loud from above. Luke hated how slowly they moved forward, and their skirmishes came closer together, some of the cultists clearly fleeing from above rather than making coordinated attacks. Did they seem less organized? More scattered?

They surrendered more easily with every floor, until the guard was halfway up the building and the noise from above seemed markedly less. The stairwell door at the end of the hall flew open and it wasn't cultists who spilled out.

"Alasie!"

Only one person called Captain Luke *that*, and it wasn't one of her dragon prince cousins or anyone else she wanted to hear it from. She braced herself and lifted her face shield.

"It's Captain Luke to you, Majorca," she snarled back, slamming the butt of her harpoon down on the tile floor with a clang.

"So formal," Drayger said with a note of disapproval in his lilting Majorcan accent. "We've got Amara. Have you found Raval, or the kids and their teacher?"

"No. We're still searching this floor," Luke said flatly. "Did Fask already meet you?"

"He's up a level, stealing all the glory," Dragyer said, and he glanced behind Luke. She had her team drop back and spread out to check the remaining rooms with a few quick gestures and they melted away out of earshot.

"Any injuries?" Luke asked in a low voice.

Drayger's voice dropped to match. "Leinani got hit with something. Tray's fussing over her like a mother hen. Any of yours?"

"Stevens got nicked by something that made him spout gibberish for a while and he had to be restrained. Chevy got grazed by a bullet. Nothing that won't wear off or heal."

"And *you*?"

Luke didn't want to admit what Drayger's voice full of concern did to her belly, let alone his gentle touch. She knew that half the castle thought that her continued public refusal of his ridiculous over-the-top flirtation was fabricated to hide the fact that they were a hot, secret item. No one dared say it to her face, but Luke knew all the rumors. *The lady doth protest too much.*

"I'm fine," she snapped. "None of this blood is mine, but if you don't get your hand off my arm, some of it is going to be *yours*."

Drayger lifted his hand from her arm a taunting inch, so that she could almost still feel the heat of him through her leather armor.

As crazy as he made her, the truth of their relationship was actually something considerably worse.

## CHAPTER 2

Drayger didn't like to admit how much the sight of Captain Luke bothered him. It was one thing to know that she was a warrior of impressive prowess, it was quite another to see her at the end of a pitched battle, her black leather and Kevlar armor puckered with shots she hadn't quite dodged, reeking of blood and sweat. Though she claimed she was uninjured, his dragon's night vision was keen enough to see that she was limping slightly.

Even now, she was all business. "Any surprises?"

The biggest surprise, Drayger thought, was how much he wanted to brag about what he'd done. He was a brilliant strategist and skilled fighter, and he had enjoyed the chance to use his talents for good…for once. He'd been invaluable in the assault, taking down more than his share of cultists and making several daring saves. He was more experienced than the Alaskan princes, and the battle might have gone badly without him.

But as much as he wanted to impress her, Luke wouldn't appreciate bravado, so he feigned nonchalance. "Nothing we couldn't handle."

Luke frowned and Drayger wished they were somewhere more private, for several reasons. It was too risky to speak openly even here, where a listening device might be set and there were shifters with keen hearing everywhere. He'd have to share his true observations with her later.

He was also feverpitched from the conflict, the thrill of victory, and the blood on his hands. He had never wanted to kiss her quite so badly.

Her smudged face was beautiful, the planes of her Inuit face absolutely perfect under her helmet. Her eyes flashed in the dark, and Drayger thought her full lips were inviting even when they frowned. "There's no sign of His Highness or the kids?"

"None. Not even a place they might have been held. No trace of them at all."

Luke gave a growl. "The raid was pointless then."

"Not so pointless," Drayger felt obligated to say. "We got Amara, and a huge chunk of her cult and magic arsenal. Without her, the rest will likely fall. It is a triumph. We *succeeded*."

It wasn't that he was expecting warmth from Luke, but Drayger found himself longing for any approval. It was infuriating how much this woman got under his skin. His theatrical obsession in her had been part of his objective at first, then a casual habit, and had blossomed into something deeper and more true than he'd ever intended.

"Not a failure, maybe, but I wouldn't call it a triumph," Luke said coolly. She looked up the stairwell beyond him and drew to attention. "Prince Fask," she called more loudly than was strictly necessary. "We've secured the levels below this. We didn't find Raval, Katy, or any of the children."

Drayger moved to the side so that Fask could pass down the narrow stairs. The aged apartment building did not ascribe to current fire safety or accessibility standards. "You did good work," the oldest prince said with all of the kindness that Luke's voice lacked. "We've secured the top and Amara is in custody. We found Leinani's listening ring in a safe." He patted his pocket. "Tray, Leinani, and Toren have already left."

Leinani's injury explained her early evacuation, and Tray would never let her go alone. Toren had probably been sent back because he was technically still the crown prince, despite being the youngest; he was diplomatically the person who ought to be caught here the least.

"Excellent," Luke said crisply. "We can coordinate our immediate retreat, before the local authorities arrive."

"The rest of us will cover you from above to the airfield," Fask agreed. "Let's get out of here while we can."

Luke saluted, but before she could turn away, the prince added, "I'm glad you weren't hurt, cousin."

She did actually smile then, just the faintest little twist of her gorgeous lips. "Same, cousin." She bumped Fask's shoulder with a fist.

Then she was turning and jogging back down the hall, whistling for the rest of the guard.

Drayger watched her go, wrestling back his jealousy and desire, and caught Fask giving him a speculative look.

"She's got a nice ass," Drayger said with a careless shrug.

It wasn't a lie.

Fask gave a cough that didn't really hide his laugh and clapped Drayger on the shoulder. "Let's get out of here, before the local *polizia* arrives and dragons and ninjas are all over the front page of the Ecuadorian tabloids."

"Front page?" Drayger scoffed, giving an exaggerated bow to gesture to Fask to climb the narrow stairs first. "After all that's been going on, that's going to be buried in the back of the gossip section. Dragons and magic are so *last month.*"

With Amara's increasing and increasingly poorly hidden activity, magic had become a hot media topic, and video evidence was going up as fast as the Small Kingdoms spy network could take it down. Legitimate newspapers and networks were starting to seriously address the topic, and efforts to continue secrecy were becoming strenuous.

The two hurried up the stairs for what was left of the top floor and Drayger found himself glaring up at Fask's far less mesmerizing rear as they went.

Even with Amara in custody, there was still the matter of a traitor in the Alaskan palace. Drayger knew that it wasn't himself, and he was positive that it wasn't Captain Luke. Beyond that, he had no particular trust for the royal dragons. He only knew that sometimes rot went all the way to the top and being Alaska's oldest prince and most esteemed diplomat didn't save Fask from Drayger's suspicion.

It had been a hard fight with Luke to get her to promise not to take Drayger's evidence to Fask himself when Drayger had brought it to her.

Not that that was the only thing that was *hard* with Luke. His libido wasn't all an act.

"Let's go, already!" Kenth called from above.

Fask took stock of the situation and Drayger thought for a moment that he was going to take the time to make a victory speech. Kenth didn't wait for it, only took off up through the hole they'd battered into the apartment building without waiting for his older brother's agreement.

His brothers looked uncomfortable, like they were divided from following immediately after Kenth and waiting for Fask's order to go.

"I gues we're going then. I'll tail Luke's group on the

ground," Fask said, returning to the stairwell, and Drayger told himself that he had no right to resent him for that choice.

"Who's carrying Amara?" Rian wanted to know, but Fask was already gone. Rian's tone of disgust suggested that no one really wanted to touch her.

The woman was standing, wild-haired and spitting mad, between Mackenzie and Rian. She had zip-tied hands and ankles, and there was duct-tape over her mouth that she was worrying at like a dog.

Maybe she was genuinely trying to chew through it.

Drayger thought that she looked a little like a drug addict; there was an unhealthy cast to her skin and a hyperfocus to her eyes. She was glaring most ferociously at Fask, which made sense because he was the voice of the Alaska royalty. Her vendetta against all of the Small Kingdoms had done considerable damage, but she seemed to have a particular hatred of Alaska.

And now her reign of terror, her history of kidnapping royalty, stealing dragon powers, and forcing children to write spells for her, was finally at an end.

Drayger tried to feel some kind of pride for playing a role in the capture as he shifted and went to scoop her up, but mostly he felt sorry for her. She, like him, was only a pawn in all of this.

## CHAPTER 3

Luke knew that there were dragons overhead, even though a glance up didn't reveal them. There was a glimmer to the cloud, a shifting uncertainty to her sight, a little dance of light that might have been an aurora in the kingdom she'd left the previous day.

But they were near the equator here, far away from polar lights.

She returned her full attention to getting all of her guards safely back to the tiny airfield where an unmarked plane waited to take them back to Alaska.

The trek back through the old city was much faster than the journey there had been. They stayed to back alleys and side streets as they could, but flat-out ran without a care for true stealth.

Useless. She'd been all but useless here.

The dragons had done all of the heavy lifting. Without the guard, it might have have been a longer fight to search and secure the entire building, but they would have captured Amara eventually. Luke wasn't entirely sure why Fask had insisted the guard come and she tried not to let

Drayger's suspicions color her reasoning. Fask had suggested that they might be needed for the evacuation of the children and had insisted on accompanying her team personally.

Luke was keenly aware of her limitations. Even her handpicked team, mostly shifters and exceptionally athletic humans, was barely the equal of one dragon. And they couldn't fly. Fask clearly thought her team needed his *protection*, and the whole operation galled Luke.

She wasn't sure which part bothered her more: unnecessarily putting her men and women at risk, or being coddled when she did.

The private jet was more empty on the return trip than they'd hoped it would be; the only additional passenger was Amara, now sedated. Luke tried not to look at the colorful lunch bags they had optimistically packed by the empty seats. They had anticipated finding and freeing the children that Amara had enslaved, as well as Raval and his mate.

The flight from South America to Alaska was hours long. Luke's first priority was to triage the injuries they'd sustained. Stevens slept off the spell he'd been hit with and Chevy hadn't lost a lot of blood before the wound was sealed up. He was already crowing about the scar that he'd have. The rest of the scrapes and strains they'd gotten were quickly cleaned and bandaged.

Luke ran a thumb over some of the letters on her harpoon, frustrated with their failure to find and rescue Raval and the others. The prince must be held in some other location, and there was no way to know where that was, or how he was guarded. If he hadn't made contact after this long—nearly a month and a half!—it was also possible that they had all simply been eliminated. If they had still been in Amara's clutches, why wouldn't she be *using* them?

Luke reassured herself that it had taken almost as long for Tray and Leinani to escape from Amara's grips, that it was too soon to give Raval and his mate up for truly lost.

To her annoyance, Drayger flopped into the seat next to her halfway through the flight, interrupting her train of thought.

"What are you doing?" she hissed.

"Taking an empty seat next to the most beautiful passenger on the plane," Drayger said. He'd mopped off the worst of his battle-grunge and Luke was keenly aware that she must smell sweaty and rank compared to his intoxicating musk.

Men were supposed to have that wild scent. Women were supposed to be delicate flowers and smell accordingly.

She had to admit that sitting beside her, one arm slung across the back of her seat as he leaned close, was in character for him. He always gravitated to flirtation in social settings, and she was usually the only unattached female in the room. *That* was why he picked her at first.

That, and the fact that she was Captain of the Alaska Royal Guard—and the ticket to his freedom.

She remembered entirely too well the day that their relationship had changed.

~

Luke had assumed when he sauntered into her office several months earlier that it was more of the same: sit on her desk, flatter her, try to make her laugh. Surely his continued flirtation was only because she was a *challenge*.

"Oh!" he'd exclaimed, giving her guards a little wave.

"Oh, your door has a *lock*." Everything he said sounded like an innuendo.

"It's for keeping people I don't want out of my office," Luke pointed out sourly. Her guards would remove him if she so much as gestured, but Drayger was usually harmless and gave up quickly when something more interesting came along. She didn't want to encourage him by acting like he was important enough for her attention. She certainly didn't want him to think that she *liked* it.

None of them were entirely prepared for Drayger to swoop to the door and close it, twist the lock, and then turn with his hands up in a serious gesture of truce. Luke rose to her feet.

"What are you doing?" she demanded.

"Hear me out!" he said. "Give me a chance and if you don't believe me, you can have them throw me in your prison or extradite me to wherever you want, but you are my only chance to get out of this. I need your help and I can help *you*."

His change in demeanor was so complete that Luke was actually angry. She had believed his carefree playboy bastard prince guise completely. Not only was she irritated that she'd been fooled, there was also something incredibly disturbing about a serious, sharp-eyed Drayger, standing at sharp military attention with his hands raised in a gesture of peace.

"Talk fast, Majorca," Luke snarled. She wasn't afraid to be locked in a room with him. He'd have to shift to have any physical advantage over her, and her office wasn't large enough for a dragon.

"I didn't get the flash drive that cleared Carina's name and implicated Amco Bank from a thief who escaped," he said crisply.

"Did you steal it yourself?" Luke tried to think of how else he might have gotten his hands on it.

"Shadow—his codename was actually Ben, just so you know. He gave it to me."

"He *gave* it to you? You were *working* with him?" Luke was outraged, mostly at herself for being conned into believing Drayger's original story.

The guards were knocking on the door, probably not sure how seriously to take Drayger's action. The office was protected by the magical lock; they wouldn't be able to break in and they wouldn't be able to hear anything that happened in here.

"So that you would trust me. So that I could get close to the royal family."

"You tried to kill Carina and Toren." She could probably neutralize Drayger, unlock the door, and let the guards in to arrest him. She could also rip him apart as a polar bear, and that was tempting, too.

"Only a little!" There was a hint of the Drayger that Luke thought she knew, just a quirk of laughter to his voice.

"You were only trying to kill them a little." The guards were pounding on the door in earnest now.

Drayger lowered his hands slowly. "Look, I'm not going to pretend I'm a squeaky-clean character, Captain Luke. I *was* hired to kill them, and when I chose not to, I was given a second chance by my...employer."

"Amara?" The leader of the Cause had tried to steal pages of the Compact, infiltrating the castle itself, and Luke was ears-deep in investigating the cult at that time.

"*Above* Amara."

That was news to Luke, who thought that the madwoman was as high as it went. "Who's that, then?"

"I wish I *knew*." Drayger's voice was disarming and

plaintive. Luke reminded herself that he was clearly a masterful actor and he was probably only playing her now.

Drayger produced his phone from a back pocket and handed it to Luke.

"What do you want me to do with this?" She had inspected and searched it multiple times, and allowed him to keep it with the understanding that he would hand it over at any point that she asked for security reasons. It was an ordinary phone, and he used it to contact some of his less savory contacts.

"Tilt it back and say *receive*."

Skeptically, Luke did, and then tipped it back up in astonishment as tiny writing briefly appeared on the screen with fiery letters. They were gone before she could really register what they said, but there was a text dialog that had not been there before.

"I scanned this phone myself," Luke protested.

"It's a very sophisticated spell," Drayger said without apology. "You weren't *supposed* to find anything on it."

Luke scrolled back through the conversation. Much of it was clearly coded, but enough was obvious to build a strong case against Drayger's loyalty to Alaska.

"I should have you arrested," Luke said coldly. The guards had stopped pounding on the door and were probably following protocol to report the incident to Fask.

"Look, I want out. I want out of this whole dirty business, and I want my leash cut, and I can't do that if I don't know who's controlling me, and I can't do it without your help."

"What exactly do you expect me to do for you?" Luke demanded in outrage. "Why should I trust you? How *can* I trust you?"

"I'm not asking you to do anything that you wouldn't already do," Drayger insisted. How was he so convincing and intense? Luke was having to reevaluate him rapidly. "You want to protect Alaska, the Small Kingdoms, the royal family. I want to figure out who it is that wants me here and what their goal is. I want *you* to stop *me* from doing whatever it is that they want me to do here."

"Why come to me? Why not Fask?" Drayger seemed friendly with the oldest Alaskan prince. Maybe that was just an act, too.

"I haven't eliminated Fask as possibly the guy with my puppet strings," Drayger said.

"But you've eliminated *me?*" Luke wasn't sure whether to be insulted or flattered.

"I'm good with people," Drayger said without humility. It wasn't the way he bragged about his libido or his looks, just a flat statement of the facts. "I read them exceptionally well and that's what makes me such a valuable player in this game. You are the most genuine, unselfish, goal-oriented, capable person I've ever met. You aren't here for politics or pleasure."

Flattered, Luke thought. She definitely felt flattered, and just a little dubious.

That was the moment that Fask flung the door to her office open with the magical power of his full name and Drayger all but oozed into a sleazy, surprised slouch in the chair facing Luke. "Manners!" he complained. "Haven't you ever heard of knocking?"

"Is there a problem, Captain?"

Luke told herself that she was annoyed to be rescued by Fask because she didn't need to be rescued, not because she was flustered by Drayger's whiplash changes in demeanor.

"Drayger wanted…privacy," Luke said in icy tones. "Apparently, he didn't realize that it would set off certain protections. Or that he wasn't going to have any more luck in private than he does anywhere else."

It was close to the truth, and if Drayger *was* right, there might be someone else at work. Someone *close.* They knew there was a mole somewhere in the castle—someone with access to the vault and to their private rooms who had planted portal anchors that allowed Amara admittance.

Luke didn't think she was actually giving the idea that *Fask* might have colluded with Amara any weight, but some instinct told her that she ought to keep the information Drayger had given her tightly guarded for now, at least until she'd figured out what to do with it. There were ears everywhere, and information was power.

~

Her truce with Drayger was as annoying as their continued fictional friction and, even now, Luke still had painful doubts about her alliance with the illegitimate Majorcan prince.

They couldn't speak freely here on the plane, any more than they could at Amara's compound, so she didn't have to feign a look of annoyance. She caught Toren's amused smirk out of the corner of her eye. Drayger's continued pursuit gave him every opportunity to make contact with her, and she wasn't surprised when he dropped a paper wadded up like harmless trash into her lap as he stretched and then withdrew his arm at her glare. She covered the paper deftly and waited until he had exhausted his efforts to flirt with her and moved on to one of her equally uninterested guards.

She smoothed out the paper with one hand, using her other to pull out her phone and pretend to read something on it while she shielded the message. Drayger often gave her ideas to run with, both because sometimes Luke was the ideal candidate to execute them, and so that he wouldn't look too clever.

*We got Amara's portal spells. Traitor must have anchors. Follow them to mole. Who wants them destroyed instead?*

Portal spells, long scoffed at as being too hard and time-consuming to bother with in the age of jets and high-speed trains, had a lot of magical rules. One of those rules was that they required a piece of the spell as an anchor at the portal's destination.

Drayger, for all his faults, was smart, and right to conclude that if they had Amara's spells, activating a portal would take them straight to whomever had that anchor. Who was going to be invested in not having them used?

Luke glanced over the people in the plane. The Compact itself, a complex spell that had actually transcended to sentience, had assured Luke in person that the traitor in the palace was *not a dragon*.

That eliminated her cousin princes, plus Mackenzie, Leinani, and—to her mixed frustration and relief—Drayger himself. But Drayger was not convinced of the Compact's accuracy on that point, even though it absolved him, and even Luke doubted that the information was complete. Mackenzie had said that the Compact was dying, and that it was more critical than they realized to Renew it at the impending allotted time, because it defined and controlled magic itself.

The Compact had as much as admitted that she had been damaged in some fashion when individual pages of the document that spelled the magic that had created her had been stolen and presumably destroyed. There might have also been alterations made—alterations that had already caused multiple mates to be called for a single kingdom. If she could falter like that, could she be wrong about the person responsible for repeatedly betraying Alaska to Amara…and perhaps controlling her?

Luke couldn't let how much she *wanted* the culprit to not be a dragon change her commitment to finding the truth.

"Who has the spells that we liberated?" she leaned over to ask Toren.

He was texting busily on his phone, probably to his mate Carina, who was human and had remained back in Alaska. "I think Rian has them. He wanted to go over them with Mackenzie and Tania." His face took a sudden look of puppy-dog guilt. "I wish we had Raval back. He knows spells really well."

"We'll find him," Luke snarled, so viciously that Toren looked taken aback. "I promise," she added more gently. Toren was the youngest of the brothers, though he had been tapped first with a mate and was a *de facto* crown prince while they sorted out what the mate malfunction really meant. He'd stepped up to the job with surprising steel and done a better job than anyone expected, so it was sometimes hard to remember how young he still was. Because she was several years older than Fask, who was the eldest, Luke knew him least of all of the brothers.

She waited for a break in the air turbulence and switched seats to settle in next to Rian. "Do you have the spells that we relieved from Amara?" she asked in her most neutral voice. She looked casually around, gauging the reactions of the others sitting near.

"Fask has them," Rian said briefly. "He found Leinani's ring, and a bunch of artifacts. Mackenzie is looking over some of them." Mackenzie could no longer read a spell and know what it did intuitively, but she had a great deal of experience with magic and had seen many of them while she still worked for the Cause.

## CHAPTER 3

Fask was sitting near the front and Luke got up and strolled up the aisle towards him.

"Good work, Captain," he greeted her. "Would you care for a drink?" He raised a hand to summon the flight attendant, then dropped it when Luke shook her head.

"I'll wait until after the debrief," she said. "I assume we'll meet immediately after we land."

"I think there will be time for a quick cleanup first," Fask said in his perfectly neutral voice.

Luke remembered with chagrin that she must smell terrible. There was a shower on the private jet, but they were over Alaska now, and it was too bumpy a ride for grooming. "Thirty minutes after we're down," she said, not making it a question. She didn't want to leave more time than she absolutely had to, and she could clean up quickly.

"Sounds good," Fask said easily. "I trust your judgment."

But did Luke trust his?

## CHAPTER 4

*D*rayger invited himself to as many family meetings as possible, so no one raised as much as an eyebrow when he waltzed in for the debrief of the raid on Amara's stronghold.

And why should they?

"Drayger! You *bastard*, stealing all the glory." Kenth's grin suggested that he wasn't actually angry as he stood and shook Drayger's hand with one strong pump.

"Hero of the hour!" Toren said, toasting him with a steaming drink.

"Is that *hot chocolate*?" Drayger scoffed. "What, are you twelve?"

Carina looked like she might ride to his rescue, but Toren only shrugged. "I like it."

Drayger's estimation of the young man went up another notch. He wished that drinking hot chocolate fit in his own image, because it actually sounded delicious and comforting. He was at the sidebar pouring himself a glass of wine as Tray and Leinani came in. Leinani had one arm in a sling and went straight to sit down at the table.

Tray came to the sidebar to snag a plate of food for her and gave Drayger a friendly punch in the shoulder. "Thanks."

"Just being my usual amazing self," Drayger said. "Part of the team and all."

As casually as he said it, Drayger had a jolt of longing. He wanted a *real* team. A team where they trusted each other and someone would always have his back. He felt so close to that here…and so bitterly far away.

He reminded himself that his goal was to be free, not fettered, and punched Tray back in the arm.

Drayger took the seat that he usually claimed, far enough down the elegant table that he didn't look like he was implying his own importance, but close enough to Fask's chair at the head to suggest that he deserved it.

They'd gotten so used to having him there for the boring discussions about weddings and engagements and press conferences that they didn't think hard about his presence when topics grew more invested and urgent. And he'd been a part of the attack in Ecuador. A vital part, even. They might all be dragons, but they didn't have the experience that he did of *fighting* as a dragon. He'd led the charge, once Kenth's initial impulsive attack had gone sideways, and made several critical saves during the battle itself.

And it wasn't just his combat prowess that helped.

The bastard Majorcan prince was also a valuable source of what appeared on the surface to be idle gossip, keeping a finger on the social temperature of all the Small Kingdoms and dribbling relevant tidbits of political insight in with sensationalized scandals. He wished that the act matched his nonchalant body language and languid attitude, but it had all been one long, deliberate exercise in trust.

# CHAPTER 4

Trust was the theme of his entire residence in the Alaska palace.

He'd turned himself in with the peace offering of Carina's stolen flash drive, handed to her with the story of stealing it from a red-haired thief. He'd begged for asylum, and turned on every ounce of his charm. He'd been given a diplomatic prison, the spells that would keep him there and from harming others not obvious, and he'd done a masterful job pretending to recognize the thief, Shadow, and trying to save the princess Carina.

The gambit hadn't turned out exactly the way that his mysterious handler had desired, but Drayger's place in the Alaskan household had solidified nicely, especially as Drayger found the little tells and weaknesses of each prince.

Like a golden retriever, Toren was desperate to have anyone tell him he was doing a good job. Rian wanted to talk philosophy and books, and had a weakness for sophisticated humor. Tray could be distracted with sports or dogs, and Kenth would happily snark about Fask's ego to anyone who would listen. Raval had been a tougher nut to crack before he disappeared, but Drayger didn't think he liked many people, so he didn't take it as a failure that they weren't chummy.

But Fask had baffled Drayger outright.

On the one hand, the oldest brother had been kind and welcoming, in a very straight-laced bureaucratic way. He was the one who first suggested that Drayger was trustworthy. Luke said that it was Fask who convinced her to relax the security protocols with him, and if the oldest prince sometimes sighed and looked put out by Drayger's more outrageous statements, that was to be expected.

Fask was friendly to him, almost to a fault, and entirely hospitable.

But Drayger's attempts to gently pry *actual* conversation from the man hit a bland wall of small talk unlike any he'd ever had to wade through. He'd tried several angles of attack, trying to garner sympathy, offer false vulnerability, spark outrage, and use surprise.

Nothing seemed to crack Fask's demeanor. He was, to all appearances, a dutiful politician, a dedicated brother, and a tireless advocate for Alaska and the royal family. He was smart and quick-witted, but his answers to everything were the same: a long-suffering sigh or an overplayed look of rapt attention that Drayger knew from cocktail parties and poker games.

There was absolutely nothing *genuine* between them.

Drayger was a player who knew when he was being played, and instinct told him that Fask was out maneuvering him at every turn, even though there was absolutely *nothing* he could put his finger on.

It was the same instinct that told him that Captain Alasie Luke was the person who could save him.

She came in, then, like a gorgeous storm cloud and Drayger remembered the hardest part of this whole charade as he had to will himself not to react too obviously to her entrance.

Her long black hair was behind her in a damp ponytail at the base of her neck, and her round cheeks had a fresh-scrubbed look. She was all business, like always, her face serene and slightly cross, her jaw set firmly, and her uniform buttoned up to her tattooed chin.

She was not the last to arrive—Fask's chair at the head of the table was still empty. Luke made a circuit of the table, stopping to speak briefly with nearly everyone. She gave Leinani a gentle hug after inquiring about her injury, and ruffled Toren's hair like he was a child.

"Captain," Drayger greeted, as she got around the table towards him.

"Drayger," she replied skeptically.

"Oh, are we being informal now?" Drayger said impishly. "Can I call you Alasie?"

"I'd prefer you didn't," she said severely.

"Then you may address me by my title," Drayger said loftily.

"You don't have a title," she said, momentarily looking confused.

"I'm the deposed Lord of Tramuntana," he reminded her, "but you can call me the Prince of Pleasure."

Luke didn't bother answering, only glowered and skirted well around him before she took her seat to Fask's right.

Drayger blew her a kiss down the table and she ignored him and turned to speak with Kenth.

Was her irritation with him sometimes overdone? Drayger always enjoyed their banter, but he caught himself wishing that there was some middle ground between their public animosity and their secret conspiracy.

He would love the luxury of talking about things that weren't politics and murder attempts, to convince her to relax and laugh and enjoy herself. Maybe he could get to know who she was behind her beautiful face and starched uniform. What would she be like if it wasn't all betrayal and business between them? What would she be like in *bed*?

Drayger forced his thoughts back to reading the room. He hadn't meant for this flirtation to take on any truth. He'd known from the start that she wouldn't accept his advances or take them to heart, but his grudging respect gradually bloomed into genuine regard.

And the attraction had always been there. He joked

about his libido, but Luke was everything he found appealing in one incredibly competent package. She had legs that went forever and ended in an ass so sweet that he didn't have to pretend to stare lustfully after her at every opportunity that presented itself. She was strong and graceful. She had eyes like wells of dreams and hair like silk. Her face was full of sweetness that she compensated for with scowls and glares.

And when she smiled, as she so rarely did, it was like she had just invented sunshine.

# CHAPTER 5

The mood in the informal dining hall was mixed, and Luke found herself analyzing each person, trying to decide if any of them looked more or less satisfied with the outcome than they ought to. None of them offered any clues.

They hadn't found Raval or the others who were missing, but they had successfully captured Amara. Her cult must be demoralized and broken and there was no political backlash from their raid…yet. The news so far reported that there had been an explosion of unknown cause in the area, but nothing seemed to have been pinned on Small Kingdoms or Alaska specifically.

Luke wasn't sure how much of the news had been fabricated. It bothered her that the video and photos showed a smoking hole where the apartment structure had been. Had it taken more structural damage than she realized? Or had Fask cleaned up the evidence after they'd left, before meeting them back at the airfield? Luke didn't like to think about the deluded cultists they'd left restrained.

They hadn't been *good* people, but everyone deserved impartial justice, and Luke suspected that they were more weak-willed than truly wicked.

Fask finally made his appearance, smelling fresh and looking showered, just as Luke was beginning to wonder what was keeping him. She checked her watch and realized he was just on time.

"Ah, Luke. Let's get started with your report."

Luke gave her piece efficiently, not lingering over her doubts or the disappointment of failing to find Raval and the children. She was careful to give everyone their due. "Our intelligence was accurate," she said, trying not to sound grudging. "Everything went according to plan."

"Our thanks to Drayger of Majorca for that," Fask said diplomatically, when she did not.

Drayger, of all of them, looked like he was at a party, not a mission debrief. He leaned back in his chair with his feet on the table, drinking what looked like wine despite the seriousness of the meeting and his still unkempt state, and he grinned rakishly at Luke from down the table. When he caught her glance, he blew a kiss in her direction, though it might have been aimed at Fask. "I still have a few underground contacts," he said merrily. "And one of them came through, what can I say?"

He could have said a lot more, Luke thought, unable to keep from scowling, but she knew why he was keeping the secrets that he was.

Luke didn't want to linger on his role, and moved to spring her next move, before any bad actors had a chance to cover their tracks. "I understand we have some of Amara's portal spells. I suggest that we activate one immediately and see where the anchor is."

"Oh, yes of course!" Tania said, sitting up straighter. Rian's mate was a librarian who had been studying the

Compact long before she knew it was a magical spell. "It would lead us to whoever here has them!"

"There were several that we think are portals," Rian agreed, shuffling through the papers that were piled between them. "And another of those shield spells. A few for healing, and a whole bunch we just aren't sure about."

"I'll look over them with you," Mackenzie offered shyly from across the table.

Tania smiled warmly across the table. "We were hoping you would. Do you think this one is a portal? Can you help us figure out the trigger sequence?"

Mackenzie was still growing into her new power as a dragon, and Luke was sure that she still felt ostracized for having been Amara's Hand in the Cause. The other mates had welcomed her whole-heartedly, but she had a lot of childhood trauma of her own to overcome, as well as feeling responsible for the kids who were missing.

Mackenzie frowned as she looked over the page of childish, cramped writing and Luke used the moment to study everyone else sitting at the table. Whose rooms sheltered the anchors? Who would want them to *not* succeed? No one moved to stop the procedure or cause any delay.

She caught Drayger doing the same thing, his own gaze so lazy and careless that Luke realized she must look highly suspicious by comparison. She was already wondering if the culprit had covered their tracks…possibly even prior to the raid. If Drayger's information came from the same person who had controlled Amara, the whole thing might be orchestrated.

But she didn't have a better plan.

"Here!" Mackenzie said. "Amara used one like this before. You'll just need to say *pigaíno* and tap your pointer finger into your opposite palm."

"Piano?" Toren said skeptically.

"*Pigaíno*," Rian corrected. "It's Greek for *go*."

Everyone looked to Fask, who gestured to the largest clear spot in the dining room. "Let's do it," he said crisply. "I want to get to the bottom of this."

"Should I call in my guard?" Luke wanted to know.

"We should be more than enough to meet any challenge," Fask said easily.

Chairs scraped back as they all scrambled into their places. Luke strode forward to take point, flanked by the dragon princes as they took protective positions in front of their mostly human mates.

"You don't have to baby me," Leinani hissed to Tray as she elbowed to stand beside him. "I'm a dragon, too."

Tray half-heartedly tried to coax her back. "I don't want you to get hurt again," he murmured.

"Maybe I don't want *you* to get hurt again," she countered. It was easy to forget that Leinani, with her polished princess manners, was as tough as any dragon prince, but Luke knew better than to underestimate her.

Luke caught Drayger watching their interaction with his usual idle amusement as he slid into the half circle they were forming. Then, to her annoyance, he saw her watching *him* and winked and wiggled his eyebrows.

Fask took point next to Luke, accepting the spell from Mackenzie and confirming his hold on the paper with her. "Like this?"

She nodded, and looked for a moment like she wanted to hide behind Kenth before she raised her chin and faced the window with the rest of them.

"*Pigaíno*," Fask said firmly, driving his pointer finger into his palm.

There was a swirl of light and wind, and a pinpoint of darkness opened in front of the window before them, air sucking between the two spaces that were suddenly connected.

As soon as it was large enough for a full person, Luke charged through, confident she would have time to shift if she needed to.

She drew up in consternation as she came through the portal on top of a desk and found herself looking into a familiar room.

"Nathaniel?!"

Familiar, trustworthy Nathaniel, keeper of the dog yard, was sitting up in shock from a couch where he'd been reading with a retired husky who came howling to four feet at the interruption.

The dog's assault was entirely in affection and Luke shoved him aside and vaulted down from the desk as Fask followed her through the portal.

"Nathaniel?" she repeated in horror.

"What's this, then?" he asked. "A portal? Captain Luke? Your highnesses?"

"Oh," Fask said mournfully. "Oh, Nathaniel. I would never have believed it."

Luke turned to see Fask kneeling on Nathaniel's desk, holding up a pile of scorched papers, and a mirror etched with tiny writing all around the frame and almost invisibly over the glass.

"I've...I've never seen that," Nathaniel protested. "What's going on?"

"We found another of these during our raid on Amara's hold," Rian said as the other brothers crowded through the portal into Nathaniel's suite of rooms. "And these are definitely the anchors for the other portals."

"Nathaniel?" Toren sounded younger than ever.

"I can't believe it," Kenth said gruffly. "After all these years."

But it was Tray's silence that was the worst.

Tray had always been closest to Nathaniel, always following him around in the dog yard asking questions and bonding with the dogs.

And Tray was the first one kidnapped by Amara and tortured with his mate Leinani.

As keenly as Luke felt this betrayal, she knew that Tray must feel it a hundred times worse and watching Tray's face fall felt like a knife-twist in the gut.

Luke had a sudden stab of doubt. Was it just a knee jerk refusal to believe ill of a man who had been in service of the Dragon King even before Luke's own appointment? She felt like she was being forced to play a role in a drama as she reached for the restraints at her belt.

"Tsk, tsk," Drayger said, slipping into the increasingly overpopulated room. "It's always the trusted family friend."

"I thought it was always the butler," Toren said weakly.

"We don't have a butler," Kenth said. "It's Alaska. We have a musher."

Tray still said nothing.

It pained her to think that Drayger might have been manipulating her this entire time, her trust in him badly misplaced.

Or had they both been played? By whom? Someone here in this room? One of the mates watching in horror through the portal? The glowing circle was starting to smoke and some of the things on Nathaniel's desk began to smolder.

Rian, frowning in concern, said, "*Alto!*"

Nothing happened.

"Amara might have altered subsequent spells so that only the activator could stop them," Mackenzie suggested shyly.

"*Alto!*" Fask cried, and the sudden closure of the portal made Nathaniel's room seem even smaller than ever.

"Nathaniel," Luke said, keeping her voice neutral, "have you been here all day? Could someone else have been here?"

"I took the dogs for a run late this morning," Nathaniel said, furrowing his brow. "Brought Pickle in to get ice balls out of his feet at about three and we've been here ever since."

Pickle was doing an old dog dance around everyone's feet, pleased as punch to be—as far as he was concerned—the center of all the attention.

Luke toyed with the magical handcuffs, loathe to put them on her long-time friend.

"I don't understand," Nathaniel said, and his eyes went around the room and sought out Luke's. "Are those necessary?"

"I wish it wasn't," Luke said honestly, reaching for him. If Nathaniel really had been the mole in the castle, he might have other magic he could use, and he might try something desperate. "You'll get due process," she promised. She hoped it was a promise she could keep, and wished the evidence wasn't quite so damning.

He looked defeated and betrayed as he obediently extended his hands to be cuffed, and Luke steeled herself to do the unthinkable. She didn't believe for a moment that Nathaniel was a traitor. He had no interest in politics, no burning passion beyond dogs and service and honoring his elders. He'd been a dear friend of the Dragon King, and Luke knew his heart was good.

He'd been set up to take this fall, and Luke still had no clue to who might have done it. Drayger was the one who had suggested this course of action, had he planted the evidence and planned this outcome? She clipped the cuffs on Nathaniel's strong wrists and kept her face cool and distant. Her best chance at uncovering the truth was to play along for now. She had nothing to go on but her gut instinct that this was as wrong as it was possible to be.

## CHAPTER 6

Drayger had always been brilliant at reading people. He was a masterful card player not because he could count cards or had particularly great strategy, but because he was so good at understanding gestures and tiny tells. He knew how people worked, why they got nervous under pressure, what made them tick. Most people were unknowingly expressive with body language, even if they schooled their faces. And they were predictable, barely more than animals with their stimulus and reaction responses.

Luke was an exception, though, because she was so attuned to her entire body. Not only was her face distractingly beautiful, she was amazingly athletic, and she controlled every inch of herself with a militaristic level of discipline. She was as smart as she was strong, and she was careful.

Drayger had known that much about her before meeting her. He had studied her records and everything the media reported about her, and there was a rich base of information out there. Her mother was the sister of the late queen, but Luke had never used that blood connection with the royal family to her own advantage; she'd won her rank with her own merit.

She wasn't always top of her class, and she wasn't always first in her competitions, but she was solid in *everything*. She didn't take flashy risks and make the showy decisions that attracted attention. Hard work and plodding effort pushed her success from behind, and she let other people take the credit and stepped up to take the blame to protect those in her care.

Which wasn't to say that she wasn't ambitious. She knew what she wanted and she went for it; she just went for it with intelligence, patience and persistence.

Drayger had known from the start that if he wanted his own freedom, he would need someone as savvy as her, someone as doggedly true to her own moral compass. Someone who might *get* him and understand his long game.

He saw right past her stony expression now and knew that she was grieving for Nathaniel's betrayal. It felt too easy, and Drayger was beginning to suspect a setup, even though the idea had been his own. Had someone else simply realized that this was the best way to catch the traitor and acted accordingly? Any of the brothers could have accessed Nathaniel's rooms in the window of time between their return from the raid and their meeting to plant the anchors and the communication mirror under a few papers. But wouldn't Nathaniel have mentioned if one of them had been in his room so recently?

They made a sad procession on the short trip from the wing where Nathaniel's rooms were back to the main castle, through halls that felt weirdly empty of the noise of children. No one spoke, but the sounds of their boots were loud and echoing. Nathaniel himself stepped proudly, his chin firm and his head high.

The others who hadn't come through the portal met them in the back hall, each falling into step with their mate.

Luke's guards stepped aside at the top of the stairs leading down to the prisons and Drayger hung back with the rest of the mates. Only the royal family was allowed below…and Captain Luke, apparently. He filed this information as useful.

"Have we ever had two prisoners down here?" Toren asked as the princes descended down into the tall stone passage.

"I can't remember a time when we even had one," Kenth said.

"I remember once," Fask said grimly. He didn't volunteer any details.

"Well, ladies," Drayger drawled, as the sounds of the arrest party grew quiet with distance. "This wasn't much of a victory celebration. Hopefully the afterparty will be a little better."

No one looked amused by the quip.

"It doesn't feel like much of a victory," Leinani said thoughtfully, rubbing her arm where she'd been injured.

"Are you hungry?" Carina asked. "We could stop by the kitchen if you'd like a snack."

"I'm starving," Leinani agreed.

"I'd like something," Tania agreed. "I'm not hungry, but I need some food in my stomach for my medication."

Mackenzie was the last to linger, standing with her arms crossed as she gazed down the stairs.

Drayger didn't need any special abilities to read the conflict on her face.

"It must be pretty strange, knowing that Amara is in

custody down there," he said gently. "You have a lot of history."

"She sometimes made me call her mother," Mackenzie said quietly. "And sometimes she acted like one."

"Mothers, like all people, come in a range of shapes and kinds," Drayger said. "Some are better than others."

"I'm a mother now," Mackenzie said in wonder, referring to Kenth's daughter Dalaya, who was already calling her maternal pet names.

"And a dragon!" Drayger pointed out cheerfully.

Mackenzie blinked at him as if she'd only just remembered that fact, and gave a dry laugh. "It stretches credibility," she said.

With someone else, Drayger might have offered to share a celebratory drink, but Mackenzie was sheltered and cautious. He knew *that* wouldn't work. Since she'd been treated as a pawn for most of her life, he knew that the way to loosen Mackenzie's tongue was simple—just to listen.

It wasn't often that he got a chance to speak with her without Kenth lurking around protectively or little Dalaya in earshot, so Drayger boldly stepped forward and hooked his arm into hers. "Let's go upstairs and admire the view that these Alaskan snobs are always bragging about. You can tell me what they've discovered about your *real* mother. Captain Luke said they found some promising details. She confides in me, you know. She pretends she's not crazy about me, but she really is."

Mackenzie looked more than a little gobsmacked and uncertain about his attention, but Drayger kept it casual and nonchalant and she didn't resist when he led her around the main stairs up to the throne room.

"See, this view is *nice*, but it's a little cold and monotone, don't you think? Too much blue. It's fine if you like mountains, but it could be broken up with some color. Majorca has these teal waters and white sand beaches. Flowers, too, and orange roofs everywhere. Now, tell me what they've found in the search for your parents."

It didn't take much prying to get Mackenzie to talk.

"The younger brother of the king of New Siberian Islands responded to Fask's queries," she said, looking down into her lap. "He said it was a possibility that he… ah…*knew* a woman in Milan who may have been my mother. The timing is right. There's going to be a blood test, but it could be a while before we have those results."

"I don't imagine there are that many royals running around indiscriminately making little dragons," Drayger said. "My own father was pretty outside of the norm for collecting bastards."

Mackenzie flushed, but smiled. "Some people collect postage stamps," she said wryly.

Drayger chuckled. "Tell me more about Amara raising you." He guided her conversation to Amara's associates, trying to gently tease out details about who the cult leader might have communicated with.

He served Mackenzie a drink from the bar that she took very hesitantly, then visibly relaxed when she realized it was only a soda. Drayger poured something stronger for himself, confident in his ability to stay on top of the effects of the alcohol. They took seats—not in the thrones, but in some of the padded wood chairs that edged the grand room, looking across it out the tall windows.

"I've told Kenth and Fask and Captain Luke everything I know about the people Amara worked with," Mackenzie said at last. "I'm sorry I can't be of any more help to you. She was careful to keep the cells compartmentalized, at least at first."

Drayger bumped her with his shoulder in a friendly

fashion. "Saw through me, did you? You're a clever woman."

No one was immune to flattery, and Mackenzie flushed happily as she sipped her drink.

She didn't ask why Drayger was so interested, but he already had an answer ready. "I need to make sure the Alaskan family thinks I'm useful, you know," he said humbly, like he was giving her insight into a great secret. "There's some connection between Amara and the people who hired me to kill Carina, and if I can figure out what that was, maybe we can get this problem at the source."

The very best lies were actually the truth.

## CHAPTER 7

Luke had no qualms imprisoning Amara. She had been non-stop trouble for months now, and her influence went back even further. She had kidnapped and tortured Leinani and Tray, forced children to write dangerous enchantments for her, and stirred up political unrest using both magical and mundane methods. She was on a fast-track to expose magic and secrets that had been safe and protected for centuries, without any care for the safety of the people at risk.

Luke was happy to see her behind proverbial bars.

Locking up Nathaniel took every ounce of Luke's self-control.

"It's done," Toren said, in his very smallest voice, as they left the sublevel. "Amara won't be trouble any more."

"She'll need to be fairly tried," Fask insisted.

"And we've still got to find Raval," Kenth said stubbornly.

"And the kids," Rian added.

No one mentioned Nathaniel, but Luke's heart hurt, and she knew that the brothers were *all* thinking about the man who had been such a close part of their family. She didn't want to believe it was true, but she couldn't find a way around the evidence they had. Nathaniel swore that he had been alone in his rooms since the raid, and Luke couldn't figure out how someone might have planted the evidence without him noticing.

The other princes scattered at the top of the stairs, in pursuit of their own rooms and rest, but Luke went with Fask up another level to the throne room. "We'll need to reevaluate the security systems," she said. "Do we want to stay at this level of alert? Should we dial things back now that Amara is in custody and we've caught…Nathaniel?"

Fask nodded in agreement. "That's reasonable."

As they entered the throne room, she felt a flare of annoyance to find Drayger, who looked like he was flirting with Mackenzie and plying her with drink. Did he have no class whatsoever, or sense of self-preservation? Kenth would certainly not take kindly to him making a play on his mate.

Mackenzie, flustered, rose to her feet and gave Fask a courteous half-curtsy. "Your Highness." She looked like she didn't know what to do with her drink, like she'd been caught stealing it from the bar.

Drayger only slouched further, giving Fask a jaunty grin and raising his glass ironically. "Your Highness," he echoed.

Fask, ever the diplomat, ignored Drayger and was swift to set Mackenzie at ease. "Your help was very much appreciated today."

"My pleasure," Drayger said, though Fask's words were clearly aimed at Mackenzie. "I'm just a part of the team. The sexiest part, no doubt."

Mackenzie looked doubtful and Fask frowned crossly. "Your information was invaluable," he agreed, addressing

## CHAPTER 7

Drayger. "And you played a vital role in the attack itself. I was happy to have you at our side."

Luke personally thought that was laying it on a little thick, but Drayger waved him off. "All in a day's work."

"I'm certainly ready to call it a day," Fask said.

Mackenzie gazed at her hands and said in a small voice, "I promised Dalaya I'd take her sledding today if I could." She cast a desperate glance at the exit. She was always a little awkward in royal company, but Luke had observed that she was particularly uncomfortable with Fask. That wasn't unexpected, given the tense animosity between Fask and her mate, Kenth.

"Give my niece my regards," Fask said easily.

Mackenzie bobbed another half-genuflection and stammered, "Yes, of course. Thank you. Your Highness. Sir."

When she had fled, Drayger observed candidly, "She's a nervous thing, isn't she?"

Was he trying to cast suspicion on Mackenzie? The woman had worked for Amara and the Cause since she was a child, but Luke trusted her gut that Mackenzie's conversion out of the cult was complete. It helped Luke's level of trust that Mackenzie was a dragon herself and she had risked everything to save the children from Amara.

Children that were still missing, along with their teacher, Katy, and Prince Raval.

"I have work to do," Luke said, glancing at Fask for permission to go. "I'll get the security levels stepped down."

"You could take an evening off," Drayger pointed out. "Amara's in your very capable prison, and you found the traitor. Relax! Have a drink!"

Luke ignored him, but Fask gave a tolerant chuckle. "It can wait until morning. Call it a night."

"That's what I'm talking about," Drayger said. "Have a nightcap! Unbutton the uniform a little!"

"I'll move to level delta first thing in the morning." Luke saluted Fask and gave Drayger a quelling sideways look before she left. He tended to ham it up a little too much, in her opinion, overplaying his flirtation with her. She was glad that he didn't follow her, but was not surprised to "accidentally" run into him a short time later outside the informal dining hall.

"The lovely Luke!" he said cheerfully. "Still in uniform!"

"It's what I have in my closet," Luke said dryly.

"I bet you have some stunning gowns in the very back for formal events," Drayger said. "Something slit way up the leg, maybe?" He put his thumbs and pointer fingers into a frame and made a show of whistling at his imaginary portrait of her.

"I can just picture it," he observed to the nearest guard. "Can't you? Alasie in something slinky!"

Luke could not remember the last time she had attended a formal event in any capacity but as Captain of the Guard. She could not remember the last time she did *anything* in any other capacity. The job consumed her life so completely that she was nothing but her last name anymore.

Except to Drayger.

And she had no idea how much of that was only an act.

Drayger hummed a few bars of music and danced forward to drag her into a few reluctant steps.

Luke extracted herself by twisting his hand back off of her arm. He stepped back ruefully and rubbed his strained wrist. "Fine, fine, I'll find another partner."

He attempted to dance with a flustered guard and then

went laughing away, leaving the hallway considerably more peaceful without him.

And there was a slip of paper tucked up Luke's sleeve.

She kept it there and went, ostensibly, to look out over the celebrated view towards the mountains and make sure that no one was watching her.

The paper discretely unrolled to read: "Quietly leave the security measures up a few extra days - have an idea."

It unhelpfully did not say what the idea was.

Luke crumpled the paper and dropped it into the fire cracking in the fireplace.

CHAPTER 8

It was a little over a week later that Drayger woke suddenly to the sound of alarms blaring through the castle. He didn't have to feign confusion as he joined the Alaskan family in the hallway.

With Amara's capture, Captain Luke had stepped down the most *obvious* security; the guards throughout the castle had thinned out considerably, but he wasn't sure if she had left up any of the magical wards that would have been deactivated at the delta level she said she would implement.

"What's going on?" Toren demanded, trying to pull a uniform jacket on over his pajama top. He seemed to be having difficulty identifying his sleeve, possibly because Carina was clinging to him in alarm.

It was dark outside, which Drayger had come to learn meant absolutely nothing about the time at this latitude. His phone said it was four in the morning.

"I don't know," Drayger said as the sound of running footsteps announced the arrival of a handful of guards, Luke at their head and sprinting towards the back stairs.

Drayger impulsively fell into stride with her. Keeping up with her took more effort than he wanted to admit. "Do you never sleep?" he asked, taking in her uniform. "What's the alarm?"

"Wards in the vault," Luke said sharply, then she looked like she wished she hadn't. Drayger had to drop away with the guards as she bolted down the stairs to the sublevel with the royal brothers tagging after her.

"Isn't this a special circumstance?" Drayger asked, when he started to follow and the guard at the top moved to stop him.

"No one down there who isn't family unless Fask says," the guard said, not terribly apologetically.

"Get that door open!" Luke shouted, arriving at the vault before any of the princes. "Faster!"

Nothing else was clear of the conversation below over the sounds of the alarm, except for shouts that Drayger couldn't make words out of. The mates crowded at the top of the stairs, waiting anxiously.

"Well, here we are again, ladies," Drayger said drolly. "Left out of all the real excitement."

"You'd think that being the Crown Princess would grant me access," Carina groused. "Does *anything* good come with that stupid crown?"

"What on earth is happening?" Fask arrived last, looking ruffled, like he'd just come from bed. "Will someone please cut that alarm?"

He started down the stairs, and met the others coming back up. The alarm finally stopped and Drayger made a point of pretending to clear out an ear.

"Sorry, Your Highness," Luke said. "I couldn't deactivate the alarm remotely from downstairs."

"Report, Captain Luke."

## CHAPTER 8

"There was an attempt on the Compact," Luke said grimly.

"I thought the extra vault wards were down," Toren said in confusion. "Amara is in custody, there's no more threat."

"As did I," Fask said. "Those spells have a limited lifespan, there was no reason to waste them."

"I left them up," Luke said without apology. "And added a specific one for the Compact itself." She avoided Drayger's gaze as she faced Fask.

If the oldest prince felt any guilt or surprise at Luke's statement, he didn't give a single hint of it, only frowned. "And someone tried to break in," he growled.

"Someone did break in," Luke corrected him. "There are scorch marks from a portal, but it was closed before we could catch them. They weren't able to damage our pages of the Compact."

"Someone planted a portal anchor in the vault?" Rian exclaimed.

"Again?!" Tania added.

"They must have," Luke said.

*Unless...*

Drayger didn't voice his suspicion out loud. He made a show of yawning. "Well, I'm really glad that your security system is so robust, but I think I'm going to go back to bed now that all the comotion has passed. Whoever tried to break in must know your security is still in place and I need my beauty sleep." He patted his own cheek. "It takes a lot of work to look this good."

Luke ignored him, but Drayger imagined he could feel a ripple of her hidden amusement. He'd always suspected that she found him funnier than she admitted and it was the most ridiculous of the things that he could feel proud of.

The princes and their mates dispersed and Drayger trailed slowly back to his room while Fask and Luke went to inspect the vault together.

Drayger honestly tried to return to his bed, but if it had felt empty before, it was cavernous now.

Luke had done as he suggested. She hadn't acknowledged that the trap was his idea, and he hadn't wanted her to, so he couldn't figure out why it felt so hollow to be right and why he yearned for her acknowledgement.

He caught himself imagining what she would be like in his arms, how it would feel to kiss her. It wasn't like he hadn't fantasized about her before, but this seemed different. It wasn't just that he wanted a quick release, he was more invested in imagining what it would be like to hold her, to tuck her up against him in that big open bed. What would her hair feel like against his skin? How warm would she be?

He'd always been attracted to her, but it felt like something was changing, like she was an itch that he couldn't quite scratch.

*She is important,* his dragon agreed.

*Why do you care?* Drayger asked suspiciously, but his dragon gave the equivalent of a shrug and left Drayger to wrestle with his sleepless desire.

## CHAPTER 9

Luke found Drayger lurking in the informal dining hall late the next morning, looking less rested than even she felt. She had pinched her cheeks so that the circles under her eye would be less obvious, but knew that she still looked like her sleep had been badly interrupted. She wasn't youthful enough to bounce back from that kind of stress anymore.

It was some consolation that Drayger looked even worse, like he'd drunk heavily that morning instead of sensibly returning to bed.

Maybe he had. Luke told herself she didn't care what Drayger did with his days or his nights.

*Especially* with his nights.

"Good morning, Alasie," Drayger drawled, like he wasn't nursing a single plate of food for an unreasonably long time just so that he could run into her.

Luke wasn't sure why she was so confident that was what he had done.

She only grunted and went to see what was left over from the breakfast spread. There were trays out with fluffy buns and hard cheese, smoked salmon, and cranberry preserves. She set herself to spreading some of the jam on a split bun. The staff had never really gotten out of the habit of cooking a lot of food, even though they had no idea if they'd find the kids.

*When.* Not *if.*

Luke spent long hours every day pursuing dead end after dead end, but she was absolutely determined to track down the kids even if it meant never having another night of sleep.

*That* was why she was so cranky, because she'd been burning the candle at both ends. She refused to acknowledge any other reason.

Drayger, completely in character, got to his feet and stretched to make sure that his white shirt, always unbuttoned halfway down his pecs, was showing an appropriate amount of chest hair. Then he came to stand directly beside her to select more food for his picked-over plate, never mind that there were perfectly good offerings further away.

"Do you have no concept of personal space?" Luke asked more crossly than she meant to. She wished there was a way to ask Drayger to button up his shirt that didn't admit it was terribly distracting to her.

"*Personally*," Drayger said in his best European drawl as he eased himself even closer, "I think it's overrated."

Then he dropped his voice. "It could have been Fask in the vault."

Luke glanced around. They were alone in the room, but the door was wide open. And listening devices could be anywhere, if someone was paranoid enough.

"He portaled into his own vault?" she hissed back. "Why would he?"

"He probably didn't portal in," Drayger pointed out. "He wouldn't need to. But when he triggered the protections you left on the Compact, he panicked and used one to get out before he got caught. Which, by the way, good work on that and making sure they *didn't* have exceptions for the royal family. He had plenty of time to wander down from his rooms like he'd just woken up to join the rest of us."

"How do you know I did that?" Luke asked mildly. She *had*, quietly adding that request to the royal caster. It had taken several extra days of his work.

Drayger smirked. "Because it's a smart thing and I assumed that you would do that because you are as clever as you are beautiful."

Luke reminded herself not to give his wild flattery any weight and forced herself back to the topic at hand. "If Fask had gone down to the vault, my guards would have seen him on the way down. They *said* no one had been down there that night."

"I can't explain that," Drayger admitted. "But I'm sure we could think of a way around that if we put our heads together." There was his innuendo voice again. "Maybe in your office with the door locked?"

"We're starting to look suspicious," Luke hissed. "I don't have a valid reason to *hang out* with you." She wasn't sure it was *better* to talk here, but it wasn't quite as obvious as ducking into her locked office under the scrutiny of her ever-present guards. It was, however, perfectly normal to have a conversation over food in a room with an open door. "Fask actually asked me why you'd been to my office so much just a few days ago."

"We could just start having sex," Drayger suggested slyly. "That would give us a great reason to hang out more. I mean, you've been after me for months now, it makes sense that I might give in eventually. Out of pity, if nothing else."

Luke choked back a laugh and smothered it with a scowl. "I think we can find another cover," she said dryly.

"Yeah, but would it be as much fun?"

For a moment, Luke could imagine *nothing* that would be as much fun, and she had to yank her thoughts back to the problem at hand.

## CHAPTER 10

*D*rayger hadn't actually intended to propose an affair. Usually, he was good at keeping his baser instincts under control when they weren't operating with an audience and sticking to the business at hand. His flirty act was mostly just that: an *act*.

But suggesting it out loud gave Drayger a sizzle of hope that he immediately squashed.

Did he think for one moment that he had a chance with this amazing woman? It was just ego that suggested he might. Ego, and his dragon, who, for some reason, was unusually interested in her.

"Let's focus, Casanova," Luke said severely, proving that his humor had fallen short with her. "I'm very sure that Nathaniel was framed, but the evidence is rather damning. I got the data from Nathaniel's personal accounts, and he got a large deposit that goes straight back to one of the sham accounts that Carina uncovered. We might have caught him that way eventually, even if we hadn't found the portal anchors in his rooms. And he has no explanation for that. No one was in or out of his rooms, that he remembers."

"I thought those accounts had been closed," Drayger said. "Is it a usual practice to leave laundered money out there?"

"Fask pulled some strings and got the American investigators to let Amco reopen them so that activity could be tracked on them. Mackenzie said that Amara knew that Carina was behind freezing their accounts and we were hoping to use them to trace her location."

"Doesn't that indicate that Amara knew that you would be watching that money?"

"Maybe she forgot? Maybe she got desperate? A slip-up? There were too many proxies on the transfer to *actually* use it to track back to her, so maybe she just considered it a worthwhile risk when they became available. Maybe she's just insane and we're trying to apply reasons to someone who has none. Why are you so sure that Fask is the one we're looking for? All of the vault incursions have been in Alaska. If he wanted to destroy the Compact for some reason, why wouldn't he be making these attempts on the *other* Kingdoms?"

"To negate suspicion?" Drayger proposed. "Who's going to guess that he's sabotaging himself? It could also be that the Compact's protections are strong enough to keep him out of other countries, but they don't extend to his own Kingdom."

Luke frowned, clearly considering the implications but not accepting them.

"Do you really believe in coincidence?" Drayger asked seriously. "Is it a coincidence that it was *Fask* who got the accounts reopened? Maybe he knew he'd need it personally for something like this."

"I find it hard to believe that *Fask* used that account to

frame Nathaniel," Luke said. "That would be so ridiculously convoluted. Easier solutions are *usually* right."

"So do you believe that Nathaniel is the traitor?" Drayger pressed. "That's the simplest solution here: Amara bought his loyalty with cold, hard Small Kingdom dollars."

Luke had too much self-control to actually flinch at Drayger's hard words, but her lips tightened and her eyes took a cast of sorrow and anger. "No, I don't believe that Nathaniel is a traitor," she said firmly, her voice rising. "But I find it hard to believe that—"

Drayger saw Toren sauntering into the informal dining room just over Luke's shoulder as she started a sentence that could only end in blurting out their suspicions. Drayger didn't think that Toren was an enemy of the Kingdom, but he was such an obedient little pup that he'd go running straight to Fask with Luke's mistrust, and ruin everything they'd tried to keep quiet. He had to silence Luke…*and* disperse suspicion.

Drayger had a split second to decide what to do and it wasn't entirely logic that made him swoop forward to lean Luke back onto the table and press his mouth against hers.

"Wow! Captain Luke! Prince Drayger! Wow! Sorry! I didn't know this room was taken!"

Toren backed out again as fast as he'd come in and Drayger braced himself for a fist or a knee. Luke wouldn't settle for a girlish slap, she was going to throw him across the room or neuter him on the spot.

Then he realized with astonishment that the ridiculous lust that he was feeling wasn't his own at all. Or at least, it wasn't *only* his own. "You liked that," he said in triumph, gazing into Luke's fiery eyes. "You liked that a *lot!*"

# CHAPTER 11

Luke should have kneed him in the groin the moment that Drayger made a move. That was the only appropriate reaction to his impulsive advance, even if she knew that he'd only done it to dispel suspicion when Toren caught them.

And she *knew* that was why he'd done it. She didn't have to guess his motivations because she could feel his emotions as clearly as she could feel her own.

More clearly, if she had to be honest, because her own emotions were a tangle of red-hot desire and confusion.

"Get off me," she hissed, and she should have pushed him off, or thrown him to the floor, or punched him in the eye, but she was weirdly weak and worst of all, he wasn't *wrong* when he claimed that she liked it.

The touch of his lips on hers had set off a wave of lust like Luke had never felt before, white-hot through her entire core like the burning tingle of frozen digits fighting off frostbite. She liked having him pin her down, wanted more of him up against her, with much less clothing.

"You don't actually want me to," Drayger said, his voice full of wonder. "You're...I'm...what is going on?"

That was the moment that they both realized what was happening and he scrambled back up off her.

"*Fertile ground*," Drayger said, strangled, quoting the Compact.

"*And great need*," Luke added.

"*They will know each other.*"

"*Fuck.*" Luke didn't often swear, vastly preferring stony silence to make a point, but this seemed like an appropriate time.

"I'd be happy to," Drayger offered, and if his cheeky grin usually made him look dashing, it was a hundred times worse now. "And I *know* that you would, too."

Then he was closing the distance between them and Luke was craving the touch of his hand even before it reached her shoulder.

Luke acted without thinking, twisting his hand back from her shoulder and leaning her whole body into her leading knee, straight at his groin like she should have when he first kissed her.

Unfortunately, the wretched, unwelcome mate bond—because that was clearly what was happening—meant that Luke nearly fell to her own knees when he staggered back, her eyes watering.

"Ow," Drayger wheezed.

For a split second, Luke thought that the wail of the alarm was in her own head, a reaction to the shock and pain. "There's an intruder," she said. She wrenched her phone from her pocket and confirmed. "In the garage."

"I'll catch up!" Drayger promised between gritted teeth as he clutched at the back of a chair.

Luke had a moment of wondering what she must look like when she met the gathering guard and joined them on the sprint for the garage. She welcomed the blast of the outside air to cool her cheeks and bring her attention back to the matter at hand. Someone had violated the wards of the palace, and this was far more critical than the kiss that was still blazing on her lips.

The garage was in chaos, the alarms blaring, and she was distantly pleased that the early wave of her guards were following protocol to the letter, even as they were faced with a smoking car and a familiar figure.

Raval's beautiful car was a lot less beautiful now. It was dented, scratched, and more than a little on fire. Luke barely recognized Raval himself; he'd grown a full beard, and his skin had darkened several shades while his scruffy hair had gotten even lighter. The teacher, Katy, was climbing out of the other side of the car with a lanky, half-grown dog. She had changed in coloring and hair somewhat less, but they were both dressed in worn rags. There was no sign of the missing children.

The dog yanked the leash from Katy's hands and made a beeline for the nearest royal guard. Luke had a bad moment when she feared that she was going to watch a tragic accident; no one seemed to recognize the prince or his mate and everyone was intensely on edge, most of all herself.

"Hold your fire!" Raval roared with more authority than Luke was accustomed to from him.

"That's my line!" Luke said over the noise, but she followed it with a firm, "Lower your weapons!"

She made it between them before anything terrible could happen in the heat of the moment and bowed her head to Raval. "Your Highness."

She got the security alarm turned off, just in time for the fire alarm to replace it. Someone found an extinguisher to use on the car and there was a flurry of activity as the big garage door was opened to clear out the smoke. The rest of the royal family arrived and the broad strokes of their adventures were exchanged.

"We went back in time, twice," Katy explained. "We spent two months, give or take, roughing it with the kids on an abandoned beach on Mo'orea, and then we went back even further, to the writing of the Compact, met the first dragons, saved the world from a magical war, and might have invented the scientific method.

"We found the traitor and captured Amara," Kenth countered. "You missed a lot of excitement."

*And I'm Drayger's mate*, Luke remembered, with a flash of shock and dismay as they returned to the castle. If five Alaskan princes having mates made no sense, this made even less. Drayger was a bastard son, not even remotely in line to inherit the Majorcan throne, and while Luke was a cousin of the Alaskan line, it was only by marriage and she'd never so much as considered that she'd be tapped to rule.

Was it a joke? A flaw in the code of the Compact? Why them? Why *now*? Luke knew who to trust less than ever, and she glanced at Fask as they all returned to the palace to find that he was scowling ferociously at no one in particular.

He said all the right things, Luke thought, as he ordered the staff to get hot food for the returning couple. What purpose could he have to betray his own kingdom, his own family?

Drayger was waiting at her office door and she let him in so they could speak privately.

"We should talk," Drayger said, and Luke could feel the mischief behind his words. He didn't really want to talk, and neither did she, but there was no way that she was going to indulge in her impulse to step into his arms and let him hold her. She had come to trust him, despite all of her reservations, but what she felt now, thanks to the mate spell, was something even deeper and trickier to navigate. It was an insistent echo of their possible future feelings, complicated by their long antagonism and the sizzling attraction that she couldn't deny she'd always had. Not now, with him feeling the things that she did.

"You should go sit in on the family meeting," Luke said, focusing her attention on the other problems that still loomed. She didn't have time to indulge in foolish yearning. "They're used to you crashing the party and you can get more details about Raval's little romp back in time and watch Fask for clues."

"That wasn't what I thought we should talk about," Drayger said, catching her hand and bringing it to his mouth. It wasn't the first time that he had kissed her hand, but it was the first time that she realized how much he relished the feel of her skin on his lips.

"This doesn't change anything," Luke protested, taking her hand back. "We still have a traitor to uncover and a Compact to renew. I don't know what she's up to and if she were here I'd give her a piece of my mind, but I have to assume that it's some kind of twisted joke at this point."

"Is it so bad?" Drayger asked wistfully, but he didn't make any effort to recapture her hand. "This?"

Luke drew in a breath and was forced herself to examine her churning emotions. It was futile to lie to him, and it wouldn't do either of them any good to let it go unexamined. Even if it was some kind of cruel prank, wishing it hadn't happened was a waste of time.

"I don't know," she said honestly. "I don't even know what it means. I'm not giving up the stars of Alaska for a crown in your country, and I'm not giving up my free will for some possible pretty future."

"You have to admit that it's a *very* pretty future," Drayger said. "A very sexy, pretty future."

"I don't have to admit anything," Luke snapped. She hated that Drayger could see the longing under her words.

If the magic wasn't lying, they could have a future love like Luke had never even imagined was possible. She could feel the pressure in her head and in her heart, to trust this man, to open herself completely to him, in every way counter to her instinct to hide her true self away and maintain her professional facade.

Trusting Drayger politically, which she'd finally realized she could, was nothing like knowing that she could trust him with everything that she was inside, all the cold, buried parts of herself that no one else knew, all the fears and uncertainties that she barely acknowledged herself.

"Luke," Drayger said gently, because he must know how she was wrestling with herself. "Alasie."

Her real name, like her real self, was almost too much to bear. She almost shifted on the spot, a gut-deep instinct to protect herself with claws and thick fur.

"Alasie," he said again, and then he was drawing her into his arms to kiss her, and she was lost.

## CHAPTER 12

Drayger felt like he was dreaming. How many times had he imagined kissing Captain Luke, loosening her hair, making her strong body soft against him? This wasn't like their first kiss, hard and desperate and only partly for deception.

This was surrender and slow release, the barest brush of lips at first, a shaky intake of breath in a way that was so vulnerable and sweet that Drayger couldn't tell what was magic and what wasn't. Some of it was *now*, the sizzling anticipation of touch, and some of it was something far in the future, a joining of such depth and truth that it made Drayger whole.

"Alasie," he said again, at a natural pause in their kiss, because he loved the sound of it in his mouth, and he loved how it felt like twanging a rubber band in her head.

No one else called her that. No one else knew her like he did now, or ever could. He felt vindicated, seeing the light of her soul, all the way through her, unmarred by any darkness. He'd always guessed that about her, been sure that she, of all people, was genuinely good behind her tough exterior and scowling walls.

It gave Drayger a moment of regret, because surely she must see him just as clearly, all his murky morals and painful scars. She'd been loved and nurtured. He'd been used and neglected. What did he have to offer her in a partnership?

He drew back in dismay, and she made a little noise of displeasure and clutched him harder, followed by a shove at his chest that sent him back a step.

"We don't *have* to do this," she said, between clenched teeth.

Drayger could feel her trying to quench her sizzling desire, wrestling with her pride and her confusion. This felt a lot like losing free will, and that was something that didn't sit well with either of them.

Drayger dredged up some semblance of his usual nonchalance. "We don't *have* to," he drawled, "but wouldn't it be *fun?*"

They stared at each other, both imagining that fun in glorious detail. At least, Drayger was certainly thinking about peeling her out of that uniform, bending her over her desk, picturing how tight she'd be, the helpless sounds she'd make, the scratches she'd leave on his back if he took her on the floor. He guessed that she was dreaming similar things, from the white hot lust she was fighting with.

She'd be a wildcat.

"You should go," Luke said.

"Really?" Drayger said, trying not to sound whiny even though he guessed that she could feel his disappointment. "Are you…sure?" What would she do if he reached out and touched her now? One casual little caress at her hairline, just a brush of fingertip on skin to see if he could set her on fire…

## CHAPTER 12

"The family will be in the library talking about Raval's revelations," Luke said between clenched teeth. "This will be a brilliant opportunity to do that people-watching thing you claim you're so good at, and you don't want to miss it."

Everything about her was a challenge. *Prove it*, her voice said.

Drayger had never wanted to prove anything so badly in his life. He wanted to prove that she wasn't wrong to trust him…that he was worthy of *her*.

*Was* he?

Drayger didn't know how he could convince *her* of that fact when he wasn't sure himself. She was everything he admired, and he…he was a bastard prince who sold his morality to the highest bidders.

"I'll go do my super spy thing," he agreed, but when he decided he had to try to touch her, she stepped back with a hiss.

It was gratifying to have his suspicions confirmed; she *did* desire him. The depths of her lust were everything he'd ever hoped, and having that bare between them was a source of both relief and consternation. He couldn't take advantage. He couldn't even tease her about it.

Well, not much.

"Someone framed Nathaniel," Luke reminded him. "Someone with power and deep pockets. We've got to catch them in a lie."

"I'm the expert on lies," Drayger said. He let his hand drop back to his side and stuffed it in his jacket pocket before it could betray him by reaching for her again without his will. "Miss me!"

He whistled his way to the library, and the guards exchanged skeptical looks but didn't try to stop him when he went in, straight to the bar.

Fask was already there, frowning at a tumbler of

watered whiskey in his hands, and Kenth and Mackenzie were close together at the opposite side of the cozy little seating area.

Drayger did a quick count of seats, assuming that Raval and Katy would join them and that four could crowd onto the couch, and made a show of dragging a reading chair into the circle and pouring himself a drink as the rest of the royal family straggled in.

All of them were in various stages of shock. Tania shook her head and settled into the most comfortable chair, Rian beside her.

"Time travel shouldn't be possible," Tania said. "Not by the rules of magic as I understand them."

"Could their memories have been altered?" Drayger posited, not because he thought it was likely, but because he wanted to insert himself into the conversation as soon as possible. "Maybe they didn't *actually* go back in time."

"You think it was some kind of elaborate charade that they lived in for several months?" Rian said skeptically. "To what point? And where would the kids be, then?"

"I can't believe I didn't see it," Mackenzie said, dazed. "Eleven of them. All different nationalities."

"Where did Amara *get* them?" Fask wanted to know. "How did she find them?" It was a question he'd asked before, many times during their attempt to reunite the children with their families.

Mackenzie still didn't have answers. "I don't know. She never told me. They didn't come into the Cause all at once, but over the space of nearly a year as she realized what they could do for her. Sometimes, she got other children that didn't work out, but they didn't stay long."

Tania used her cane to rise to her feet and disappeared into the rows of books to return with an aged leather-bound book. "This is one of the oldest paintings we have of them," she said, opening to the frontispiece.

Mackenzie pointed to each one and named the children. Some of them were easy to identify—Cindy with her dark skin, Lon's crooked grin. "Jamie looks like…me."

"That might narrow down our search for your lineage," Tray said. He'd come in with Leinani and poured them both drinks. "Anyone else want something?"

Drayger did his very best people-watching, observing at once that Leinani was only pretending to sip her wine. Tray was more worried about Leinani than the conversation. Mackenzie was a tangle of emotions that was transparent on her face and Kenth was scowling generally so that no one would know how much he wanted to comfort her.

Tania and Rian acted more like they were trying to solve a fascinating puzzle, teasing at the technical details of magic. Toren was keyed up like a sugared and overtired toddler, and he and Carina had a lot of questions about who was going to attend the Renewal now that Raval was an option again.

And then there was Fask. Did he look more frustrated than usual? Who *wouldn't?*

Raval and Katy came in at last, like ragged returning heroes. If Raval was unshaven and both of them looked slightly haggard, they were happy and healthy, and they were welcomed with tears and hugs. Drayger bowed over Katy's hand and kissed it and winked at her, but if Raval was annoyed by the greeting, he didn't show it.

Katy sat beside Mackenzie and they pored emotionally over the portrait of the kids and exchanged stories of all their excitement.

Drayger downplayed his own part in Amara's capture with exaggerated humility.

The mood in the room changed starkly when Fask revealed that Nathaniel had been caught red-handed with portions of Amara's spells and a communication device.

Fask reported, "We checked Nathaniel's accounts and found that he'd received a large chunk of money. Millions of dollars that could be traced back to one of Amara's laundered accounts."

Drayger watched each of them avidly, looking for signs of guilt or remorse, but regret was the closest thing he could identify. Nathaniel had been popular with the brothers. None of them liked the idea, but agreed that the pile of evidence was damning.

When Katy excused herself to the restroom, Drayger might have tried to steer the conversation back to Nathaniel to try to pressure someone into betraying something, but the women immediately guessed at Katy's gravid state. Raval solemnly confirmed it, and there was no changing the topic from *babies* until Katy herself returned.

Drayger noted with interest that Leinani, the first to ask out loud whether Katy was pregnant, had still not actually drunk any of her wine, but had subtly traded glasses with Tray partway through the evening so that she was toying with an empty one. She gracefully refused an offered refill.

Raval insisted on taking a yawning Katy to bed, and Drayger circled the room making targeted small talk wherever there was an opening. Kenth glared him away from Mackenzie, Rian and Tania simplified their conversation to include him briefly, assuming he would not keep up with their technical magic speak. Drayger let them believe he was too bored or stupid to follow along. Toren and Carina joked with him a while about being lost on tropical islands. Leinani and Tray left first, hand in hand.

Fask was the last to leave, which was very like him. It wasn't that late, but it had been a lot of day, even for people who hadn't traveled in time…or had a mate bond triggered. The other brothers were glad to retreat to the privacy of their suites with their mates.

Drayger eyed Fask's nearly empty glass. "Pour you another?" he offered casually.

Fask looked at it like he'd forgotten he was holding it and he dashed back the last remains of amber liquid. "No, better not. I'm not sure what all of this means, but tomorrow is going to be a long day trying to explain it to the other royals. I need my rest."

"Alas," Drayger said, making a show of draining the last of his already-empty glass. "I was only looking for an excuse to refill my own."

Fask chuckled as he stood and returned his tumbler to the bar. "You haven't really needed excuses to lean into our hospitality."

"I feel I more than pay for my stay with the sheer pleasure of my company," Drayger said.

Fask sobered. "More seriously, your help is always genuinely appreciated. You have been a great help to us in several *less diplomatic* situations these last few months. *Keep it up.*"

Was there a slightly knowing barb there? Did Fask guess that Drayger suspected him of being the puppeteer on the other end of his strings? Whatever else the prince might be, he was not *stupid*. Perhaps this was his way of reminding Drayger that he was on a short leash, and being observed himself.

Or perhaps it was only genuine gratitude.

"I'm happy to help," Drayger said sincerely, and then he went to gather up a few forgotten glasses like a good little houseguest.

## CHAPTER 13

It had been a mistake to kiss Drayger, Luke decided.

A *huge* mistake.

"What are you doing, *Grandmother*?" she asked thin air when the door closed behind Drayger. She'd known about the spirit in the castle for as long as she could remember, and always assumed it was an ancestor of some kind, a spirit looking after the royal family, the way some spirits guarded waterways or wind.

It hadn't changed anything for Luke to learn that this spirit was actually a spell, and not just any spell, but the Compact itself, a casting so complex and powerful that it wrote the rules of magic itself. She was still a pain in the ass, always acting mysterious and cryptic, giving half-answers, and never showing up when she was actually needed.

Like now, when Luke was desperate for answers. Why had she and Drayger been chosen as mates? Who could she trust? What kind of future could they possibly have together? Why *now*, with the Renewal pounding down on them? She wished she had a friend—maybe a girlfriend—that she could vent to. Someone she could trust, that she knew wouldn't judge her for thinking back over their kiss—kisses—with hunger.

She was kind to her guards, and thought their respect was both genuine and mutual, but they were not friends. She trusted them, but had always maintained a level of professional aloofness that isolated her at the top. She was not going to talk about *crushes* with any of them.

The closest thing she had to a true friend was Fask, as the oldest of her cousins, and she was beginning to believe Drayger's once-outrageous suggestion that he was somehow involved in the attacks on Alaska and the Compact.

And the second closest thing she had to a friend was *Drayger*.

And now, they'd kissed, and she had no idea what that meant. The possible future that the mate bond showed her was dizzying and dear, and it terrified Luke how much she wanted it to be true and how much she dreaded that it wouldn't be.

She dumped a folder of paperwork out on her desk with determination. She still hadn't gotten through the official sealed records for their assault on Amara's stronghold, and Raval's return would mean even more to document.

Luke was able to bend her mind for the task only a short time before she caught herself remembering the heady pressure of Drayger's lips on hers, and she was so angry with herself that she swept all of the papers off of her desk in frustration, knocking over a box of evidence as well. Artifacts went spilling onto the floor, and a ring rolled away under the desk.

Luke gathered most of them up and had to crawl under her desk for the ring. She nearly dropped it when Fask's voice came from the engraved circle, and sat up so fast that she cracked herself on the head on the underside of her desk. "Raval, what's wrong? You look agitated."

It took her a moment to remember that Fask had pocketed the ring during the sting on Amara's stronghold. It must still be in his uniform pocket, and something had activated it now. What had Mackenzie said about the ring? It was only on when the bearer needed to hear something. Luke rubbed her stinging scalp. She was probably going to have a lump there.

Was *Luke* the bearer now? What did she need to hear?

"Fask, you sonnuvabitch, I know what you've done." Luke might not have recognized Raval's voice if she hadn't heard his command in the garage. Whatever trials he had endured in the rescue of the children and their madcap race into the past, it had strengthened and hardened him considerably.

"I have no idea what you're talking about." Fask had perfected that bland tone, ideal for diplomatic occasions when he didn't want to admit that he was rattled. Luke had witnessed it enough times to know that he didn't use it lightly.

*"You know what you did!"* Raval snarled. "How could you!? He is—"

"*Forget it*," Fask said firmly.

The ring went red-hot in Luke's hand and she tightened her grip so that she wouldn't drop it in shock. It cooled almost at once. She'd have to ask Mackenzie or Leinani what that meant.

"Fask?" That was Raval's voice again, but it was completely different than it had been. All of the urgency had leached out of it and he sounded confused. "How did I get here?"

"I don't know," Fask said smoothly. "I assume you went to the vault for something. You've had a long, hard time of it. You must be more tired than you realize."

Luke shivered at the carelessness of his voice and felt as if she'd just been handed a beautiful gift and turned it over to find that it was full of spiders.

"Yes," Raval said, dazed. "Yes, that must be it."

Luke guessed that the heat in the ring meant that magic had been used. Fask must have done something to Raval's short term memory. A spell of some kind, used defensively because Raval had *known* something. Something dangerous to Fask.

"You've had a really trying journey," Fask said kindly. "Your mate is waiting for you in your rooms, you should go to her."

"Katy," Raval said thoughtfully. "Katy is my mate."

Did Luke imagine that he shook himself then, like a dog after a swim? She desperately wished that she could see with the rings as well as hear; there were so many conversational cues in body language. But if the ring was in Fask's pocket, there would be nothing to see anyway.

There was a standard hail from guards and Luke thought that the brothers must be at the top of the stairs to the understory where the vault and prisons were.

Then the ring went quiet and still, cutting out right in the middle of a word. After straining at it for a few moments, Luke put it down on the desk before her. Mackenzie had warned that it only had a few uses left, when she still had the power to understand spells simply by looking at them. Luke suspected that it was useless now.

Drayger had been right; Fask's loyalty was compromised.

She was equal parts crushed and relieved.

Fask *was* the traitor.

And Drayger was right. He'd been honest and truthful, and this pretty much proved it.

Luke had no idea why that filled her with relief, but she knew that he was the only person she could talk to now.

## CHAPTER 14

*D*rayger was outside on one of the back porches of the palace having a late afternoon smoke, trying to make sense of the new order of the universe, and he knew that Luke was nearby, and very upset, just moments before she crashed out onto the porch. She slammed the doors behind her and stalked across the frosted planks to the railing where he was leaning.

"Do you have another one of those?" Luke hissed.

"Are you sure?" Drayger asked in his most annoying practiced drawl. "It's a nasty, awful habit that you hate."

"Dire times," Luke said, extending an imperious hand.

Drayger fished another cigarette out of the package in his pocket and leaned close to light it from his own as Luke took a surprisingly practiced drag. Drayger had never seen her smoke before and hadn't guessed that she actually did.

"Tell me all about it, honey," he teased, leaving a proper amount of space between them along the porch rail. There were cameras installed on the porch now, and if half the castle was more sure than ever that the two of them were sleeping together than ever, Luke was still like a feral cat with him, keenly aware of him and dying to be petted even though she hissed and clawed to keep him at arm's length.

He could actually feel her start to relax as they shared a moment of silence. It wasn't just the nicotine, Drayger knew. It was him, and he was glad that he could be some comfort to her, even if she wasn't willing to admit it in words or let him touch her.

He could be patient, knowing now what they would someday have.

"*Possibly*," Luke said out loud. "It's a *possible* future."

She'd been thinking the same thing he had.

It wasn't just that they were compatible, it was that they were deliciously in sync. He could guess exactly where her thoughts were by the emotional flavor of her in his head.

Right now, she felt more than mere surprise by all the day's revelations. Time travel. Amara's kidnapped children being the first kings and queens. Being his mate.

That alone would be enough to unsettle a normal person. But Luke wasn't normal, and something else had alarmed and dismayed her. Drayger guessed that she'd learned something that she hadn't wanted to. Something that had solidified her trust of him, and her crumbled feeling of betrayal with the Alaska princes. Had one of the brothers done or said something truly incriminating at last? Drayger wished he could protect her from the harsh realities of the world, where everyone was out for themselves and even family was suspect and untrustworthy.

*Especially* family.

For all that Luke projected an image of self-sufficiency and cold efficiency, she was soft inside, gentle and caring. The royal family was more than her responsibility. It was her calling, and she loved and belonged to them. Knowing that one of them had betrayed them all must be a bitter pill.

But when Drayger tried to project his desire to comfort and protect her across the frosty, formal distance between them, he feared he only projected his *desire*.

Even bristling with outrage and ill-concealed distress, she was the most gorgeous thing that Drayger had ever seen in his life. Every line of her face was art, from the planes of her forehead, to her short, straight nose, to the lines tattooed on her firm, round chin. Every bit of her was beauty and strength.

The sex would be *amazing*.

"Knock that off," she hissed.

"This is your fault," Drayger said. "You clearly find me impossibly sexy. It's a sign of your excellent taste."

"I swear to my ancestors that if you say anything about *fertile ground*, I will make sure that you *aren't*," she added.

Drayger chuckled.

She glared at him and glanced back at the cameras.

"It's a lot to take in," Drayger said. "Those kids. All the first kings and queens. The Compact. Raval and Katy going back in time."

"That's not what's bothering me," Luke said, confirming his guess. "I know for sure now that Nathaniel wasn't the traitor."

"Because you know who it really is?"

Luke's silence suggested she did.

"Who is it?" Drayger asked more quietly. "I'd offer to thrash them, but then you'd have to arrest me, and I'll do you more good if I'm free. Not that I'm not up for restraints, if that's to your taste. In fact, let me take that back. Please arrest me and have your dirty way with me."

Luke's brown eyes danced briefly and Drayger felt a confused mix of interest in his proposal and a wave of amusement and gratitude.

"Who is it?" Drayger asked again, not really wanting the answer.

He wasn't surprised by it, or by Luke's despair as she quietly shared it. "Fask."

"Rotten all the way up at the top," Drayger said, wishing he could reach out and tuck her into a comforting embrace.

"I overheard him talking to Raval," Luke said. "Leinani's listening ring is still in his pocket. Raval found something out and was about to accuse him of...I don't know what. Fask cast a spell on him and he forgot it on the spot."

"Where did Fask get a spell?" Drayger asked. "Was it from Amara's arsenal? How long will it last?"

"I don't know," Luke spat. He could tell that a big part of her ire was that she didn't have the answers she wanted.

"A memory spell might explain why none of your guards remembered anyone going down to the vault the night the protections were triggered," Drayger realized.

"Don't think I haven't thought of that." Of course she had.

Something else occurred to Drayger. "The Compact said it wasn't a dragon."

"She must have been wrong. Or there's more than one traitor? Or maybe this is something completely different."

"Or Fask isn't a dragon."

Luke stared at him. "Fask is one of the *dragon princes of Alaska*." Her voice was flat, but he could feel from her mind that she found the idea morbidly curious.

"When did you last see him shift?" Drayger wanted to know. "He wasn't part of the first wave when we captured

Amara. He stayed in human form the entire time, as far as I saw. He wasn't part of the rescue of the children originally, and he didn't volunteer to go in Raval's car to save them the second time. It's funny how he's always sending one of the others off to do the dragon things. I've *never* seen him shift."

"He's dragon strong," Luke said, but as confident as her voice was, she didn't *feel* convinced. "I've watched him play hockey with his brothers as recently as Tray and Leinani's not-an-elopement."

"If he's got the kind of magic to make portals and memory wipes, maybe he's got a spell for that, too."

Luke took a long drag of her cigarette. "I saw him shift plenty when they were young. He and Kenth were always doing races and competitions. And later, as a young man. The last time I saw him shift for sure was…probably fifteen years ago, before their mother died."

"How *did* their mother die?" Drayger wanted to know. He knew the official story, that she'd been drowned in a spring breakup along a river, but details of the event were vague and Drayger didn't need magic to know that it was a contentious point between Fask and Kenth.

The feeling of Luke in his head took a shade of sorrow. "Aunt Esme was human, not even a normal animal shifter. It was spring and she was working to tidy up a winter camp on the shore of a river when an ice dam upstream suddenly gave out and swept her away."

"Why does Fask blame *Kenth* for it?"

Luke gave him an appraising look. "You picked up on that?"

Drayger decided that he liked the feeling of her grudging respect. "I keep telling you, I'm really good at people. Practically a genius."

He was rewarded with a snort that bordered on a

laugh. Drayger was a little chagrined that she'd know how much her esteem meant to him.

"Kenth was *supposed* to be the one doing the job that Aunt Esme was doing. Fask already considered Kenth a screw-off, constantly shirking his duties, but this was a new level of not-where-he-was-supposed-to-be. It's understandable that Fask took this failure really personally."

Drayger thought about that as he blew out a trail of dragon-enhanced cigarette smoke, trying to put the information into some kind of world order with everything else he knew about Fask. "Fask is really good about taking responsibility. It's part of what makes him such a natural leader. He wants the glory, but he's always ready to take the blame when something doesn't work out."

"He and Kenth have always had one of those close brotherly rivalries," Luke said, but Drayger could feel her considering his words. "Maybe this is different because Kenth was involved, and because his mother died. There are a lot of emotions tied up in it."

"Maybe *he* feels responsible." Drayger proposed.

"How does that make sense?" Luke wanted to know. She wasn't dismissing the theory, only chewing over it curiously.

"I understand people pretty well," Drayger repeated. "There's a point for most of them where there's something so horrible that they can literally not handle the truth, and they have to twist the blame somewhere. They distort the facts in their own heads and cling to that falsehood desperately."

"You're speaking from experience," Luke said, with a burst of unwelcome pity.

Drayger thought he should hate her raw sympathy, but somehow, it was only a relief. "I spent a lot of time pretending I could justify what I do—what I did—because it was a lot prettier to think that I had morals and standards than to realize that shitty actions are shitty actions and it doesn't matter why you think you're doing them if they are the wrong thing to do."

## CHAPTER 15

It would have been so much easier to dislike Drayger, Luke thought. Her attraction for him didn't bother her—it was annoying, but not really much different than being hungry or thirsty or having aching muscles after a satisfying workout. But *liking* him, respecting his clarity of thought and his cleverness and wanting to unlock the complicated layers of him like a nested puzzle box…this was dangerous ground.

She certainly didn't want to admire him.

And she never wanted to love him.

That was a *possible* future. A potential, not even a probable. It was the meddlesome work of the Compact, trying to fix up a "granddaughter" with entirely the wrong guy by supposing some outcome that neither of them wanted.

It wasn't any easier to think about Fask, and Luke was running out of cigarette *and* calm. It tasted like ass and bitter old tea and she ought to stub it out, but she didn't want to leave Drayger's stupidly addictive presence.

He was the only one she could trust right now, even though she could feel the echoes of all his regrets and remorse. He didn't think he was a good person, but Luke was finally realizing that *good* wasn't an easy label that she could just slap on someone. Drayger worked hard to be *better*, he didn't let his mistakes lead his future. He wanted to atone, and he was willing to do the hard scrabble that got to high places. He played a role, but now that Luke had seen beneath his carefree, playboy mask, she would never be able to think about him without knowing the *truth* of him.

He didn't look at her, and Luke kept her gaze to the view. To all appearances, they were sharing a smoke on the porch and talking about the weather. It was cold for the season, but they were both shifters.

After a moment, Luke stubbed out the last of her cigarette. "I've got a lead to follow," she said unhappily. "Even if I might not like where it takes me."

"Something I can do?" Drayger offered. He sounded lazy, but his mind was always quick.

Luke's traitor brain immediately went places it shouldn't and Drayger shot her a grin of pure mischief. "Not *that*," Luke said sharply. "Just keep your ears open, Majorca."

She took the cigarette butt in with her to the trash so the landscaper wouldn't give her grief and brushed her teeth before going to find Mrs. James. It was the longest of shots that Luke had ever followed up on. "Do we keep old cellphones?"

Mrs. James looked at her like she had just asked for a caterpillar or a dust bunny. "Like, *antique* cell phones?"

"When one of the princes upgrades their phone, what happens with the old one?"

Mrs. James blinked at her. "Well, we don't toss them right away, just in case there's a problem. There's a storage room behind the kitchen where we put their things when they outgrow them. It's due to be cleaned out in the worst way, but we've got so much space in the palace that it's never been a priority. Of course, that might be different now, with all of the boys finding their mates and having babies. You've heard, haven't you? Katy's pregnant and I have my suspicions about Leinani. The way Tray's been since she got hurt, you know. It was so nice having the castle full of kids for a little while! Wouldn't it be lovely to have that again?"

Luke let Mrs. James blather on about the joy of children in the palace for a short time before realizing that it was a conversation that she couldn't get out of without drastic measures. "I have work to get back to," she said, nearly rudely. It was hard to overcome her ingrained habit of deference to elders.

Mrs. James waved her away. "Let me know if you find baby things in the storage room!" she exclaimed.

The storage room behind the kitchen was opened with Luke's master key and she felt the spell that protected it wash over her with recognition.

It was a room crowded with dusty computers and printers, with boxes of cables and adapters and cartridges that might or might not actually fit anything. The labels were largely unhelpful: "Cables." "Stuff." "Toren's room cleanup." "Kenth's old crap." "Don't throw this away."

The box of miscellaneous old phones was the size of a suitcase, a geological trove of phones that got bigger and clunkier as Luke dug down into it.

They were all dead, of course, but she found adapters for most of them in the "Cables" box and lugged it all back to her office, locking the door behind her.

It was a tedious job, charging each phone and checking the messages for a date. She kept the strata of the box itself intact so that she could narrow in on the dates that she was looking for. Each one required the use of an unlocking spell that she had carved on a flat stone disc, and Luke felt like she was watching the letters grow fainter with every pass.

But finally, she found what she was looking for…and dreading.

Fask had texted Kenth in the evening. "Job for you at winter camp. Clean up shore. Be there first thing in the morning."

The text showed as viewed but wasn't answered.

Fask had *sent* Kenth to the very place that their mother died, the morning that it had happened.

Luke scrolled back to see if there were examples of more of this level of micromanagement, but Fask's other communication with Kenth must have been in person or by phone. There were a few records of short calls between them, and they were in a few group texts together, but nothing else.

By itself, it would have meant nothing. It didn't indicate any wrongdoing. It just assigned Kenth a task.

A task that turned deadly.

Luke put the phone down and stared at her wall.

It wouldn't have been fatal to Kenth if he'd been caught in a flash flood. He was a dragon, able to shift and get away. The worst he'd get was wet, maybe tumbled in some ice. Embarrassed, maybe.

Was it meant as a prank?

And how could Fask coordinate a flash flood?

Luke turned over possibilities in her head as she got up to pace. Could he fly upstream and loosen an ice dam? It seemed unlikely that there was a convenient jam that he could unleash at exactly the right time. Morning wasn't the time those usually happened—it would be later, at the hottest point of the day. And why would he *kill* his mother?

## CHAPTER 15

Luke was missing something.

There was some vital piece of information that would tie this all together, make everything make sense, in this puzzle where *nothing* made sense.

Who could control a spring thaw? Should she dismiss this as merely coincidence? What role did Fask play in the betrayal of the kingdom?

Luke's frustration was so keen that she was unsurprised when there was a knock at her door.

Drayger.

"Booty call!" he sang, because of course he would.

## CHAPTER 16

Drayger was drawn to Luke's office like he was on a fishing line, her despair and frustration cutting through even her desire.

The guards outside her door tried to stop him. "Captain Luke doesn't want to be disturbed," one of them said grimly.

"Oh, she definitely wants to be disturbed by me," Drayger assured her, reaching past to knock on the door. "Booty call!"

Both guards snorted to hide their surprised laughter.

The office door opened. "What do you want?"

"I'm here to show you pleasure you've never so much as imagined," Drayger said.

Luke didn't laugh, just crossed her arms and waited for a better answer.

"I guessed that you hadn't paused for dinner, with everything that was going on with Raval's return, and I snagged you a ham croissant from the kitchen," Drayger said, glad that he actually had.

Luke thawed a fraction and stepped aside. "For a ham

croissant, you can come in. I have some questions I want to send along through your sources."

Drayger grinned broadly and wiggled his eyebrows at the guards. "She'lll be *interrogating* me for a good long while," he assured them as he backed into the room. "Don't worry if we're in here for quite some time. Don't interrupt. No matter *what* you hear!"

"Drayger," Luke said warningly, and then he was shutting and locking the door behind them and settling down to business.

As much as he would have loved to use their time the way that he'd implied to the guards, Drayger's first order of business actually *was* to get Luke to eat. "I know you skipped dinner," he scolded her. "I endured nearly an hour of political nonsense and it's Renewal this and Renewal that, and who's going from each country and what all of this means diplomatically. Fask thinks that the New Siberian Islands are going to pull out of the Small Kingdoms treaty altogether."

"That would complicate the Renewal," Luke said with a scowl, refusing to let Drayger hand feed her. "What are you doing? Stop that. It's not romantic, if that's what you're going for. I can feed myself."

Despite her cross words, she was genuinely touched by his offering of food and Drayger vowed to find out all her favorite treats and bring them to her.

She took the ham croissant and Drayger had to remind himself that flaky French bread products were not supposed to be that sexy. Or maybe they were; the French were celebrated lovers, after all.

"Pull yourself together," Luke snapped. "I don't have time for smutty distractions."

"I think I'll add that to my titles," Drayger said. "Drayger of Majorca, Deposed Lord of Tramuntana,

Smutty Distraction. Handsome in Exile. I'll have business cards made up."

He could feel her soften with humor that didn't make it to either her face or her shoulders as he settled in the chair across the desk from her and propped his feet up. Was there just a hint of a smile at the corner of her eyes? He wouldn't have noticed it if he didn't feel it in his head.

"What did you find?" he asked, when she had inhaled the croissant and washed it down with whatever was in the bottom of her coffee cup. Probably not booze. She was better than him.

"Do you know what my people said about the first king?" Luke asked, toying with an older model phone.

"Ladranyikayer," Drayger said. He liked to shrug off the idea of book learning and history, but only because he wanted people to underestimate him. He knew all the kings of the Small Kingdoms back to the beginning and still felt foolish for not recognizing the children as the first ones. To be fair, time travel had not been considered possible. "He united the Native people of Alaska and was accepted as their ruler without bloodshed."

"The Real People gave him three impossible tasks, according to our traditional stories. They charged him with filling our stores with food and our seas with fish, with proving his loyalty to our ancestors, and to making it possible to span long distances without moving.

"I assume he did so, since he was accepted as your king? Did he use magic?"

"He taught us techniques for agriculture and harvest that we still use today, to get the most from our land without stressing it, scaling up to account for a population that seemed mythical at the time. He united all our tribes by giving us a common language and bringing the technology of print, which allowed us to communicate over great distances. And he walked among the ancestors in the sky and sea and changed his shape to fly and swim with them. We let outsiders believe that it was just a story, of course, but my people have always known that our rulers bridged the spirit world and our own."

"All of Alaska?"

"All of the Real People. We let the history fade to fanciful legend."

"What do you think of the fact that the spirits came from another place and brought about the Compact in order to prevent a war with dragons?" Drayger asked.

"It is not more of a revelation than finding out that what I thought was a spirit ancestor was the sentient form of a complicated spell," Luke said frankly. "All the things I thought I knew, all the truths that seemed so clear...now none of it is. I don't know who to trust, or where to turn. Fask, my cousin, he's done something awful, something I don't think I want to know."

She pushed the phone across the desk at him and Drayger read the message.

"Fask *sent* Kenth to the place their mother died?" It didn't make sense.

"*Nothing* makes sense," she snarled, like she'd read his mind. Drayger didn't think their bond went that far—certainly he couldn't pick words from the feeling of her in his head. It was just that she knew him that well.

"It's not enough to build a case," Drayger said thoughtfully. "This doesn't prove anything. It raises more questions than it answers. Was it just a coincidence?" He scrolled back through the texts, but there wasn't much there.

"I'm starting not to believe in coincidence," Luke said dryly, and there was a sudden shift of tension in the room that Drayger wasn't sure was hers or his.

## CHAPTER 16

"Luke—" Drayger started. He could feel how keyed up she was, how turned on and tuned in she was.

"Don't..."

"Alasie, then." He put his boots down on the floor and leaned forward over the desk to her. "You said you didn't know who to trust or where to turn. I don't either, except for you. I trust you. And you can trust me." He reached forward and tapped her on the forehead. "And we can get to the bottom of all of it before the Renewal and get the Compact back in order and all the magic back in the genie bottle because there are no two people in the world like you and I together."

"You want to be the hero," Luke said softly, gazing back at him in a way that looked straight into his heart. "You feel like you have things to make up for."

Drayger had a moment of sizzling hatred for the mate bond that made him so transparent to her, terrified that she would see more than he wanted her to.

"If I stay in here any longer, your guards are going to think things that aren't true..."

Luke sighed. "You're right."

"We could just *do* those things..." Drayger suggested, not entirely teasing.

"Get out," she said.

CHAPTER 17

Everyone wanted to talk to Raval the next day, making it frustratingly hard for Luke to catch him alone.

"Your Highness," she said, jogging to catch him in the hall. "May I have a moment of your time?"

"I promised Mackenzie I'd get those photos downloaded for her," Raval said bluntly. "Will it take long?"

Raval appreciated concrete and quantitative answers. "Give me five minutes," Luke said. "It's a matter of kingdom security."

He considered, nodded, and followed her to her office without further comment.

"I wanted to ask you about your conversation with Fask last night," Luke said as soon as the door was locked behind him and the privacy spell was activated. There was no reason to beat around the bush, and sometimes weak spells that went in sideways about things could be circumvented with direct pressure.

"In the library?"

"After the library. You went to the vault and he met you there. You were *angry*."

Luke was looking hard at his face and even Raval, who could be hard to read, was completely transparent. He had no idea what she was talking about. "I overheard you arguing," she said gently, "but I couldn't tell what you were arguing about. Do you remember?"

Raval shook his head slowly. He wasn't dismissing her words outright, but he clearly didn't believe them, either. "I don't remember seeing Fask after the library. I tucked Katy into bed, and I went…I went…I had to…"

Raval's eyes went distant. "There was something…"

Luke tried to breathe quietly and not disrupt him. All spells faded, and if he could shake this off…

"I went to the vault," Raval said thoughtfully. "I checked my hoard and then I went to bed. It was early, but I was very tired. I'm not sure how time zones work when you're time traveling, but it feels like there's jet lag involved."

"Do you remember what you did in the vault?" Luke prodded. "Did you see anyone?"

Raval shook his head. "I didn't see anyone. Why? Was something stolen?"

*Your memories*, Luke thought, but she didn't say it out loud.

"Nothing is missing," she said. "But if you remember anything else, any tiny little detail, anything that doesn't seem to fit the rest, please come tell me."

It had been close to five minutes. Raval stood. "I will, Captain," he promised. Did he look slightly dazed and distant? The expression wasn't that out of character for him.

When he left, Luke pulled up the duty roster and found the guards who had been patrolling the stairs to the secure area underground. She texted each of them in turn, knowing it was their off hours, and was pleased by their prompt responses anyway.

"Did you see Raval leave the vault last night?" she asked each one. "Was anyone with him?"

Both of them confirmed that Fask and Raval had come up the stairs together, just as Luke had overheard.

Luke's immediate desire was to share the results of her conversation, unsatisfying as they were, with Drayger. But she was already spending too much time with the infuriating man and she knew that it was inviting gossip to seek him out unnecessarily. He could gather his own intel and she could gather hers and they would exchange information when circumstances made it convenient.

She *certainly* wasn't trying to find an excuse for another kiss.

Had Toren told his brother about catching them? Luke wasn't sure what to think of Toren anymore. At one point, he'd been young and annoying and would tattle on anyone, but he wasn't that little boy anymore, and he'd matured rather impressively in the past several months in particular. Carina must know, and Luke found herself *hoping* that she had told the other mates.

She was so *tired* of secrets.

Had it started with Kenth's secret child? Or before that, trying to keep Tray and Leinani's elopement a secret? Of course, that had turned out to be a kidnapping, not a willful flight.

Why was this so complicated? she wondered, steepling her forehead on her hands. It was bad enough that she was embroiled in ugly politics and treachery.

But why did her heart have to get involved?

She could feel that tantalizing promise of the mate bond, that possible future of perfect happiness with

Drayger, in Drayger's arms, in Drayger's heart. She'd been attracted to him before, and she had reluctantly started to trust him, even to *like* him, but this was far more dangerous. This was more than having a common goal. This was like having a common *soul.*

*It has been a long time since we had a good tumble in the snow,* her bear reminded her wistfully. *It always makes you feel good.*

If she let herself, Luke could be swept up in passion and partnership, and she was afraid of how much she longed for that outcome. It wouldn't work out that way. It *couldn't* work out that way. Their bond made no sense. It was a mistake, a flaw in the broken code of the Compact, and if she hoped for a happy ending too hard, she would only be disappointed.

She wasn't the heroine in the fairy tale, she was the sidekick, the trusted advisor.

This was supposed to be *Fask's* story.

And it looked like Fask was the *villain.*

## CHAPTER 18

Drayger resisted his dragon's urge to find Luke and comfort her.

He could feel all of her prickles and despair, even if he couldn't tell what had set her off. He wanted to wrap her up in his arms, tease her into laughing, and lay her down on a soft bed and strip off her clothing to make sweet, sweaty love to her.

Dammit, he always circled back to that, even when he was trying his hardest to stay professional in his own mind because she would pick up what a terrible, horny, base creature he was.

*I don't understand your reluctance*, his dragon scoffed. *Your urges are natural to your flesh and you are meant to be together.*

*It's not that simple*, Drayger protested.

In some ways, it was better if she thought he was only dreaming about the sex they might have, because otherwise she might see how much he craved her in purely cerebral ways.

Let her believe his needs were only carnal, not that he was desperate for her affection…and her friendship.

"Ah!" Drayger sprang to his feet as Kenth came in. He'd been lurking in the informal dining hall, where Mrs. James usually had a modest spread of between-meal snacks to graze on. It had been started when the castle was crawling with hungry children, but she had continued it out of optimism or habit. "It's my favorite disgraced brother!"

Kenth scowled at him. Maybe that scowl came from his mother's side, because it was eerily similar to Captain Luke's. "What do you want, Majorca?"

"Same as you, Alaska," Drayger said flippantly. "A decent cup of coffee and a strip of fish. I'll give you that, your Pacific salmon beats our Atlantic salmon."

Kenth took a piece of the smoked fish from the buffet and put it on a plate, not looking amused.

"I was thinking about heading out for a short flight today," Drayger said chummily. "My wings haven't been stretched in far too long."

"Good for you," Kenth said shortly.

"It did make me wonder, though, when was the last time you saw Fask shift?"

Kenth stared at him like he'd gone mad, which wasn't entirely unwarranted. Drayger did feel slightly crazy, like everything was flying out of control.

"Who cares?"

"No really, think about it," Drayger persisted. "When did you last see him shift?"

"He was at the raid on Amara's place in Ecuador," Kenth said dismissively.

"But no one saw him as a dragon there. He went in with Captain Luke on the ground level."

Drayger reminded himself not to have any stray thoughts about Luke as he said her name.

"To *protect* the captain," Kenth said. "As a *dragon*."

"Which proved unnecessary," Drayger pointed out. "So when was the last time you *actually* saw him shift?"

Drayger watched Kenth's scowl turn thoughtful. "Huh. I can't remember. We did all the time as kids, but…it's been a few years now, at least. It's not like we've been chummy." Then he seemed to remember who he was talking to and looked irritated. "Not that it's your business."

Drayger put his hands up peacefully. "Just making conversation," he said. "Seemed curious, that's all."

Kenth turned back to the snacks, loading up his plate with vegetables and cookies.

"Majorca."

Drayger had been concentrating so hard on shutting Luke out of his mind that he hadn't noticed her approach and he had to quell the rush of tenderness that her voice set off. Could he pretend hard enough that it was just lust that she'd be fooled?

Luke tipped her head to Kenth. "Your Highness."

"I'm just leaving, Captain," Kenth said. "He's all yours."

"Just what you always wanted," Drayger quipped.

"It's like Christmas," Luke said sarcastically. "I'm going over the notes from the raid and I want your testimony in some form that wasn't written like a soap opera."

"Hey," Drayger protested, "I spent a lot of time on that write-up."

"I am not putting a file in the official records that uses the phrase *glorious manhood*."

"It does have a ring to it, doesn't it?"

"Just come to my office and give me a clean version of the account that won't shame the kingdom."

Luke didn't wait for him to follow, but turned on her heel and strode away.

"She can't *wait* to get me alone," Drayger observed slyly to Kenth. "Coming, Captain, darling!" he called, springing after her.

## CHAPTER 19

As dangerous as Drayger had always been, now he was a hundred times more, because Luke couldn't keep her feelings safe from him.

But to her surprise, although he teased her mercilessly, and made it clear with his grin and the arch of his eyebrow that he knew whenever she felt that zing of lust that she'd always tried to deny, when her office door shut behind them and ensured their privacy, he was all business.

They both knew what was at stake, and how short their stolen time together was, and they used it wisely, exchanging what they had discovered and trying to make sense of the betrayal in the castle. Luke told her about her efforts with Raval, Drayger confirmed that no one he'd talked to had seen Fask shift in recent memory.

Luke pursed her lips. "We have to assume that Fask can use his memory-erasing spell at any point, and there's no point in confronting him directly."

"Would it work on more than one person at once?" Drayger asked. "It's possible that if we were both there we could overpower him."

"There's an equal chance that it would affect everyone in range," Luke countered. "And we'd still have to convince everyone *else* of his betrayal. We need evidence beyond our own testimony before we try something direct."

"Raval knew something," Drayger mused. "If we knew what that was…"

"I've tried questioning him," Luke said, pacing in frustration. "He doesn't remember anything about that trip to the vault. I don't have access to the vault, and you certainly don't."

"Do we know for sure he was in the vault?" Drayger pressed. "Could he have gone to speak with Nathaniel or Amara?"

Luke cast back over the conversation she'd overheard, wishing she'd thought to write it down while it was fresh in her mind, or record it on her phone somehow. "Fask *suggested* that he had been," she said suspiciously. "When Raval wondered what he was doing there."

"But he's an unreliable witness," Drayger said. "Maybe it doesn't have anything to do with the vault at all."

"Amara or Nathaniel might have the answers we're looking for," Luke said, trying not to feel hopeful. Was it her own hope, or Drayger's? If she had ever thought to imagine it, she would have expected a mate bond to be unpleasant, particularly with him. She had enough in her head without someone else crowding in with their own doubts and sensibilities.

But Dragyer was a breath of fresh air there. She'd always thought he was self-centered and egotistical, but the truth was that he was constantly thinking of others, and he had a sunny sweet optimism that he hid with his crude jokes and rough humor.

So much of his carelessness was an act, and Luke recognized that she was exactly the same way, hiding her sensitivities and insecurities behind a facade. If she chose cool distance and he chose hamming it up and making a clown of himself, they were still remarkably similar in their methods of sheltering behind a social mask.

She shook herself back to focus. "Maybe Raval confronted one of them with some new facts from the past. Maybe they confessed something to him. He would have access to any of those rooms, and he's a caster, he might have brought some kind of truth or conviction spell. Maybe it's still in effect."

"Spells fade," Drayger reminded her. "We might not have much time, if that's what happened."

Luke nodded. "I'll go down and question them both as soon as possible."

Drayger snapped to attention and saluted her. "What are my directives, Captain, sir?"

Luke told herself not to laugh or let her expression soften, then remembered that he'd know that he'd amused her anyway. "See if Mackenzie knows anything about forgetting spells," she suggested. "Find out whether there are any in that ream of spells we got from Amara. They should have been documented when they came in, see if something's missing. And see if you can find a way to neutralize it."

"Sir, yes, sir, Captain Hotpants, sir!" Drayger said, wiggling his eyebrows.

"You are an *ass*," Luke said, and if it didn't sound particularly fond, Drayger would know that it was.

## CHAPTER 20

"Ah, Mackenzie!"

Mackenzie was helping Dalaya get snacks in the informal dining room, and she startled at Drayger's loud greeting and looked around as if she'd been caught doing something naughty.

"Hello, Dalaya," Drayger said. "Done any drawing lately?"

Mackenzie looked as cross as Drayger had ever seen her look, and a little afraid.

Dalaya, on the other hand, split into a giant grin. "Mr. Drayger! I can draw if Mackenzie is there and I'm very, very careful."

Drayger made a show of crouching and tiptoeing closer very carefully and Dalaya giggled.

As the only remaining child in the castle, she was getting very used to a lot of extra attention, but Drayger thought that between Mackenzie's caution and Kenth's protectiveness, she was probably not going to suffer too much for being slightly spoiled. "What's good to eat?" he asked, straightening.

Dalaya showed him all of her favorites, and tried to sneak a second cookie onto her plate. Mackenzie made a noise of disapproval and the cookie went onto Drayger's plate instead.

"Thank you, darling," he said easily, ruffling her hair. When Mackenzie turned away to pour herself a drink, he slipped the cookie back onto Dalaya's plate to her wide-eyed delight.

He was stuffing a replacement cookie into his mouth when Mackenzie returned and he gave her an innocent look. "I actually had a few questions for you," he said winningly. "About a forgetting spell."

Mackenzie glanced at Dalaya, who was doing a terrible job of hiding the new cookie on her plate behind a carrot stick.

"Why don't you go eat at the little table," Drayger suggested. "I've got super boring questions for Mackenzie and we can sit over here in the grown up seats."

Dalaya quickly picked up on his hint and went scrambling to the little table that had been set up for her near a window while Drayger herded Mackenzie just out of easy earshot.

He guided her to a seat where she could watch Dalaya from a distance and took the seat next to her. "I've got a friend that I'm worried about. Not so much a friend as an associate, really, but they've lost a really selective memory and I'm concerned that a spell might have gotten them. Did Amara have anything that could do that?"

He liked to use just enough truth, a structure of honesty shrouded in misdirection. It didn't feel quite so much like a lie, even if it was.

Mackenzie relaxed a little as Dalaya waved a cheerful carrot stick from her table. "She didn't have a spell," she said. "But she did have an artifact. Her attempts to copy it with the children were unsuccessful but it had many uses left."

"What does it look like? Did we get it from Amara during the raid?"

Mackenzie flinched and Drayger realized he'd let himself get too intense. He slouched more deliberately and made a show of accidentally dropping a crumb in his lap; acting embarrassed about tiny social slip-ups would often invite sympathy and put someone else at their ease. "Oh goodness, I'm a barbarian," he said, fishing the crumb from his lap and popping it into his mouth. "It's amazing they allow me in polite company."

Mackenzie gave a nervous little chuckle.

"I'm sorry, ma'am. You should not have to suffer my ill manners. I'll try to keep my food in my mouth herewith. Come, what were we talking about before I betrayed my poor upbringing?"

"A memory spell," Mackenzie reminded him with a giggle. "Amara's artifact."

"Right. Maybe I'm under one!" he laughed. "I clearly have a memory like a goldfish."

"I drew a fish." Dalaya had gotten bored at her table and had come to his elbow. "It came to life. Can I have another cookie?"

"We're careful not to do that anymore," Mackenzie reminded her.

"You can have one more cookie if you sit at your table and eat the rest of your crackers first," Drayger told the little girl before Mackenzie could deny it. "Just one," he said, smiling winningly at the child.

Dalaya wasn't going to question her good luck and scampered to the buffet to touch every single cookie that was out before deciding on one to eat.

"What did the artifact look like?" Drayger asked casually.

Mackenzie was back to watching Dalaya, giving Drayger only half her attention at best. "It was a bracelet, an etched brass cuff. About this thick."

The Alaskan castle wasn't nearly as cold and drafty as many old European palaces, but most of the inhabitants wore long sleeves, even if they weren't actively wearing uniforms. It would be easy to wear a bracelet without being detected, and Fask in particular was never caught in something as casual as short sleeves.

"How selectively does it work?" Drayger asked casually. "My friend doesn't seem to realize they're missing half their memory of that night, and they weren't drinking, so I can't even blame it on that."

Mackenzie licked her lips self-consciously, then seemed to remember the napkin in her lap and gave her mouth a lady-like pat. "It's, ah, a fairly complex enchantment. Memories are tricky, and they have roots in so many things. The spell attacks whatever the person is thinking of most strongly at the time, and tries to erase all the things that lead to it."

"Are the memories actually erased?" Drayger asked, careful to keep his voice gentle and his eating casual.

Mackenzie shook her head. "Imagine that they are muffled in cotton. And of course, it's a spell, so it can't last forever. Bits and pieces peek through, like a dream at first, and eventually, in a few weeks or a month, they are all back."

*A ticking time bomb*, Drayger thought. But maybe Fask didn't need very long. He only had to keep his nose clean for a little while, until he'd secured power.

Until the Renewal.

Whatever Fask's plan was, it clearly centered around the ritual that rewrote the Compact.

"Do you know if we found that bracelet during the raid?" Drayger asked. "Could it be here?"

Mackenzie gave a helpless little shrug. "I don't know. It probably would have been kept with the listening ring and the control stone and Amara's other most valuable artifacts."

Fask had the listening ring. He probably had the bracelet, too.

"I wonder if there's a way to break the memory spell early," Drayger said, as if he was simply musing out loud. "My friend lost something they'd really like to get back and it would be nice not to have to wait a few weeks for him to find it."

If they could unlock whatever information that Raval had found, maybe they could stop Fask before the Renewal.

Mackenzie looked at him thoughtfully. Did she believe him? There was a distrustful look to her transparent face, but that was very much in character for her...and no wonder.

"Sometimes, if you can present the victim with evidence, it can be enough to break through the momentum of the spell. A photograph or recording of them doing something they don't remember might work."

That didn't help Drayger. If they had a photograph or recording, they wouldn't need Raval's memory at all.

"Is there a way to block the artifact from affecting someone else?"

Mackenzie considered, then reluctantly said, "I don't remember for sure, but it required touching the bracelet, so if you could stop them from doing that, I suppose?"

Drayger decided to change the subject. "Oh, say, have they made any inroads on finding your father's identity?"

Mackenzie's whole face changed from wary to anxious and excited and eager. How had she survived so long in the cult without learning to hide her feelings better? Drayger wondered. Maybe she had tried not to *have* them.

"It's been confirmed," Mackenzie said breathlessly. "The second son of the king of New Siberian Islands really *is* my *father*. Fask is going to see about arranging a meeting."

Drayger impulsively hugged her and kissed her on each cheek. "You must be so happy!" he said expansively.

He guessed the danger of his rash expression of easy affection as Dalaya shrieked, "Daddy!" and bolted for the door behind them.

Drayger turned to face Kenth, keeping a friendly hand on Mackenzie's shoulder. He rarely admitted he'd done something wrong, finding that brash certainty was the best move every time. "Your gorgeous mate might meet her father!" he exclaimed. "This is such exciting news! *Princess* Mackenzie!"

Kenth glared at Drayger's hand as he scooped a dancing Dalaya into his arms, but looked a little uncertain behind his scowl. He'd obviously expected Drayger to regret his forward touch and now he was doubting his own reaction.

Mackenzie rose to her feet, gathering up her empty plate, and Drayger picked up her forgotten napkin from the floor for her. "We just finished a snack," she said, looking flustered as she accepted it.

"Speaking of snacks," Drayger said, "I'm going to go make myself presentable for supper. You would not believe how much work it takes to look this good."

## CHAPTER 21

Luke resisted her urge to drag a hand along the cool stone wall of the hallway below the castle. She remembered visiting her Aunt Esme as a child. The Alaskan princes were several years younger than her, and she'd resented having to play childish games with them. Security had been considerably more lax then, and she had sometimes escaped the tiresome brothers and diplomatic duties by hiding down here.

It wasn't much to explore, exactly, being just one long hallway with no turns, but the sealed door to the vault were inset just enough to feel like a secret little private space. There were other doors, to the *dungeons*, but they were further down, and even Alasie (she had been more Alasie than Luke then) was afraid to go that far alone.

"We'll never need those," Kenth had scoffed when they spoke of them in hushed tones. "Alaska doesn't have bad people." He must have been ten, or possibly only nine, because Fask was not quite a teenager then.

Alasie, who was very much a teenager, already knew that even Alaska had its share of bad people, and she suspected that Kenth was only trying to pick a fight with his brother. Fask was very invested in royal guard games, catching imaginary criminals and bringing them to pretend justice with grave punishments.

She walked past the vault door now. They wouldn't open for her, and the vault wasn't her destination anyway.

The next door was the one where Amara was held, the following one was Nathaniel's cell, and the final one was the prison that had been repurposed to hide the dragon form of The Dragon King himself.

Luke hesitated at Amara's door. She had already done formal interrogations, but planned to question them both again. She was in the habit of doing the hardest tasks first, but she was not sure which of these would be the most challenging. Amara was not to be discounted, no matter how mad she'd become, and Luke would need her wits to navigate their conversation.

But Nathaniel…

Luke sighed and walked on. This would hurt worst, no matter how the conversation went.

The cells barely deserved that title.

They were not at all grim or dark. There was warm wood paneling on every wall, and thick carpet on the floor. Each room had bookshelves and minifridges. To any casual view, they were each beautifully appointed suites, with private bathing facilities and all the comforts of home. They simply had no windows, and they were uncannily, uncomfortably silent.

The door to Nathaniel's room opened when Luke spoke her name and lay her hand flat on it.

He looked up from the couch where he was reading with heartbreaking hope on his face that faded when he took in her expression.

"Come in," he invited politely. "Make yourself at

home."

"Is there anything you need?" Luke asked, drawing a chair from the desk to sit across from him.

"Nah," Nathaniel said with a shrug of one shoulder. "They aren't starving me. Plenty to read. There's even beer." Then he looked wistful. "How are the dogs?"

Luke updated him on all of them, from Phoebe, who was quite over her own puppies, to Trixie, who had escaped a dozen times, to the unexpected return of Lancelot with Raval in the time-traveling car.

"He grew into those big paws?" Nathaniel said eagerly. "Good coat?"

"He lost most of the coat growing up in the tropics, but it will probably come back."

"In spades," Nathaniel agreed with a sad chuckle. "Those dogs are champion shedders."

There was an awkward silence then, and Luke finally said, "I wanted to ask you some questions."

Nathaniel's face shuttered. "I told you everything I know. Everything I remember."

Luke knew that it stung his pride that his word wasn't enough alone to clear his name. "Not about Amara or her spells. About Prince Fask."

Nathaniel's brows knit suspiciously. "What about him?"

Luke picked her words carefully. "Do you remember the last time you saw him shift?"

Nathaniel frowned. "He's been busy running the country. Hard to book a lot of flying time for fun."

"Think about it though," Luke encouraged. "When was the last time you saw him shift for sure?"

"Been a few years now," Nathaniel said, tapping his fingers on the spine of his book. "Before Kenth left, I think. Maybe before that. He kind of throws himself into his work."

"Do you know what happened with Kenth and Fask the day their mother died?"

Luke was careful to watch his face as she asked the unexpected question, but Nathan didn't betray anything but sorrow. "That was a true tragedy, that was. Your aunt was a good woman, kind and strong and loyal. She loved those boys so much."

"Why was she there? Kenth was supposed to be cleaning up the camp."

"He took that straight to heart, too," Nathaniel said mournfully. "I guess she just knew it needed done? It's the kind of job easier done by a dragon, but she never hesitated to do her share of any hard work." He gave her a brief smile that Luke tried to return. "A little like her niece."

"Does it seem odd to you that she got swept away in a sudden breakup flood? She grew up on the river, she knew the warning signs."

Nathaniel's shrewd look suggested he knew where Luke's mind had gone.

"You don't think it was an accident."

"I also don't know how it *couldn't* be an accident," Luke said mildly.

Nathaniel's impressive eyebrows knit thoughtfully and they were both quiet for a moment.

Luke struggled with her impulse to assure Nathaniel that she knew he wasn't guilty, that he hadn't had anything to do with Amara or undermining the country. She should at least keep some semblance of impartiality.

Was that its own kind of betrayal?

"Has Raval been to see you?" Luke asked at last. She hadn't wanted to open with that.

Nathaniel shook his head. "Toren came and told me

about his return. I'm glad he's back safely, even if it seems like a pretty wild story."

He hesitated, like he wanted to say something, then shrugged.

Luke wished she was the kind of person who could charm others, like Drayger. She wanted to set Nathaniel at ease and comfort him, and at the same time, continue to hold her cards close. She knew that this room was monitored. Drayger would be able to make Nathaniel laugh, whether he wanted to or not, and tease him to cheer without much effort.

Luke was not so charismatic.

She gave an irritated noise of frustration at her runaway train of thought and stood up decisively. "I still need to ask Amara a few questions."

Nathaniel stood with her. It was strange that he didn't have a dog to shove off his lap and Luke vowed to see what visitation rules were for animals. "Come back any time," he said gruffly. "I…appreciate the company."

Luke bit back the words she wanted to say. *I believe you.* "I'll see you again soon," she promised. They shook hands, warm and a little longer than pure politeness dictated. "Soon."

He nodded and Luke left the room and heard the door seal behind her with a little sizzle of magic. She wondered, as she left, if Tray had come by to visit him at all.

However painful and awkward visiting him was, she owed Nathaniel a great debt. His capture meant that the real traitor might slip up and she could be there to catch them.

The hallway was noisy after Nathaniel's room, even though it was quiet by any other standard, with just the barest far-off sounds of the castle, muffled by stone.

Amara's door opened just as easily.

## CHAPTER 22

If Amara had been a madwoman before, she was chillingly inhuman now.

She was completely insane, and not in a cute, funny way at all. She had scratched all of the furniture with her nails until they had broken and bled. Although she had been given toiletries, she had clearly chosen not to use them, and her long hair was wild around her face.

Raval and Tania theorized that working so much magic had a detrimental effect on someone, and that some of her madness had come from casting so much without proper magical buffering. Mackenzie had a quieter guess that losing her power and the worship of the Cause had broken a mind that was already a few cells short of a full brain.

Luke wondered if they should sedate her, but she hadn't been more than minorly self-destructive yet. The monitoring of the room included magical restraints that could be activated if necessary.

"You've all been to see me now," Amara said graciously when Luke unlocked her door and came in. "Truth, Kindness, Patience, Strength, Loyalty, Courage." She was sitting at the table, rearranging plastic cups in rainbow colors, like a little child.

"Those are the principles of the Small Kingdoms," Luke said, not sure how to apply them to this conversation. She gingerly took a seat across from the woman.

"Lies, Cruelty, Impulse, Weakness, Betrayal, Cowardice," Amara scoffed. "You will know them all," she predicted. "Sit down! There's tea!"

"I don't want tea," Luke said. "I have some questions for you."

"You have to ask the right ones," Amara said. "The wrong questions only get you the wrong answers."

She was about as helpful as the Compact was. "What do you have against the Kingdoms?" Luke asked. "You had power, money, magic. Why did you spend so much of your energy trying to defeat us?"

"Power has to be in the right hands," Amara said loftily. "The Compact should not hoard it. It is unnatural."

That tracked. Amara had spoken about how evil the Compact was before. "Why Alaska, though? Why not one of the other Kingdoms?"

She giggled. "Because I had friends here, of course."

"Who?" Luke asked sharply. Could it be this easy? "Who helped you?"

"A little voice in my head. Flowing water. A drink of tea."

It was never that easy. Even if Amara gave testimony, it was clearly mentally suspect.

"Do you know Prince Fask?" Luke prodded.

"Truth. Lies. He says he's one thing but he's something else."

That didn't tell Luke anything. "What about Raval?" she guessed.

"Kindness. Cruelty. And empty face and a full mind."

This was going nowhere fast.

"Have you *met* Raval?" Luke wanted to know. "In person? Last night, perhaps? Did you tell him something?"

Amara shook her head. "I have no interest in demons."

Her cult had called dragons *demons*, trying to spin them in an unflattering light to sow discord. If the Kingdoms had revolutions at just the right time, the Compact wouldn't be Renewed and she'd have her way, with wild magic unleashed on the world.

"You have to realize that if you destroy the Compact, the magic is chaos, that you won't have it anymore than anyone else would. No caster would need the structure of spells and it would burn the world."

Amara launched herself across the table at Luke, her fingers in grasping claws. "Wrong! You are wrong! It is the Compact that is chaos, keeping magic from the worthy people!"

Luke wasn't actually afraid of the woman's assault, but she was surprised and alarmed. It was instinct and muscle memory that had her raising a hand to block Amara's strike and use her momentum to bring her down. She twisted one of Amara's arms behind her back and knelt easily to pin her and hold her other arm harmlessly away.

"I don't want to hurt you!" she said.

Amara went limp. "Why not?" she asked in a tiny child's voice. "Why wouldn't you? I hurt the people you love."

Luke was surprised enough to answer honestly. "I don't believe in retribution as justice. There is enough pain in the world already."

"Do you think I will be punished enough in the afterlife?" Amara asked slyly, like she was trying to trap Luke.

Luke shook her head. "I don't believe in that kind of

afterlife. I would rather you learned in this life that what you did was wrong and willingly atoned for it."

"Atone," Amara echoed.

"I'm going to release you," Luke said. "Do not try to attack me again."

She stood but stayed alert and coiled to react as she cautiously let go of Amara and backed away.

Amara continued to lie on the carpet and Luke realized that she was shaking with laughter. "What's so funny?"

"That you think you will win this. All the pieces are already in play. You're too late to change anything. Magic is out of the bag. Everyone knows it, and they will blame the people who kept it from them."

Luke didn't like to think about that eventuality, but she was beginning to think that it was too big a secret to keep. Could shifters and casters live openly in the Small Kingdoms? Or would there be a purge of *different* and *frightening*, because people were afraid of what they didn't understand? They had to fight hard enough to equalize differences among non-magical humans, was the whole race simply incapable of harmony? She knew that the civil guard was strained to their limits trying to keep unrest from exploding

There was simmering resentment and fear everywhere.

Luke didn't have to answer those big questions, she just had to answer the immediate ones. "Do you know who betrayed Alaska?"

"I don't remember," Amara said, rolling to sit up and look directly into Luke's face. "Maybe you betrayed it by trusting your heart." She gave a toothy smile. "Your heart is in your chest, except when it's in your throat or your stomach. I don't remember! I don't remember!"

Was it all just nonsense? Luke felt like they were only going in circles and shutting Amara's door behind her was a great relief. It took a moment to clear the whirl from her mind. Amara was bizarrely charismatic even when she wasn't magically enhanced, and Luke felt dirty just listening to her for a short while. She started to stride back towards the steps to the castle and then paused.

There was one more door down here: the third cell where the Dragon King slumbered.

Luke turned on her heel and walked thoughtfully to it. "Alasie Luke," she said.

It sprang open like an invitation and Luke stepped in.

The dragon slept like a great mountain. Even his heartbeat was slow, and his breath was like a distant sigh of wind. The room configuration that had seemed so spacious for Amara and Nathaniel was filled almost to the ceiling and every corner with his great, gleaming form. All the furniture had been removed or pushed to the walls, but there was one chair pulled up beside him.

After only a moment of hesitation, Luke went to sit in it. The last visitor had left the light on.

"Your Majesty," she said. "*Uncle.*"

Her latest promotion had come after his mysterious ailment, but Luke thought that he would have been proud of her. He had welcomed her into his castle on her visits as a child, and encouraged her devotion to the guard. She remembered him as kind and cheerful, and as doting on his much younger wife while not ever treating her as anything less than an equal.

Even then Luke had recognized what a balancing act the man managed. He was fair but flexible, kind without being weak, and strong without ever sacrificing grace.

He was a good king.

He was a good man.

And now, for some reason, he was trapped as a dragon in a slumber that wouldn't end. What had been a curiosity had stretched into an anomaly and was now a tragedy.

Luke had come to visit him several times, not sure what her responsibilities as Captain of the Royal Guard entailed in this matter. At first, she gave him briefs of the kingdom as if she were reporting to him and he could hear her, but after a while, her visits became short courtesy calls, and finally she stopped making them altogether.

Was he still in there?

"A lot has happened since I was last here," she said, and she gave a dry laugh at the understatement.

*This* room did not have monitoring on it, and knowing that seemed to loosen Luke's tongue. She explained everything she knew as if he was listening attentively, nodding and encouraging in that way he had that never felt insincere. She told his unresponsive mass about Toren and Carina, Tania and Rian, Tray and Leinani and their kidnapping, Kenth and Mackenzie with their daring rescue of the children, Katy and Raval taking their trip back through time to the start of the Small Kingdoms. He probably knew some of the stories already; clearly at least one of the brothers had been visiting.

She explained the trouble with the Renewal and the out of control magic, and the way that the tide of approval was turning against the monarchy. She explained about Amara and her capture, which should have fixed everything but *hadn't*.

"I don't know what to do," she said plaintively. "Alaska is in trouble, the Renewal is at risk, Fask might be behind it, and I don't know who to trust or where to turn."

*Drayger.* She could trust *Drayger*. "Drayger is my mate," she confessed reluctantly. "And I know what to do with that least of all of it."

It was the first time Luke said it out loud. It was the

first time she'd really admitted it to herself. She knew what happened and she couldn't deny what she was experiencing. But it was the first time she allowed herself to realize what it *meant*.

Drayger was *her mate*. Their possible future was more wonderful and fulfilling than Luke had ever dreamed...and it didn't fit in her life in even the smallest way.

She stared at the Dragon King's hide. "I could love him," she said in wonder. "I could *love* him."

Did she already?

When she made a revelation, he was the first one she wanted to share it with. Every time she saw him, she was struck by how handsome and appealing he was. He was funny and clever and charming, and as hard as she tried to find him annoying and shallow, she knew that he wasn't, and it made her insides weak to think that all of his fake flirtation might actually be *real*.

She wanted to impress him, like she hadn't wanted to impress anyone since she accepted her calling and had her tattoos, her *tunniit*, etched into her chin as an expression of her commitment to her people.

The silence in the room was unnerving, nothing but her own words being absorbed by the walls and floors and the slow, steady heartbeat and shallow breathing of the dragon.

Luke stared across the room until her attention was caught by a chip of light that she couldn't quite explain. She stood and went to it, finding a small coin of etched glass in the carpet. It was faintly amber, but mostly clear, and had tiny lettering scratched all over it, too tiny to make actual words out of without magnification.

There were no other personal items in the room. It wasn't in a place likely to slip from someone's pocket. It looked like it had been hurled to this corner in anger.

Was it something from Amara's arsenal? Should she ask Raval or Mackenzie to look at it for her and see if they could puzzle out what kind of spell it was?

Just as Luke was about to slip it into her own pocket, a reflection caught her eye that didn't seem to be caused by anything in the room. She tilted it, trying to guess what might have caused it and just as she thought she might have only imagined it, she saw a tiny figure in the glass.

Luke turned it and drew it closer to her eye as the scene resolved.

At first she thought that it was a scrying device, that she was seeing into Fask's rooms and she had a pang of guilt that she might be spying on a private moment. Then she realized that it was a younger Fask by several years, and that the man he was facing was his father.

A recording? A critical moment in history? A moment of truth?

There was no sound with the image, but the king looked grim and appeared to be berating Fask. Then, to her horror, Luke watched Fask draw a dagger. She recognized it at once as the dragon-killing blade that was the second-most protected item in the vault.

The king looked disappointed, but not alarmed, until Fask lifted the blade in one hand and plunged it into the palm of the other. The king came to his feet, clearly yelling in surprise and lunging to stop him, and Fask pulled the blade out of his hand and drove it into the king's chest.

Luke had watched dragons shift many times in her life. It never lost its magical thrill to see a human blur into an elegant mythical form, flowing from one to the other almost seamlessly, like reality shivered in place. This was different. It was ugly and forced, and the king's dragon was dragged into physical being like an explosion of lava, the human form splitting and dissolving away with a scream of pain.

Luke felt sick watching it, but didn't dare look away and miss some critical part. The dragon thrashed once and grew still as lines of power seemed to drain from it into the bloody hole in Fask's hand. Fask wasn't a dragon, or the blade would have killed him. But it had *transferred* him his father's dragon power.

The king was dead, Luke thought, when the glass medallion went cool and still in her hand. Only his dragon had survived, crippled and constrained.

On a hunch, Luke lifted the glass and looked through it at the dragon's sleeping form. Ropes of power still pierced the creature, binding it in place.

## CHAPTER 23

Drayger was drawn by Luke's agitation to the top of the stairs down to the vault and the prisons.

"Can I help you?" one of the guards asked when he approached.

Drayger tried to think of some reason they might let him downstairs. He certainly had no excuse to be in that back hallway at all, unless... "I was invited by Captain Luke to interrogate the criminals. I can be *very* convincing, you know."

They did not offer to move aside, clearly making a liar out of him.

"I could text her?" Drayger offered, but when he did, there was no reply and his message didn't show as delivered. There was probably no reception down there.

He didn't think that straight-up charm would work on either of them, though he might have luck with the petite woman on the left if she were off-duty. There was just enough amusement behind her professional mask to suggest that she found him interesting. The grim brick on the right didn't look like his type, even supposing Drayger was his.

Was it worth trying to push past and see if they were willing to physically detain him? Desperate as he was, Drayger knew that it was a ridiculous notion. Even as a dragon, there would be safeguards in place to stop someone who wasn't of the Alaskan royal family.

Before he could test them, he heard a door shut, far below, and he would know the sound of Luke's boots on the stone floor anywhere he heard them.

"Oh, there she comes," Drayger said casually, as if he hadn't just considered charging past the guards. "I'm sorry, but I'll have to tell her how tragically unhelpful you were. I hope you don't get demoted."

"Majorca!" Luke stomped up the stairs like a stormcloud. "Stop harassing my guards!"

"Harassing? Guys, back me up, was I harassing you?"

Then Luke was springing up the last step and dragging him backwards by one elbow. "I've got questions for you, Majorca," she spat.

For a moment, Drayger was genuinely alarmed. Had one of the two prisoners pinned something on him? Would Luke believe the worst of him? Had he lost her trust? This was the moment he'd dreaded more than any other, when she'd turn on him like everyone else in his life had...

But the churning feeling of her emotions in her head didn't seem aimed at him, and Drayger quickly realized that he was part of some ruse. "I'll come willingly!" he exclaimed, putting his hands at the back of his head. He winked at the guards. "Should be fun!"

"March!" Luke snarled, prodding him before her.

"Yes sir, Captain, sir!"

She didn't let her stiff stride betray anything but anger

until they were in her office, the door shut safely behind her, when she went unexpectedly limp against it in a slump of abject despair.

"You found something out," Drayger said, lowering his hands from his head and letting his grin slide away. "Something you don't like. I'm so sorry."

"*Fask*. Fask *isn't* a dragon. But he *has* a dragon. He's stolen his father's dragon, or at least his power. I suspect it all ties in with how Amara was able to steal the dragon power from Tray and Leinani, the chaos magic she unleashed in Dalaya and Mackenzie, but it was *Fask* all along."

"He *was* a dragon," Drayger said. "Everyone agrees that he was once. What happened to him?"

Luke let her fists thump onto the door behind her in an uncharacteristic release of her anger. "I don't know," she said, drawing herself up to pace furiously. "He lost it somehow, at some point before their father slipped into his coma. After his mother died…or *when* his mother died."

"You think that's related?"

"I can't think that it's *not*," Luke said, gesturing helplessly. "I didn't want to believe this. I didn't want to think he was capable of *any* of this."

Drayger could not quite resist stepping forward to take her fluttering hands in his, hoping to comfort her. "Let's think it through. What *reason* would he have for an agenda like this? What has he got against Alaska?"

He could feel the firmness of his grip steady her. "If he'd somehow lost his dragon, he'd know that the Compact would never pick him to rule Alaska," she said mournfully. "That could be why there was that push to change and neuter the Compact. If he couldn't be the king of Alaska, he didn't want anyone else to be? Or he thought he could manipulate people into accepting him as king if it was screwed up enough?"

"Do you think he hired me to kill his brother?" Drayger said in sympathetic horror.

"It looks like he was capable of killing his mother," Luke said darkly. "And I know he killed his father."

*His mother was her aunt*, Drayger remembered.

But the worst of it, of course, was Fask's betrayal. "I'm so sorry," he said again, helplessly. "I know you didn't want it to be true. Hell, I didn't want it to be true."

"You warned me," she said. "You told me not to trust him."

"Yeah, but that's me," Drayger said, desperate to lighten the situation. "Who trusts *me*?"

He momentarily forgot that Luke would see through his bluster, and he was surprised by the rush of warmth and affection through their mate bond. He was still holding her hands but he let her go when she made the slightest tug for freedom.

Then she caught him completely by surprise by stepping into him and catching him up in a ferocious embrace. "*I* trust you," she murmured against his neck.

"Luke," Drayger said into her hair. "*Alasie*."

Luke was the uniform she wore. Alasie was the woman underneath, vulnerable and beautiful.

He wanted her, rather desperately, but he wanted this more. He could survive without food and air if he could hold her in his arms like this and soothe away the sharp edges in her mind. When she relaxed in his embrace it was like an orgasm all in itself, a sweet release, a surrender.

She fit there so perfectly, her head resting against his, her body snugged up to his. One leg was against his, and she was so *warm* and strong and long against him.

His body wanted more, and he had to shift just a little

so he wasn't too obviously pressing his erection against her, but his heart could be content with this. She was his safety and security, his shelter in a storm, his inspiration. He thought that he understood why poetry was written, because ordinary prose could never capture the swell of emotions that he felt.

Even poetry seemed lacking, like words were incapable of defining something so precious and pure.

He loved her like he'd never imagined love could be, and he didn't think it was the mate spell showing him what might be—those future impressions were dreamy and distant, but this was immediate and raw. He loved this woman now and always, even if she never let him get any closer than this.

And then, to his surprise, she twisted in his arms and was pulling his face to hers for a kiss.

It wasn't like their first kiss, full of deception and sparked by magic. It wasn't like their second kiss, cautious and sweet. This was a kiss of claiming, and Drayger knew that he was hers, completely.

"What are you doing?" he asked, drawing back and desperate for her answer.

"You know what I want," she growled. "You can feel it from me."

Drayger held her face just apart from hers, a momentary power struggle as all of their boundaries and borders fell into new shapes. "Knowing what you want isn't the same as knowing what you're *doing*," he reminded her. "I want you clear-headed and complete. It can't be...angry or impulsive. Alasie, I love you. Not later, or maybe, but now, and I'll wait, if that's what it takes, for you to feel the same."

She froze in his hands, her eyes as big as her heart, and seemed incapable of speech. Drayger questioned his resolve. He was an idiot to miss this opportunity. This might be all they ever got. He should have just taken the sex and treasured the memory of it forever and he'd blown it being *noble* and what was even *wrong* with him?

*She's the one*, his dragon reminded him, drunk on the magic of the mate spell. *The one forever.*

But *forevers* were like happy endings, things from fairy tales meant for heroes, not screwups like him.

Then she was close again, her nose next to his as she said, "I *want* you. I want you to kiss me."

Drayger kissed her until he was dizzy from it and her lips must burn like his. He tangled his fingers into her hair, loosening it, but not quite releasing the bun. He kissed her deeply, dreadfully, fumbling like a virgin afraid of second base, tasting her, tantalizing and teasing until she pulled away again and panted, "I want you to touch me."

He got her uniform jacket off of her as slowly as he could manage, button by button, sliding it off her wrists and holding her pinned there, just for a moment with one hand, while he put his other hand down and cupped her. He ground his palm against her clit, testing the pressure she liked as she went incandescent in his head with excitement.

She was wearing a simple white t-shirt under the jacket, and her bra followed it to the ground. Drayger left lower parts to caress her modest breasts with both hands, teasing the nipples to hardness before he pulled her close up against him. This time, he *wanted* her to feel how hard he was for her, to press it just so and make her writhe against him.

"I want you to take your clothes off," she murmured.

She didn't have to say it twice.

Drayger shucked his shirt off over his head without bothering with any of the buttons, and heard stitches pop as he struggled with the clasp of his pants and she dealt with her own. They almost fell over, eager for every inch of uncovered skin, and then he was pressing her down on the couch and sliding in between her spread legs at last.

Drayger was a dragon, so he knew hot, and *Luke* was hot. His cock had never felt so alive and so desperate as it did now, thrusting deeper and harder and sweeter with every stroke. "Luke," he growled. "Alasie…"

The couch was awkwardly narrow, and after he'd brought her once to pleasure, he stood up, causing a cry of dismay and grasping hands, because she wasn't any more finished than he was. He pulled her up to her feet effortlessly and had to hold her there and kiss her and feel how their bellies fit together before turning her towards her desk and bending her over it.

Luke had a tidy desk, but even tidy desks had *things* on them. There was a name plate that went skittering onto the floor, and a dozen sticky notes that crumpled beneath them. A carved cup of pens fell over and rolled, hitting the computer monitor with a clatter before it fell off. A folder was shoved away to flutter into her chair.

She was even tighter this way, and so slick, and Drayger could feel how this angle gave her even sweeter sensation. He wondered how many times he could do this, bring her rolling through waves of tension and release, until she had one final crest that had her crying out and clenching around him and he was helpless to do anything but join her in a final, perfect pleasure. It felt as though the orgasm would never end, the echo of her satisfaction and his like a spiral of euphoria.

They lay on the floor afterwards, laughing and panting and petting each other.

"Told you," Drayger finally managed to say. "I *told you* it would be amazing."

Luke propped herself up on one elbow and grinned down at him. "You are insufferable," she said, but she leaned over and kissed him anyway, slow and lazy and full of all the things she'd never say.

Things like, *I love you.*

Even if he knew it.

## CHAPTER 24

Luke caught herself smiling at her guards three times the next morning, only realizing that she was when they looked puzzled and doubtful.

*Told you so*, her polar bear rumbled in satisfaction.

*You're as conceited as he is*, Luke retorted.

But her bear wasn't wrong. She felt *better*. It wasn't just dopamine from mind-blowing sex, she thought, when she tried to analyze herself. That definitely played a role in her contentment, but when she thought back over her sweaty encounter with Drayger, it wasn't the physical release that left her feeling like she was floating. That had been amazing, and it would be foolish to deny that her body had needed it, but it was his words that made her feel like she was suddenly complete.

*Alasie, I love you. Not later, or maybe, but now…*

He *loved* her.

She knew it was true, and she knew that the remaining doubts she had about being his mate—his *soulmate*!—were rapidly crumbling.

He *loved* her.

Luke had never thought to crave romantic love. She had a family's love, and her bear, and her job and her service to the kingdom. There was no *space* for more *love* in her life, until Drayger showed her all the holes she hadn't known were there in her heart. He filled them to overflowing, until she was dizzy with happiness and hunger.

He completed her.

He *loved* her.

She had to jerk herself back to the problems at hand several times throughout the day, and the biggest problem of all was *Fask*.

It felt disloyal to feel so happy when she knew that everything else was flying out of control. The Renewal was still charging down on them, the other kingdoms were at a level of political animosity that Luke was not sure she had ever seen. Fask was locked for hours in teleconferences with other royalty, sometimes with Toren at the younger prince's insistence, but mostly alone, often emerging like he'd gone rounds in a ring.

Luke had all of her usual duties on top of that, and her guards were not immune to the increased tension around the castle. She had personality conflicts to defray, and she still needed to speak to Fask about taking Nathaniel's favorite dog down to him. She was behind on correspondence and paperwork.

And despite all of that, Luke couldn't stop thinking about Drayger, about his clever fingers and hot mouth, the way he touched her with reverence and care.

She was ridiculously hungry, but she went past the informal dining hall straight for the throne room that afternoon and wasn't surprised to find Drayger lounging on one of the thrones.

"Those are reserved for the royal family," she said crossly.

He moved like a dancer, flowing out of the throne and stalking across the hall towards her. He always wore distractingly tight pants, but Luke found herself wondering if he hadn't shrunk these even more than usual.

Luke glanced down the hall behind her to ensure that the nearest guards were out of both sight and earshot and had to catch her breath when she looked back and caught sight of him again. Did he *have* to be so sexy?

He didn't slow down as he reached her, but swept her straight up into his arms the way that Luke had desperately wanted him to but hadn't actually thought he would.

"What are you doing?" she hissed, twisting from his embrace before he could kiss her.

"No one is watching," Drayger assured her as they danced apart. "We could do it right here, on one of the thrones. Fask's throne! It would serve him right."

"Cool your nuts, Majorca," Luke told him, trying not to laugh. "You are not getting laid in the throne room today."

"How do you know?" Drayger countered, striking a pose. "There are a couple of new housemaids who would be very willing."

Luke knew he was trying to make her jealous, but it worked. "Don't you *dare*."

To her surprise, he must have known the depth of her possessiveness, because he sobered and stepped forward to take her face in both hands. "There is no one for me but you," he told her. "I am yours *forever*."

Luke was a hot inch from taking him right there on Fask's throne after all when she heard noise in the hallway behind them. They bolted apart and she had to clench her hands into fists and control her breathing with effort.

"Are you two arguing again?" Tray wanted to know.

"Give it a rest, Drayger! Luke is never going to let you unbutton that uniform."

Luke felt her ears heat and hoped the flush wasn't noticeable. Maybe Tray would write it off as anger.

"Your Highness," she said respectfully through her clenched teeth, turning to tip her head.

"Fask has some questions for Drayger," Tray said. "He wanted to see him in the library. Something about Majorca pulling out of the Small Kingdoms. It's all very confusing and no one knows what that would mean for the Renewal."

Luke forced herself to stop thinking about Drayger unbuttoning her uniform. "We were done," she assured Tray shortly. "He's all yours."

"Lovely Luke," Drayger teased, clearly feeling the chaos in her core. "We will continue this *conversation* another time."

He paused to give her one of his oh-so-formal kisses to the cheek and whispered near her ear, "Fask will be out of his rooms for a time."

This was an opportunity, Luke realized, squashing her libido as she made a show of shoving Drayger away impatiently. "Don't waste your charm on me."

As Captain of the Guard, she had access to Fask's rooms. It was a privilege she had never had to use before, but this was her chance to check it for answers or some kind of concrete evidence that she could use with the other brothers.

She waited for Drayger and Tray to leave and found herself staring at Fask's throne, imagining what they could have done there. It was deeper than her couch, but the arms might get in the way…

Luke shook herself and stalked back down the hallway towards the wing where Fask's rooms were.

## CHAPTER 24

Her guards were at the door. "I need to get something for Fask," she said off-handedly and they didn't hesitate to step aside.

Fask's rooms looked as they always had—Luke had been in them many times consulting about security topics and even just catching up on castle gossip. Fask liked to have a hand in what was happening, and they often commiserated about the burdens of their duties over a glass of wine or whiskey.

They were friends, Luke reminded herself mournfully. They were friends and cousins. He was *family*.

And it all had been a lie.

She thought about the cold expression on his face when he stabbed his father. He wanted *power*, and he would stop at nothing to get it. Including befriending his cousin, the captain of the guard. Was her appointment his work as well? Luke was angrier at the idea that she'd been given some kind of favoritism because she might be easy to manipulate than any other part of his betrayal.

She surveyed the suite, analyzing all the hiding places. Fask liked a spare aesthetic, so it was free of clutter, which saved her that much headache at least.

She gave the desk a cursory rifle—she didn't think that Fask would be foolish enough to leave anything incriminating out, but it was possible he'd gotten sloppy. A locked file drawer obeyed the same unlocking spell that had opened his old phone, but there was only some token money, a non-magical gun, and top secret files that appeared to have nothing to do with the Renewal. One of them, a folder about the murder case that Carina had been accused of, did make Luke pause, but a quick flip through it didn't reveal any details that Luke didn't already know.

She tried the bedroom next, flipping through the reading material on his bedside stand and checking beneath the pillow and mattress. No confessional journals fell out and there were no burner phones with tell-tale numbers or bloodied daggers or artifacts to be found.

Luke could feel her frustration rising, and had a weird echo of Drayger's concern for her in her ears, but she blocked that out, taking her search to the bathroom. The cabinets were all quite tidy, with no unknown medication or bloodied grooming tools. There was nothing out of place, and she was running out of time.

"Can I help you find something?"

No, she *was* out of time.

Luke straightened from looking in the bottom bathroom drawer and quenched her stab of panic.

"Fask," she said evenly.

"Cousin," he replied. "I'm pretty sure you weren't looking for a spare hairdryer."

There was no point in lying, but Luke wasn't going to offer him any help, either. She remained quiet, waiting for Fask to draw his own conclusions. She looked beyond him and saw that the door to the hallway had been shut silently behind him.

"You talked to Raval," he said flatly.

"Is that a problem?" Luke asked mildly.

"It might be. It depends on what he told you."

Luke wondered how long they could dance and kept her silence.

"You've been different, cousin," he observed. "Distant."

"It's been stressful," Luke said blandly. "With the Renewal coming up. Attempts on the Compact. You know how it is. The security of the kingdom is in my hands."

Fask slipped a hand into his pocket and Luke flexed her fingers. He drew out Leinani's ring. "I didn't remember that I had this until much later, and then I realized that you would have the other one."

Luke didn't answer.

"How much do you know?" he asked. He still sounded so…reasonable. As if it was the most normal thing in the world to talk about betraying the kingdom and damaging the Compact. "Have you told anyone else?"

*Drayger.* Luke had a stab of concern. It was one thing if Fask got ahold of her, it was quite another if she implicated Drayger. Let him continue to think that Drayger hadn't slipped his leash, even if that meant taking a dive herself.

"I haven't said anything to anyone," she lied to his face. "It was hard enough to believe it myself." Were they talking about the same things? What did Fask think that she'd overheard?

She watched his hands and tried to look like she wasn't. Would she have enough warning to stop him from casting the memory spell? Should she attack him now, without any evidence? He wasn't a dragon, but he had his father's dragon strength and power. And above all, she had to protect Drayger…

"Good," Fask said, touching the cuff of his uniform. *"Forget it."*

## CHAPTER 25

"I have a burning question," Drayger said, after Fask left the meeting in the library. He tried briefly to warn Luke that Fask was coming, but the mate bond was at best an emotional mess, and he felt her annoyance followed by her very firmly shoving him away.

Luke was smart and she was savvy. She'd get out of the way or concoct a good story. She was probably already done in Fask's rooms. Drayger had to *trust* her.

Drayger wasn't particularly *good* at trust.

Tray and Rian were standing like reflections in a mirror at the bar and Drayger was draped in his chair, finishing a finger of bourbon that he hadn't wanted and didn't feel. "What's your burning question?" Rian politely asked.

"If it's from Drayger, I don't want to know what parts are burning," Tray quipped. "You should see a doctor about that."

"So, what *was* the bet that had Rian wandering the castle nude for a week when he lost?" Drayger asked.

Rian groaned. "I don't want to talk about it."

Tray looked smug. "I'm sworn to secrecy," he said proudly.

"The world deserves the answer," Drayger insisted. "There are entire webpages dedicated to the mystery."

"Ask Captain Luke," Tray suggested.

"Don't ask Captain Luke," Rian protested.

"She knows? The plot thickens!"

"She'd never tell you," Rian said, like he hoped it was true but not certain. Was his look a little suspicious? Had Toren told his brothers about catching them kissing?

Drayger had to yank his traitor mind back from thinking about kissing her again, about how she had kissed him back, how she had—

"What exactly is going on between the two of you?" Tray asked suspiciously.

Drayger didn't have to act to keep his expression full of mischief. "I'm sure I have no idea what you mean."

Rian and Tray exchanged identical looks of skepticism.

"You've been spending a lot more time together than you usually do since Raval got back," Tray pointed out.

"But you're being less outrageous than you usually are," Rian added. "And I haven't seen you making moves on any of the staff."

"Maybe the captain has just finally realized what a treasure I am," Drayger said smugly. He gave them a cocky smile that suggested he had gotten everything he wanted.

"He's pulling our leg," Rian said to his twin. "They aren't together. There's no way. I trust Luke's common sense."

Tray looked at Drayger with narrow eyes. "I don't know. He doesn't seem quite as desperate as he usually does."

"Desperate?" Drayger sputtered, sitting upright. "I have never in my life been *desperate*."

"You might be right," Rian said, scrutinizing Drayger. "He does seem less twitchy than usual."

"*Twitchy?*" That was even worse. "I am *wounded.*" Drayger got gracefully to his feet. "You know what, I don't have to take this kind of abuse. I'm going to find Captain Luke and tell her how mean you've been to me."

Rian and Tray laughed, as he'd intended them to, and turned back to the bar as Drayger made a show of storming from the library.

Drayger's fake outrage faded immediately as he remembered all over again Luke's sweet surrender in his arms, and he struck out in the direction of her office. She wasn't there, but Drayger went by instinct for the informal dining hall, where she was loading a plate of salmon and savory rolls.

"Alasie!" Drayger strode up to her. "Tray says that you know the bet behind Rian's week of nudity. I simply must have the whole story."

"Captain Luke to you," she reminded him crossly. "What do you want? I have things to do." To Drayger's shock, her mind was as cool as her face. There was no hint of warmth to her, none of the underlying yearning that he'd become accustomed to. Had the mate bond faded so quickly? Drayger was struck by his disappointment in the idea. He loved having her close in his head, like a constant caress.

"What's wrong?" he wanted to know, reaching for her arm because he couldn't help himself.

She shook him off, looking—and feeling!—only annoyed. "Don't waste my time, Majorca."

Did she want to stick to business? Was she angry at herself for letting her guard down and sleeping with him? Drayger was still confused by the very drastic end to the mate bond, if that's what this was. The princes had all made it sound like a slow fade, not a snapped rubber band.

He was completely dismayed by how chilly she was in his head, like all their potential promise of happiness had vanished. Had he screwed something up? Had she found something out about him that ruined his chance with her?

*Something is very wrong,* his dragon supplied anxiously. *It tastes like magic.*

"Were you able to get into Fask's room?" Drayger asked quietly. If she wanted to be all business, he could be all business.

She stared at him in confusion. "Why would I want to get into Fask's room?" she snapped.

"To see if he had any of Amara's other artifacts or spells," Drayger reminded her. "To try to find evide—"

He realized as he spoke what had happened.

Fask had caught her and released the memory spell on her. She'd been thinking about Fask's betrayal, which had wiped it from her mind...but she'd also been thinking about Drayger and their secret mate bond, so her recollection of that was gone too...right along with the bond.

"Alasie," he breathed in horror.

"I'd appreciate it if you'd stop calling me that," she said impersonally.

## CHAPTER 26

Luke knew that something was *off*, because Drayger was worried for her.

She wasn't entirely sure how she knew that Drayger was worried, because it didn't make sense that his feelings were in her head.

Not understanding what was happening always made her particularly cranky. If she didn't know what was going on, she couldn't *fix* it.

Drayger was still hovering around her, which was altogether out of character. Usually, he made an obvious play at her, turned her rejection into a joke, and danced away before she could be genuinely annoyed by his persistence. His expression now was no part humor and no part flirtation, only determination.

"Was there something that you needed from me?" Luke asked impatiently.

"Come have a smoke with me out on the back porch," he said.

"Why would I have a smoke with you?" This went past

annoying and straight into baffling. "It's a nasty, disgusting habit."

"Look, I will explain everything to you, but I can't do that here."

"Why should I trust you?" Luke said, but even as she spoke, she felt like she did, and her instinct conflicted with every shred of her common sense. Drayger was at best unreliable and at worst a mole for Majorca. She still hadn't been convinced of his pledge to Alaska and couldn't quite recall why they had ever accepted it.

"Give me a chance," he begged, and it was oddly un-Drayger-like.

Drayger was confident and brash. He was sure of himself and always optimistic. But this Drayger was desperate and despairing. He didn't seem to be flirting with her the way he usually was, all wild flattery and innuendo. Luke told herself that she didn't miss it, but for some reason, she did.

She hesitated. He wasn't asking for anything outrageous, just unexpected. "I have things to do," she said, though she couldn't quite remember what they were.

"I won't take much of your time. Alasie—Captain Luke. I really need you to hear this." He took the plate of food from her hands and put it down like he had every expectation of her agreement.

Information from his source? Something highly confidential? Luke tried to remember what they'd been investigating. Amara was imprisoned. Nathaniel had been found with undeniable evidence. Raval was back from the past with his mate and the kids were all safe in their destinies.

Mostly because she couldn't think of a reason not to agree, she finally shrugged. "I don't have long," she snapped, walking fast down the back hall towards the porch in question. "And I certainly don't want a cigarette."

Drayger scrambled to keep pace with her and neither of them bothered with a jacket.

It was an unseasonably warm day, a brief false spring when the sunlight had some actual strength for the time it was over the treetops. It was bright off the snow, and Luke squinted until her eyes adjusted. Drayger turned to face her.

"I don't have any photos or recordings, Alasie, so I'm going to have to just tell you and hope that it works."

"*What* works?" Luke hated being out of the loop more than anything else in the world, and she was keenly aware that there *was* a loop, and she *was* out of it.

"You're my mate, Alasie."

"It's Captain Luke to you," she reminded him crossly. Why was he being so insistent? Usually his flirtation was light and harmless. He teased relentlessly, but he never crossed the line, either with Luke or any of the women in the castle.

Her mind seemed to slide off the rest of what he said, like it wasn't important, and that confused her, because surely a *mate* was important. She forced her mind back to it.

There was no reason that they would be mates. She wasn't in line for a throne, and neither was Drayger. It didn't make sense, and besides, if she was, wouldn't she remember something so critical?

"There's a traitor, and you're under a spell."

"I know there's a traitor," Luke said impatiently, ignoring the rest. "Nathaniel. We caught him with Amara's spells and money."

"But you don't believe that Nathaniel is a traitor."

Luke struggled with her memory. "I don't remember why."

"Fask hit you with a forget-me spell."

It ought to be shocking, but Luke only felt irritated and it slid from her head as quickly as it got there. "What do you want, Majorca?" she said, because she was frustrated that she couldn't remember what he'd just said. "Why did you call me out here? Did you have something to tell me?"

"Try!" Drayger insisted. "Fight it! Alasie, you're the smartest, toughest person I know. You can beat this."

Of course she could beat this. Luke could beat anything she set her heart to. But she didn't *understand* her heart right now. "I don't know what you're talking about."

To her surprise, Drayger got angry, and she knew that he was even before he shattered the top porch rail with a furious fist, smashing it with one swift blow.

"What are you doing?!" She sprang forward to stop his insane vandalism and he turned to meet her, taking her by the shoulders with surprising familiarity. She should have twisted out of his grip—it was a simple hold and she knew a half dozen moves to neutralize it—but she hesitated.

Even as enraged as he clearly was, she wasn't afraid of him. She didn't consider him a threat, despite knowing that he was a dragon that had obviously just lost control of his temper.

She knew to her very core that he would never hurt her.

That he…

It slithered out of her head as quickly as she could start to think it and Luke shook her head. "What is wrong with me?" She shouldn't be standing on the porch with Drayger, she should be inside doing her work. Why was the railing broken? Why was he holding her by the shoulders? Why was she *letting* him hold her by the shoulders?

"Drayger," she said in deep confusion. "Why are we out here?" Something was *wrong*.

And she couldn't remember what it was.

There was a flash across Drayger's face that Luke shouldn't have been able to identify as hope, but she was absolutely positive that it was.

"Look," he said earnestly, "I don't know another way to convince you of this."

Then, to Luke's mixed astonishment, dismay, and complete delight, he took her face in both hands and kissed her.

## CHAPTER 27

Drayger felt the exact moment that the memory spell broke. Luke went from struggling in his embrace, to kissing him back, and then to seizing his arms in her iron grip and pushing him back to arm's length as everything flooded back into her head.

"That sunnova—"

"Language, Captain," Drayger chided her, so glad and grateful to have her feeling right again inside him that he had to kiss her again, hungrily.

"Drayger," she protested against his lips, and then she bit him hard.

"Ouch! What was that for?"

"Never kiss me without my permission!"

"That's gratitude for you!" Drayger complained, making a show of rubbing his throbbing lip. "I just broke your memory spell and all I get is grief."

Neither of them was actually mad, and her bite had been more exciting than off-putting. She had to know what she did to him by now, how every moment made him fall even harder in love with her.

"Alasie—"

As swift as a shift in the wind, her mood changed. "*Fask*," she spat, turning to look out over the porch rail that Drayger had broken with his frustrated blow. "That rat bastard tried to wipe my memory of his betrayal."

Drayger pounced on her words. "He still thinks you don't remember! We can use that!"

"For what? *How?*" Her words were sharp, but the question was genuine.

"He'll trust you. We make him think that you don't know and he'll slip up."

"Spells don't last," Luke reminded him. "He must know that eventually I'll remember everything and that will be the *end* of him."

Drayger could not deny how very sexy a vicious Luke could be. He didn't ever want to be at the receiving end of the anger in her eyes and flaming in her mind, but it gave her a spark of vitality that was very appealing.

"He must not need very long," Drayger said.

"The Renewal," Luke said, pursing her lips. "The Renewal is in just a few weeks, he must be planning something for around that." She gave him a shrewd sideways look. "Why *did* the Compact select us as mates? Does she need you to represent Majorca and I was the nearest woman you had any potential with?"

*No*, Drayger wanted to protest. *It wasn't because Luke was convenient, it was because she was perfect.* But if Majorca was thinking of pulling out of the Small Kingdoms, was that a possibility? He didn't want to believe that Alasie was anything less than his destiny, but there was logic in the idea. "I don't know what the Compact has in mind, but I suspect that it—she—has a plan of some kind. But Alasie—"

"Captain Luke," she corrected automatically.

Drayger risked the cameras to take her hands. He'd already done property damage and kissed her in front of them anyway. "*Alasie*," he insisted, "I *love* you. I don't care why we crossed paths or what other politics or prophecies come between us. I am yours, forever, and that's nothing to do with the Compact. I will follow you into hell, bring you back from death, and fight Fask himself for your freedom, if that's what it takes."

He was glad of the mate bond then because although Luke's face was impressively stony, he could feel the swell of feeling his words awoke. She glowed with emotion and warmth, like a nascent sun behind her iron self-control.

She loved him back, he thought. He wasn't casting his affections uselessly into a pit of disregard; she felt for him as intensely as he felt for her, not just someday, but *now*.

He doubted that she would ever admit it, and he loved her even more for that stubbornness.

"What do we do?" she asked quietly. Her hands were clasping his back, but neither of them made a move towards the kiss they both dearly wanted. "About *us*, I mean."

"Toren already caught us kissing," Drayger reminded her. "Tray and Rian are suspicious. It can't be a secret for long."

"What *is* it, though?" Luke asked. "What *are* we? Just kissing friends?"

It was the *friends* part of her proposal, not the kissing part, that hit Drayger in the gut. "We're figuring it out," he proposed. "It gives us a chance to talk privately without looking like conspirators. And I mean, geez, it's long past time you gave in to my considerable wiles. People were probably beginning to question your sanity. No one is going to be *surprised* that you finally succumbed to my charm."

"Your charm gets much weaker the more you brag about it," Luke said, the barest hint of a smile at her lips and the warmest rush of humor in her mind.

"We need to get the others on board," Drayger said, bringing himself back to the business at hand with will. As much as he wanted to drag her back to her office to practice the kissing part of kissing friends, Fask still needed to be stopped. And to do that, they needed to know exactly what he was planning to do. "They need to know what he's done. Maybe they have some pieces to this puzzle that we're missing."

"I'll ask my cousins to meet us in my office at thirteen hundred hours," Luke said. "We'll see if we can't break the spell on Raval now that we *know* what he saw and find out what they know about Fask's plans. I'll say that it's to bring them up to speed on some security changes."

"Have them bring their mates," Drayger suggested. "I'm beginning to think that the Compact has some kind of agenda, that she's picked each of us on purpose."

Luke frowned. "It's been a while since I saw her. I hope there's not a problem."

"There are a lot of problems," Drayger said merrily. "Most of them are in my pants right now. Maybe we should make the appointment for fifteen hundred hours and see if we can solve some of those first…"

Luke's frown didn't waver, but Drayger felt her in his mind with a flash of amusement and delight at the idea. "Focus, Majorca," she chided him. "And have your pants on when you show up for the meeting."

CHAPTER 28

Luke schooled her expression and steeled her nerve before she knocked on the frame of Fask's open door. "Your Highness?"

"Come in, Captain."

Was Fask's gaze particularly suspicious and slightly knowing? Luke was surprised by her sizzle of fury. He had *stolen* her memories of Drayger—memories that she hadn't even realized she treasured until they'd been ripped from her head and returned.

She reminded herself that her *feelings* were not the worst of his offenses and the vision of him coldly stabbing his own father hardened her will.

"I came to ask about allowing Pickle, Nathaniel's favorite dog, to stay with him," she said, hoping it was just the way she might have ever said it. Did she sound too warm or calm? She was keenly aware of her own guards, standing in earshot just outside Fask's doors.

Fask frowned and Luke was surprised by how grieved he managed to look. It gave her a moment of doubt, especially when his shoulders suddenly slumped. "That was a hard blow, wasn't it, cousin?"

"I find it hard to believe that he could have been working with Amara," Luke said, knowing she sounded too stiff but not sure how much to relax.

"Are you still investigating the matter?" Fask wanted to know. He asked so plaintively that Luke would have been fooled in any other case and she felt a grudging respect for his acting skills.

"I am," she admitted, hoping that her deceit was half as convincing. She feigned a look of distant confusion, trying to remember how Raval had looked when he was fighting the spell. "I haven't found anything that might point to anyone else." She remembered Drayger's quote. "Sometimes the easiest answer is the right one, even if we don't like it."

If she hadn't been watching Fask's face, she never would have noticed that tiny flicker of satisfaction. The anger she'd been suppressing surged up so hard that she could feel Drayger's alarm in reaction.

She got herself back under control as Fask stood.

"Do you mind if I come with you to fetch Pickle?" he asked. "I'd like to speak with you privately."

It was the last thing that Luke actually wanted, but she nodded. "Of course, Your Highness."

Luke had never been much of an actress, and going with Fask to the kennels put every inch of her dramatic skills to the test. Not punching Fask in the face put every inch of her self-control to the test.

"At least we don't have to worry about Pickle being a shifter," Fask said, with a dry attempt at humor. "We were there when he was born." Shadow had squirmed his way into the palace by being a dog shifter with acting skills that Luke had to look back on with awe. At one point, she'd caught him scooting on his rear across the carpet like any husky with an itchy butt, and he'd been so completely dog-like that they had all been fooled.

"Ha ha." Luke knew that it was a very poor approximation of a laugh, but perhaps the grim times explained it.

"Are you feeling alright?" Fask asked solicitously as they kneed aside the dogs who came howling out of their houses to greet them at the dog yard.

Pickle was in the furthest kennel, disconsolately refusing to get out of his straw like his more rambunctious younger teammates. Luke paused to scratch offered ears and chins as she and Fask made their way through the yard to him.

"I'm a little tired," Luke admitted after a moment, hoping that was the correct answer for a working memory spell. "I'm looking forward to catching up on my sleep after the Renewal." She knelt by Pickle, who whined happily when she petted him, but didn't volunteer to get out of his kennel. She glanced up at the oldest prince.

Fask looked satisfied with Luke's answer. "It's possible the Renewal won't even happen."

"How could the Renewal not happen?" Luke asked in surprise. Too much surprise? Should she seem more dazed? This was a *minefield*.

"The Compact is clearly broken," Fask pointed out. "We don't have a clear line of succession. There is more animosity among the Small Kingdoms than there used to be; some of them are even suggesting pulling *out*. Maybe it's time for a new Compact, not just a tired repeat of something that no longer works in modern times. We've been treating the person who is trying to alter it as our enemy, but maybe they aren't. Maybe they're *right* about this."

How did he manage to sound so reasonable? "You

think that the person who is still trying to damage the Compact is looking out for our greater good?" Luke said it as mildly as she could. She didn't have to fake confusion, but she had to smother her alarm.

"I'm not saying Amara was a good person or that she wasn't out for herself, but maybe she wasn't wrong about *this*."

Luke didn't trust herself to speak. The Compact was what kept magic from spinning entirely out of control. It was a pillar of their kingdom. It was a *person*. She clipped the leash she'd brought onto Pickle's collar and convinced him to get to his feet, groaning, to walk back to the castle. The other dogs howled and yipped in jealousy and lunged at the ends of their leads.

"You've had a computer go out before," Fask continued thoughtfully, as if he didn't consider it a very big deal. "Sometimes the core code gets too badly garbled and it's better to start from scratch, a completely fresh reboot."

"Isn't that what the Renewal does?" Luke was pleased by how even and unconcerned her voice sounded despite the outrage in her soul. This was blatantly suggesting that they let the Compact *fail*. She kept her breathing even and her face still. Even Drayger would be impressed by her acting.

It was ridiculous how much she wished he was there to witness it; she wasn't a child or a dog who needed constant approval.

"The Renewal is based on re-casting exactly the same spell as before, with all the same limitations and exclusions." Fask was using his soothing diplomat voice on her, like she was a fractious lobbyist, or an annoying pest. Was it supposed to be reassuring? All it did was raise the hair on the back of Luke's neck. "But times change, and it hasn't changed with the world. I am starting to believe that we need not a Renewal, but a *refresh*. A completely new Compact, that responds to our new needs and considerations."

"What changes would you make?" Luke asked. She could not quite manage enthusiasm, but she did keep her voice neutral. "Magic needs bounds." Was that too far?

"Of course," Fask agreed as they came to the door of the palace. He paused before them and faced Luke seriously. "But those bounds shouldn't apply to *all* of us. The right power in the right hands is what these times require."

Power.

It came down to power at the end of it, every time.

Power over people, power over magic. Fask genuinely thought that *he* was those right hands that he spoke of, and Luke felt a chill that had nothing to do with the weather. Her polar bear even shivered sympathetically.

"The Compact is very complex," she said, trying to sound as if she was intrigued by the idea and not only horrified. Did Fask honestly think that she would be on board with this proposal, even if she hadn't already uncovered the horrible things he'd done? "How could we make a new one?"

"We have Amara's focus stone," Fask reminded her. "And Dalaya and Mackenzie both have chaos magic."

Kenth would never agree to have his mate and daughter do something as risky as using Amara's controlling magic to guide them to create complicated spells.

But if Fask could control memories, what else could he do? What tools had Amara given him even before the raid that they knew nothing about? The mirror he had planted in Nathaniel's rooms hadn't been part of what they had retrieved. Not officially, anyway.

"I never thought about the possibility," Luke said, with all the diplomacy she could muster. "You might be right."

For a moment, she thought that she had capitulated too easily, that Fask would be suspicious about her easy agreement, but then he nodded in satisfaction and opened the door for her.

Pickle's claws clattered along the tile floor as they walked quietly down the back hall.

The guards parted for them at the top of the stairs to the sublevel.

"I'd like to take Pickle down myself," Luke said, as offhandedly as she could manage.

"I can count on your help, can't I, cousin?"

Fask's look was intense and Luke summoned every ounce of her will to smile at him reassuringly. "Alaska always, Your Highness."

Fask smiled and Luke let out a sigh of relief as Pickle plunged down the stairs with her and she could leave the prince behind her.

She wasn't sure what her face did when she let it relax at last, only knew that Drayger could probably could feel her fury and she really hoped he didn't do something stupid before they could talk.

She thought maybe that she'd done at least one right thing when she saw how joyous Nathaniel and Pickle were at their reunion.

The dog, who had been walking stiff and subdued for their entire journey through the palace, had sudden puppy-like energy when the cell door opened, leaping for Nathaniel and licking him, his tail beating against anything in its way.

"Pickle! Who's a good dog? Who's the *best* old dog?" Nathaniel knelt to embrace him and accept his kisses eagerly, looking years younger himself. "The goodest dog ever."

"You can keep him here from now on," Luke

promised. "I'll come three times a day to take him for walks and I'll bring food." It would be a task she couldn't easily delegate, she realized belatedly, because only she and the royal family could come down here, but it would be worth the extra work for that look on Nathaniel's face.

…Even while she was plotting to somehow overthrow a sociopathic prince of Alaska's plan to upend the Compact and take the reins of power himself, while also juggling a not-so-secret affair with a bastard prince houseguest.

"Alasie—"

Nathaniel sometimes called her by her child name and was one of the few people that Luke didn't mind it from.

"I know you didn't work with Amara," she blurted.

Luke had meant to keep it secret longer, in case Fask had gotten to Nathaniel, too. But she could not bear any longer that he might think that she truly believed the evidence against him, and she'd turned off the monitoring of the room even before she'd gone to see Fask.

Nathaniel's eyes, already bright from his reunion with Pickle, grew wet and he had to blink hard as he looked up at her.

"You know—?"

"I know who framed you, and I have to stop him before I can get you out of here. But I couldn't let you keep thinking I might actually believe you betrayed Alaska. Nathaniel, you are my *friend*."

He had to push Pickle away to stand up and Luke let him wrap strong arms around her. It was funny how becoming Drayger's mate and *friend* had made her realize how precious her other true friends really were.

## CHAPTER 29

Luke's roomy office was crowded to the absolute limit, with princes arguing with their mates over who would take a seat, while Drayger tried to embarrass Luke by picturing how he'd taken her on each one of those surfaces and letting the lustful memory color their bond.

She glared daggers at him and Drayger was so relieved that their connection was back to where it ought to be that he didn't even care when she elbowed him hard in the side as she locked the door and activated the wards and edged back through the crowd to her seat.

"I'll sit," Katy said, while Leinani was still protesting Tray's insistence that she take a spot on the couch. "My feet are killing me. I had no idea that they would swell before the rest of me."

Tray and Leinani both ended up on the couch next to her, squashed in with Carina. Tania looked skeptically at all of the chairs and said she'd be just as comfortable standing, even after Luke offered her own seat. Mackenzie shyly took one of the chairs facing Luke and Kenth took the other.

"So, why exactly are we here?" Toren wanted to know, perched on the arm of the couch next to Carina. Raval was hovering awkwardly at the other arm near Katy. Rian stood with Tania.

"And why isn't Fask here?" Rian wanted to know, prompting the others to look around as if they expected him to be hiding behind someone.

"Are we planning a surprise party?" Toren speculated. "His birthday isn't until May."

"This is the only place in the castle where we absolutely won't be overheard," Luke said, all business. "Drayger?"

Drayger took a certain amount of pride in surprising them all by completely dropping his careless, easy-going mask. "Fask was not invited to this gathering because Fask is the mole you've been looking for in the castle. The one who set the anchors that allowed Amara entrance to the palace."

"I thought Nathaniel—" Rian started, glancing at Tray, who was quiet, his hand in Leinani's.

"He was framed," Luke said firmly.

"I knew it," Toren said in relief. "He couldn't have done that awful stuff." He didn't address the accusation of Fask.

Tray's knuckles on the arm of the couch went white, but he didn't speak.

"Do you have proof?" Kenth wanted to know. "What evidence do you have?"

"The Compact said the traitor wasn't a dragon!" Carina exclaimed.

"But, Fask? He's our brother!" Raval said it like it explained everything, but his face was deeply confused.

## CHAPTER 29

Luke swiveled to face him and rolled her chair closer. "You know something," she told him gently. "Something that you can't quite remember. Fask has a spell, one of Amara's, that removes short-term specific memories. He used it on me, and he used it on you."

"I don't remember that," Raval blurted. There was a ripple of dry laughter, all of them grasping after any humor possible in this grim setting.

Luke leaned to hand him the coin of faintly-carved glass. "I don't know if you got this in the past, or if it's something you made. I found it in the room with your father's sleeping dragon, and it seems to be some kind of truth-viewer. It's used up now, but it showed me what it showed you before it burned out. The *truth*. Fask killed your father."

The last laughter died entirely.

Raval had been holding up the chip of glass, trying to tease legible letters out of the surface and he froze in horror. "He...wait, wait...I *do* remember. I *saw* it! He had the dagger from the vault! And he... I met him near the vault and I asked him how he could...how he could...but then it was all gone and I didn't know why I was there."

Katy reached up to take his unresponsive hand. "Raval?"

"He's not a dragon!" Raval realized. "He used that dagger to take father's power into himself, but it would have killed him if he'd been a dragon himself."

Luke went on gently. "When he realized what you knew, he cast the memory spell on you. But I had overheard your conversation, because he still had Leinani's listening ring in his pocket."

"Is that when you and Drayger started your little conspiracy?" Rian wanted to know.

Drayger caught Luke's steady gaze and held it, drawing

strength from her patience. "No, we had been working together considerably longer than that," he said.

The quiet that answered that was deeply suspicious.

"Fask used the memory spell on me as well," Luke said. "So that I would forget about what I'd overheard."

Was she going to tell them about the mate bond that she'd forgotten as well? Drayger caught himself holding his breath in anticipation. Did she want to acknowledge it to others, or would it remain their shameful little secret? Did it really matter to the rest of this sordid affair?

"I'm not exactly sure why we are trusting Drayger with his part in this," Kenth said. "It's a little convenient that he's been inserted into our family so completely, and suspicious that he's accusing our *brother* of sedition when he's supposedly betrayed his own kingdom. Majorca has never been our ally. It takes a rat to know one? Maybe he planted a little magical video clip for you both to find."

Drayger wasn't particularly surprised that Kenth was the most reluctant to believe that Fask might be compromised. Sometimes the relationships that were most at odds were the most intense, and loyalty was a tricky thing that was often rooted in family bonds that never really relied on logic.

Luke met Kenth's stare with her own. "*I* trust Drayger," she said firmly and Drayger was surprised how deeply it affected him to hear it out loud. "He doesn't have access to the vault or many of the places that portals have been placed. He didn't know about Dalaya. And, he's my *mate*."

If her spoken trust was a comfort, hearing her tell someone else that he was *hers* cut straight into Drayger's heart.

"I told you," Toren hissed.

"You said they *kissed*, not that they were mates," Carina protested in a stage-whisper.

"They *kissed?*"

"They're *mates?*"

"Since *when?*"

"I thought she hated him."

"He's a better actor than I ever suspected."

"Are you *sleeping* with him?"

"I honestly thought you had better taste than that!"

"How long has it been going on?"

"I need a timeline for this."

For a moment, their voices were just a distant distraction and Luke's brown eyes were the only thing that mattered in the room. She was his mate, and he was hers, completely. Drayger didn't want to look away or follow up on the pressing business of the betrayal, he just wanted to drink in the feeling of her in his head, like they were two slipped gears that had just fully engaged.

She was stronger willed than he was, and turned to address the questions as calmly and matter-of-fact as she did everything. "It happened the night Raval returned, shortly after Toren caught us talking in the informal dining hall."

"They weren't just talking!" Toren blurted.

Luke ignored him. "I overheard Fask talking with Raval later that night. I found the truth-viewer the following day after I questioned Nathaniel and Amara. Fask caught me snooping in his room and released the memory spell on me the following day but Drayger broke me out of it. Now we're all caught up. And it's none of your business who I'm sleeping with."

Drayger had to bite back a snappy sex quip, reminding himself that the crude, forward Drayger they were expecting was only a front. He'd been playing it so long that it was second nature now.

"What are we supposed to do about this?" Carina asked. "Do we *arrest* the oldest prince of Alaska for his father's not-quite death? Do we have proof that isn't magical? We don't even have a body, unless you count a sleeping dragon."

"What does this mean for the Renewal?" Rian wanted to know.

"Is this related to the attempts on the Compact?" Tania asked.

There were more questions than there were answers, but Drayger felt the mood in the room gradually shift from shock and disbelief to reluctant acceptance...and then to anger. Fask was the one with his fingers in all the things. He could have easily told Amara where to set the trap that captured Leinani and Tray. He had easy and unquestioned access to the vault.

"He sent my daughter a Christmas gift," Kenth said, standing and trying unsuccessfully to pace in the crowded office. "It must have had the anchor in it. He was the only one who even knew about her."

Mackenzie tucked her legs up into the space Kenth abandoned as he charged up and down the small space, tripping on feet until Tray impatiently told him to sit down or get out.

"He had my daughter kidnapped and tampered with!" Kenth roared. "Don't tell me to calm down!"

Tray got to his own feet. "He had me *and* Leinani kidnapped and tortured! You aren't the only one he's screwed! You don't have some kind of special privilege of being the most wronged person in this room!"

Leinani rose beside Tray. "Let's be reasonable…"

"There's nothing *reasonable* going on here!" Kenth snarled.

Carina and Toren both scrambled up as Tray clearly took that as an attack on his mate and for a moment Drayger honestly thought there was going to be a fist fight.

"Alaska first!" Luke snapped.

Drayger wasn't sure when she'd stood, but she was the eye in a storm now, and Tray and Kenth both reluctantly backed away from each other.

"None of this is comfortable news," Luke said, "and I don't fault you for being angry. I didn't want to believe it, either. But this is the hand we've been dealt and now we decide what to do with it. Your father's murder is a thing in the past, but we need to look at the future now. Fask appears to be continuing Amara's agenda. He wants to subvert the Renewal, to rewrite the Compact to his *own* advantage. He said that he might use Mackenzie and Dalaya to that end."

Kenth managed to look both horrified *and* smug, glancing back at Mackenzie and Tray.

"What do you suggest?" Toren asked.

Luke gravely sat down, but her presence continued to dominate a room full of royalty. "I suggest that we find a way to stop him. We're already facing a geopolitical firestorm and the rest of the world wants answers about magic, shifters, dragons, demons. How do we maintain that secret? Do we *want* to maintain that secret? Whether we understand it or not, you five…six…*the twelve of us*… have been tapped by the Compact to be the next leaders. Ask yourselves, what does that look like? What do we *want* it to look like? *That's* what we do next."

Tray and Kenth gave each other guilty glances.

"I don't suggest we move against Fask yet," Luke said more gently. "We don't have as many answers as I wish we did and I fear there is something or someone else at work. We've still got a few weeks before the Renewal. Stay alert and see what other information you can dig up. The best thing we can do is share stories. Toren, Carina, I may want you to make diplomatic contact with some of the other Kingdoms. We can't know for sure what Fask has been telling them, but I'd like to find out. Tania, Rian, I have some questions about the Compact and its language about the Renewal itself. Has Fask found some kind of loophole? Mackenzie, Raval, I want your ideas for magic protections that might stop Fask's plan. Kenth…"

"I won't hurt him," Kenth growled. "Yet."

"I *want* you to fight with him," Luke said frankly. "Give him grief on every front. Needle him more than ever. You're our distraction. Pick a battle every chance you get."

"That shouldn't be hard for you," Tray snorted, and Kenth grinned.

"Tray, I want you to kiss his ass."

"What?"

"Go play hockey with him when he's done fighting with Kenth, be a willing sounding board for his frustration. See if he will confide in you."

Tray groaned, but agreed.

"The rest of you, I need eyes and ears. We have to move forward towards the Renewal, faster than we thought, and we have to do it quietly. I wish this had been a gathering to share happier news, but this is what we have to work with."

"Maybe someone else has got happier news," Drayger suggested, because he could tell that Tray was absolutely bursting with it.

He left it ambiguous, but Leinani immediately knew what he was referring to. "How did you know?" the princess asked in astonishment, putting a hand to her waist.

"I'm much smarter than you give me credit for," Drayger said, as the rest of the room turned to congratulate her joyfully.

"I was going to tell them!" Tray protested.

"I'll let you pass out the cigars," Drayger said expansively, "but I've been waiting for at least a week now and you were going to have an aneurysm first."

"No cigars in my office!" Luke announced, and that was the cue for the meeting to end.

## CHAPTER 30

Luke stayed in her seat as the princes and their mates left one by one. Drayger, completely back in his role as a clown, ushered each of them out. "Let's move along, now," he joked. "Out you go, closing time, last call!" He ruffled Toren's hair, to the crown prince's deep annoyance.

Luke got to her feet as Raval and Katy left last. "If you want to talk about the memory loss, it happened to me, too," she offered him. "It leaves kind of an ugly taste in your head."

Raval stared at her unblinking for a moment. "I might," he said finally.

At last, Drayger locked the door behind them and Luke was letting herself flow into his arms with all the hunger and need that she had kept banked through their meeting. She cupped him in warning with one hand. "If you ever do that again," she said between kisses, "I'll see that the fertile ground phrase in the Compact has *nothing* to do with having children. I almost jumped you across my desk in front of *all* of them. What on *earth* were you thinking about?"

"You," Drayger said honestly, nibbling at her neck. She could feel his satisfaction that he had been able to affect her so powerfully. "You, bent over that desk, you, with your legs spread on the couch, you, on the floor, the noises you make, how hot you are inside..."

Every word lit her lust up a little more, and there was a mad scramble to peel each other out of their clothing.

Luke was surprised how good it felt to let people know about them, how raw and right it felt. It wasn't just a shameful secret or a dangerous weakness. She was this man's mate. She had *admitted* it, and that surrender had been both terrifying and exciting.

He was hers, and she claimed him with her mouth and her nails on his back, drawing him down onto the couch with him, and from there to the floor when the cushions slipped beneath their assault. She was wild and demanding, and Drayger responded to her every suggestion with enthusiasm and innovation, until they were both pitched higher than she'd realized was possible, and falling together in perfect harmony.

"One of these days," Drayger panted as he rolled off of her, "I'd like to make proper love to you in an actual bed."

"I have rug burn on my back," Luke confessed, and they lay tangled together on the carpet and laughed helplessly.

"I've done my job, then," he said, a weird mix of chagrined and proud in her head.

*I love you*, Luke almost said in a moment of weakness then. It wasn't just her body that loved him, though, and she didn't want him to think that was all it was. She was still coming down from all the pleasure and physical bliss that he'd brought her, but there behind it was the singing feeling of connection and belonging that she never thought she'd find.

He was more than a lover, more than a co-conspirator. He was her partner, her equal in all things. Clever, unexpectedly compassionate, and *completely* hers.

When all of this was done and finished, and the Compact was safely renewed and Fask was brought to justice, she looked forward to…

Luke's train of thought hit a wall.

"You're wondering what's next," Drayger said, not oblivious to how her mood had been quenched.

"Yes," Luke admitted, though she didn't elaborate. Were they really in line to rule? Which country? The Compact surely wouldn't force her to leave her beloved land to rule Majorca, even assuming Majorca accepted a disgraced bastard prince as their king. And there were already five mated princes of Alaska, it wasn't like *this* kingdom was going to be looking around for a cousin-by-marriage to take the throne.

"Well," Drayger drawled. "Give me about fifteen, maybe twenty minutes, and we can do that again. Maybe we'll switch it up and give you rug burns on your knees…"

Luke had to laugh, and she sat up and leaned over him to kiss him firmly. Her hair had gotten loose somehow, though she didn't remember how any more than she remembered exactly how she'd gotten out of her uniform.

Drayger caught her by the long black locks as she would have drawn away and pulled her gently back for another lingering kiss.

"I love you, Alasie," he whispered against her mouth. "I love you so much."

Luke knew she was supposed to say it back, and she desperately wished that she was brave enough to do so. Instead, she kissed him, so hard she worried she would split her lip. "I have to get back to work," she said, as she rose to her feet. "Some of us have things to do."

"I have things to do, too," Drayger protested, taking the hand that she offered to help him up. "I've got royal rebellions to foment, and some rumors to set in motion." He rose gracefully, but didn't let go of her hand until she twisted it from his grip.

Luke was keenly aware that they were both still naked, and the hunger in his head—and hers!—suggested that Drayger might not need the full fifteen minutes he'd estimated to go again. She dampened down her own needy hunger and reached for her uniform, carelessly thrown over her desk.

The cup full of pens had been knocked over again.

Drayger didn't persist, to Luke's vague disappointment, but found his own clothing and dressed with his usual prattle of half gossip, half serious updates. "Tania's got an appointment with her physical therapist at four, we have time if we need to see her about the language in the Compact regarding that bit about multiple mates you were asking about earlier. Mackenzie has made arrangements to meet her father in two days. She'll be going with Kenth and Dalaya, because Kenth won't let either of them out of his sight. They might have an opportunity to speak candidly with the Queen of the New Siberian Islands about their withdrawal from the Compact. None of them are terribly good diplomats, but Dalaya might be able to charm them."

Luke silently absorbed his updates, concentrating on organizing the important information into some kind of pattern, not on watching how Drayger's muscles flexed as he pulled on his shirt and shimmied gracefully back into his pants.

He was so…beautiful.

She'd always known that he was an attractive male specimen, shifter strong and graceful, with a striking face and a build that was in every way her ideal, but it was astonishing how much *more* handsome he was now that she knew what lurked behind his flirtatious surface.

Her hunger for him wasn't only sexual, and it wasn't only cerebral. He was like the feeling of sunlight on her skin after a long, dark winter, and she was a plant drinking it up. He utterly completed her.

And dammit, he knew it. Luke caught his playful, pleased glance and forced her thoughts back to all the problems they were facing. She could not afford to be distracted by his pretty face right now.

"You talk to Tania about why we might have been tapped as mates," Drayger proposed, when they were both smoothing down the final fastenings of their clothing and Luke had her hair twisted back again. "I'll follow up with Toren. He's still technically the crown prince and he's going to want some guidance."

"I did not anticipate accepting you as the vehicle of that guidance," Luke said wryly. "If you had asked me a month ago whether I even trusted you, I might have said no."

Drayger gave her his best rakish smile. "I have unplumbed depths. And if you'd like to plumb them…"

"Focus, Majorca," Luke snapped. "I'll go speak with Tania. Maybe she has some ideas about why things are happening like they are, especially with this new information about Fask. And maybe Raval has some thoughts, with his information from the first Renewal."

They bottlenecked at the door. "Are we leaving together?" Drayger asked, wiggling his eyebrows at her. "Should I go first?"

"Just get out," Luke said, wrenching the door open, "before I throw you out."

## CHAPTER 31

"I know what we have to do," Drayger said when he caught Luke in the hall the next day after a midday meal that he mostly spent distracting from the princes' *terrible* attempts at pretending everything was normal. None of them were natural actors. "You're not going to like it."

Luke looked and felt suspicious, like she was expecting a joke. She waved her guards to step back down the hall out of earshot. "I know what we have to do, too, and *you* aren't going to like it," she countered.

"Ladies first," Drayger said graciously.

"I have to tell Fask about us."

That drew Drayger up and fired him full of mixed feelings. "Are you sure?"

"It's what I would do under any other circumstances," Luke said. "I'd be up front about it and report the liaison as a matter of professional courtesy. Too many people know now to continue keeping it a secret."

"Are you going to tell him we're mates?" Drayger wanted to know. On one hand, he wanted to tell the world.

On the other, it was a beautiful thing that he was jealous of and wanted to hold close to his chest.

Luke shook her head. "I think that may be more information than we want to share. We know he's working *against* the Compact herself. He only needs to know *enough*, not *everything*."

"I could visit you in your rooms?" Drayger said with a sudden zing of hope. It wasn't that he minded making love to Luke on her office floor, or propped on the narrow couch, or across her desk, but he was dying to lay her down on sheets and take his time with her.

She didn't answer out loud, but her sizzling anticipation was response enough. "What was it that *you* thought we needed to do?"

It took Drayger a very determined few moments to remember what he'd originally been thinking about and wipe out the image of what, *exactly*, they should do in her bed. "Ah, um, oh! The Compact! We should steal the Compact."

Luke's shock was an ample damper for his libido. "You think we should *what*?" She glanced down the hall and tempered her voice. "Are you *feverish*?"

"Fask wants to stop the Renewal, apparently. He can do that by destroying, or altering the Compact. We should steal it and do the Renewal first."

Luke looked at him like he'd lost his mind. "You want us to preemptively *steal the Compact?* That is a terrible idea."

"I told you you weren't going to like it," Drayger said. "But think about it. Fask is the one doing all the liaison with the other Small Kingdoms. Every scrap of it. He's been sabotaging the Renewal the whole time, even to the point of convincing some of the other kingdoms to drop out of the treaty. He probably had my father killed because he wouldn't go along with his plan and my half-brother

## CHAPTER 31

Liam was a more willing participant. He was probably behind the attempts on the Japanese royals, too. Maybe he's behind the earthquakes in Rapa Nui or the wildfires in Madagascar."

"He shouldn't be able to do any of that," Luke protested. "The Compact protects the kingdoms from being able to retaliate against each other. And how would he control earthquakes or fires?"

"The Compact has been hurt," Drayger reminded her. "It might not be able to do as much as it—she—used to be able to do. Or it might be a loophole that Fask without his dragon doesn't count as a part of the treaty. That might have been an eventuality that was never seen coming."

Luke pinched the bridge of her nose and scowled. "So we, what? Steal the Compact and host our own private early Renewal? This is the most *insane* idea you've ever had."

"You will do it."

They both turned in unison, surprised and alarmed to find that someone had come up the hallway behind them without so much as a sound.

An elderly woman with white braids to her waist stood in front of the tall windows at the end of the hall. Drayger couldn't quite focus on what she was wearing, like it was a cloak of shadows or a dress of night sky. It reminded him of the natural camouflage of dragons, just a little out of sight even right before him.

"Grandmother," Luke said quietly, bowing her head. "Ah, not that you're really my grandmother."

"I am in some ways, grandchild," the Compact said. "The ways that matter."

Drayger wasn't entirely sure what kind of respect you were supposed to give an artificial intelligence spun out of a spell so complicated that it could be alive, but he bowed his head along with Luke. "Ma'am." That seemed like a safe title.

"*Mariposa*," she replied, and Drayger was shaken to his core to hear his mother's nickname for him as a child.

Luke gave him a concerned sideways glance and Drayger scrambled to mentally mute his reaction. "You were saying that we…should steal the Compact?"

That certainly distracted Luke. "You have to be kidding."

"I am dying," the Compact said matter-of-factly. "There are factors trying to prevent the Renewal and magic will be unleashed on the world. I do not want my work to be in vain…and I fear the consequences if the wrong people get a hold of the power. You must bring my pages together and recast the spell before it's too late. Do it sooner than later. Don't wait."

"How are we supposed to do that?" Luke demanded. "The Renewal is supposed to be done by all the Small Kingdoms. Some of them are refusing to attend."

"You will have to improvise," the Compact chided, "just as I taught you. What is the most important part?"

"I don't know!" Luke protested. Drayger could feel the flutter of her panic in his mind. "I don't know what's most important! It's seven hundred pages long!"

"There is only *one* thing you have to remember," the Compact said.

Then she fell into a cloud of dark feathers full of stars that vanished when they floated to the floor.

Drayger reached for Luke and was selfishly glad to find that she was already reaching for him. They clung to each for a long moment trying to make sense of what they'd been told.

"We have to steal the Compact," Luke said, shoving him away like she was embarrassed by her momentary weakness. "Of all the impossible things. Steal the Compact and do our own Renewal."

"You should listen to me more," Drayger told her. "I'm a genius and the Compact likes me more than you."

"Clearly, having hitched *me* to *you*," Luke replied acidly, brushing herself off as if he'd soiled her shirt.

"I am wounded!" Drayger said, but he was remembering the other thing that they had decided to do.

She was going to tell Fask that they were together. They could be together in truth, not sneaking around in back corridors trying to find chances to kiss and having uncomfortable floor sex.

"Will you please keep your mind on business?" Luke snapped. "That is entirely too distracting right now. I have a heist to coordinate, apparently. No, sorry, I mean a *dozen* heists into the most guarded vaults in the world to coordinate. Whether the Compact is behind it or not, I have no idea how to pull this off."

"Fortunately, I'm a bit of a genius," Drayger said with a grin. "I have some ideas about that."

Luke skeptically waited for him to go on.

"We picked up a lot of artifacts in the raid on Amara's stronghold, and a lot of them came from other kingdoms. So…we should return them! Especially to the countries that have pulled out of the Small Kingdoms."

"Since when are you interested in repatriation of stolen artifacts?"

"When I realized that they would be put in their vaults," Drayger said, waiting for the understanding to dawn in Luke's face.

"I'm failing to see the connection—" Luke started to say, and Drayger was watching her closely enough to see her pupils widen. "You're suggesting we boobytrap them with portal anchors."

"Clever Captain Luke," Drayger said, delighted that she'd gone down the same track as he had and as pleased as a puppy to feel her grudging respect. "Once we have access directly into their vaults, we can take their pages and get out without anyone the wiser. Most of the Kingdoms haven't been hit as hard as we have and probably don't have protections as sophisticated."

"We have to hope," she said quellingly. "And hope isn't much of a strategy. Also, we don't have enough anchors for every Kingdom."

Drayger could see her contemplating the idea. "Do you have a better idea?" he asked.

"No." And it clearly frustrated her.

"I can take Majorca," Drayger said. And Leinani can get Mo'orea's just for asking, she doesn't have to fake her way in or even get it ahead of time."

"That's two," Luke said briskly. "That leaves a lot left to heist."

"We don't have to steal pages from the ones who will join in willingly."

Luke was obviously convinced. "I bet Tania and Rian could get into Japan—she's been talking about asking to see their pages of the Compact for research reasons anyway. Maybe we can use that."

"Toren can make some trips and hand out a bunch of these artifacts, he's just dying to do more of those diplomatic things." Drayger thought it was kind of cute.

"*Stealing* is not actually *diplomatic*," Luke said, but Drayger was warmed by how impressed she was with him. "We should try convincing, before we start pilfering."

"Ah," Drayger said. "But stealing is more *fun*."

## CHAPTER 32

Luke found herself at Fask's doorway again and she knocked on the frame feeling more nervous than she had as a new guard presenting herself for her rank tests.

"Come!"

Luke didn't let herself linger or lurk in the door to betray her uncertainty, but marched in with resolve.

"Cousin!"

Luke bit back her instinct to remind him to call her Captain, because she didn't want the reminder that they were *family*. "Your Highness."

"What can I do for you, Captain?"

That wasn't actually much better.

Luke stood at attention across the desk from him. "I would like to take this opportunity to let you know that I have started a…ah…physical relationship with our guest, Drayger of Majorca. I assure you it will not impact my duties or loyalty, but felt obligated to inform you of the arrangement."

Fask was either an even better actor than Luke had

already given him credit for, or he honestly hadn't expected or heard rumors of the relationship.

"Drayger?" he said incredulously.

"Drayger." Her *mate*.

"I...expected better judgment from you, cousin."

"Are you going to forbid it?" Luke challenged defensively. She reminded herself that she was supposed to be coddling Fask and assuring him of her loyalty, not contesting him.

"Could I?" Fask asked with a chuckle. "No, I wouldn't. I think it's in appallingly poor taste, but I have no doubts that you will keep your priorities in order. I wish you only happiness, and if the deposed prince satisfies you, I certainly won't stand in your way."

That was the Fask that she'd always thought she knew. A diplomat, but one with a good heart, who wanted what was best for everyone.

"Have you spoken with Raval lately?" Fask asked innocently and Luke knew at once that he was probing the strength of the memory spell.

"We discussed the succession problem at some length," Luke said mildly. "And I have debriefed him thoroughly on his little romp into the past."

"Nothing else?" Fask prodded.

Luke let herself look briefly dreamy and confused, then shook her head. "Was there something else we needed to talk about?"

"No, nothing," Fask assured her.

Luke gauged the silence as a dismissal and nodded crisply. "I'll have the weekly report on your desk in the morning."

"I'm heading out tonight to meet with the Queen of Japan in person. I probably won't be back until the afternoon, so don't rush." Fask stood and walked her to the door, chuckling and shaking his head. "*Drayger.* I wouldn't have believed it. He doesn't seem like your type, Luke. What do you see in him?"

Luke paused before opening the door. What *didn't* she see in him? He was clever and good and wildly sexy and deeply complicated and painfully vulnerable. What answer would Fask accept?

"He makes me laugh," she finally said, completely deadpan.

Fask didn't have to know that their best laughter was after the release of sex, lying together in a sweaty afterglow.

Fask tipped his head doubtfully, then smiled and seemed to accept the statement. "Then I wish you all the best," he said. "You are a free woman who can make her own decisions and far be it from me to deny you a little joy in these complicated times."

Luke left feeling like *complicated* was the theme of her life.

She'd told Fask about Drayger and Fask hadn't forbidden the relationship. Now what did they do? Did she invite Drayger to her rooms for the night? Would he show up unbidden? She certainly wasn't going to go to *his* suite. Was she supposed to text him? *Booty call,* she remembered him calling at her office door.

Toren had to hiss at her three times before Luke noticed him lurking in the doorway to the informal dining hall, she was so lost in her thoughts.

"What is it?" she asked. He looked painfully guilty, constantly glancing around. "Try to look like we're just having a conversation. We've had a lot of ordinary conversations, Your Highness."

"Yeah," Toren said in a low whisper, "but we've never done…this. I'm…a little nervous."

Luke had a moment of pity for him. He was *terrible* at this deception thing, especially compared to Drayger. And she compared everything about *everyone* with Drayger now.

"Sedition can be a little overwhelming," Luke said in a way she hoped was comforting.

Toren's silvery-blue eyes got big. "Is this *sedition?*"

Maybe comforting wasn't her strong suit.

"We're going to steal the pages of the Compact from all the Small Kingdoms," Luke said, knowing that wasn't much better.

Toren looked like he was a dog who was ready to pee on the floor. "*What?*"

"Get Carina and make some arrangements to go make some of those diplomatic visits to the other kingdoms that you've been hinting at but not really wanting to do."

"Fask was going to…"

"Right, *Fask* was going to do them all. And now I need you to do them," Luke said. "I want you to announce that we are returning a lot of lost artifacts of cultural importance to the other Small Kingdoms. We're returning some of the magical items that we collected in the raid on the Cause, and we're going to make sure that they have portal anchors in them. When they are put in the vaults, we'll be able to go in and get the pages of the Compact. Then we'll be able to put the Renewal into motion before anyone else can sabotage it."

Toren stared at her. "That's insane."

Luke might not be great at comforting, but she was great at commanding. "Listen up, Your Highness," she said firmly. "The Compact herself has set us on this mission. We're answering a higher calling right now, and this is your chance to prove that you can do it. I'm requisitioning all of Amara's spells and I need your help now."

"But won't the Compact protect…"

"We're doing this *for* the Compact," Luke reminded him. "She won't stop you. Are you up for this job, Your Highness?"

Toren visibly drew himself together and saluted. "Yes, Captain," he said. "I'm ready."

Luke refrained from patting him on the cheek or offering him a piece of cheese from her pocket.

## CHAPTER 33

*D*rayger wasn't sure what the formality was for finally being able to see Luke in public, so he played it as he always did, full of false confidence.

"She's expecting me," he told the honor guards when he got to her door that night. He'd playfully used that line a hundred times, but this was the first time it was the truth the way he implied it.

And she really was, her anticipation like a fiery sizzle in his head. Would she be wearing her uniform? Had she slipped into something that claimed to be more comfortable but really wasn't? What would Luke wear when she was privately ensconced in her own rooms for the night? Conservative pajamas? A short T-shirt with nothing under it?

The guards didn't comment or stop him from knocking and then casually opening the unlocked door to slip inside. "Thanks, ladies!" he said on his way in, and then he was sliding the deadbolt home behind him.

Her front sitting room was empty, but Drayger looked eagerly towards the bedroom and the bathroom, where she was stepping through a steam-wisped doorway. One towel was wrapped around her, she was using another to dry her long, wet hair.

Drayger had always admired her body, but there was a vulnerability to seeing her undressed that added a depth of appreciation. Those long legs! Those strong bare arms! Her smooth golden skin!

She smiled at him, just the slightest lift of the corners of her mouth, and she tossed the towel she was holding towards her desk as she let the other slip off of her altogether.

She was a goddess, an absolute paragon of beauty and power, and he was enthralled by every curve and line from her long neck to her feet, where her toes were flexing in the carpet beneath her.

That was as long as Drayger could possibly resist her, and they met halfway through the room, her arms sliding up around as he claimed her mouth and clasped her close.

"You're wearing too much," she complained, tugging at the collar of his shirt.

"Well, I *could* have arrived naked, but I was afraid I would scandalize your guards," Drayger said, reaching for the button on his pants. "And you're always getting on me about keeping my pants on."

The pants were definitely not staying on now, and his shirt swiftly joined them on the floor as they made their kissing, grabbing, touching, torturous way towards the bedroom.

"Wait," he panted, as they got to the doorway. "Wait..."

"Why?" she growled, clawing him harder.

"I want to see you," he explained, setting her at arm's length. "I want to worship you. I want to look at you and know that you're mine, for this moment at least. I want to sear your beauty in my mind."

He could feel her reaction to his words and see it in the tremble of her body. She wanted the world to respect her for her competence and her prowess, but she melted to be considered attractive. Did she think she wasn't? Drayger suddenly worried. She'd spent so much of her life and her living building an image of strength and sternness. Had she forgotten how gorgeous she was? Did she truly not know?

"You are the hottest thing I have ever seen in my life," he told her. If his words weren't ample, she could not possibly miss his physical reaction; his cock was hard and erect like she was water in a desert and he was a divining rod.

"You are like music and happiness. Your breasts. Your beautiful face. Your neck. Your collarbones. That place where your hips meet your waist. Those legs! Luke… *Alasie*…if I was going to make a perfect woman from parts, these are all the parts I would have chosen."

It was everything he could do not to touch her yet, and she was breathing hard and flexing her fingers but not offering to close the distance between them.

"Statues pale in comparison," he said. "You're even prettier than *I* am, and that's saying something."

That surprised a howl of laughter from her. "You are impossible!" she said, and Drayger wasn't sure who closed the distance between them first, only knew that she was in his arms and he could *touch* all the parts he'd been lusting after.

They made love slowly at first, then fast and urgent as he lay her down on the broad bed and showed her all the things that had been missing from their awkward office sex. Then he was slowing down again, to prolong their pleasure. It was such a luxury, not just the fine cotton sheets beneath them, but having time and space and privacy to show her what she meant to him.

He coaxed noises from her that she hadn't dared to make before, and when he was at his own fever pitch, he was not quiet himself, and they coupled and cried out in release that was both physical and emotional, because this was what they could be together and it was a supernova of everything he was as he claimed her at last for his own.

They drowsed together, sticky and spent, until Drayger kissed her forehead. "Mind if I use your shower?"

"Please do," she said, stirring and stretching against him. "I'll change the sheets and shower again after you."

As exciting as their romp had been, Drayger felt like *this* was the real milestone. She was inviting him to sleep in her bed for the night. This was a thing they were *doing*. She was his, completely, and he had never been so happy in his life.

He showered efficiently, eager to get back into her arms, and gave her a long lazy kiss as they passed at the bathroom door on her way in.

The bed had been made up again and Drayger slipped into it nude, relishing the feel of her sheets on his skin and the anticipation of holding her again.

He nodded off to the sound of her shower, dreaming of the velvet of her skin and the silk of her hair, until a jolt of fury jerked him awake.

He was still struggling back from sleep when Luke came storming from the bathroom, holding his phone like she was going to smash him in the head with it.

"You dirty, filthy *liar*!"

## CHAPTER 34

Luke should have known it was all too good to be true.

There was no place in this whole sordid, horrible soap opera of a nightmare that she was living for real happiness.

"I was an *objective*?" she snarled, brandishing the phone.

Drayger did an admirable job of looking surprised and disarmed, but Luke could feel his heart sink as he realized what she knew.

She hadn't gone into anything with an intention to snoop. She just had a flare of curiosity when she saw Drayger's phone on the bathroom counter and remembered him showing her the magically encoded communication system.

Anyway, they didn't have any secrets from each other…right?

The passcode screen melted away when she tilted the phone back, said the activation word, and the outgoing text was burned into her brain.

*Objective AL achieved.* It had been sent that day. By Drayger.

It took her a confused moment to put it together. Alasie Luke. *She* was AL. And she was *achieved? She was an objective?!*

Drayger blinked in surprise and dismay now, and Luke could feel his heart start to hammer. He should be afraid, she thought, white-hot with fury. "You were playing me the whole time?"

"I was told to get close to you," Drayger admitted, because what else could he do with her waving the evidence in his face.

"You certainly did," Luke said, trying not to think too hard about exactly how close they'd gotten. It wasn't just the sex, but her heart that she'd let him touch.

"Alasie—" Drayger started to plead. He sat up and tried to take her hands, distractingly naked still.

"Captain Luke to you," she snarled, because she couldn't stand hearing her name from his lying lips. She couldn't trust him. She couldn't trust the broken mate bond. She couldn't trust a word or a feeling from him, let alone from herself and she clung to her anger like a shield.

"I would have told you," he said quietly, "but I didn't think it mattered."

Luke pounced. "It didn't matter? It didn't matter that this—all of this!—was one deliberate act on your part? In what reality would that *not matter?*"

"It wasn't like that," Drayger protested. "That's not what *this* is about!"

What *this* did he mean? This sex? This conspiracy? This partnership of convenience? His wild flattery about beauty? This thing she'd thought might be love?

He swung his legs down off the side of the bed to stand up and Luke backed up out of reach.

Luke wasn't sure she was being entirely rational, but

she certainly wasn't going to budge an inch from her outrage at this point. "You said I could trust you. You said you'd told me *everything*. This is a pretty *giant* oversight."

"I—"

"Why didn't you tell me you were sending this message? What *else* have you sent?"

Drayger was still advancing on her and Luke was still backing up. She wasn't afraid of him, but she was afraid of how she might crumble if he touched her.

"You were going to tell Fask about us," Drayger said gently. "It was going to be out in public. I had to make a report of it, like I *would* if I were still working for him, pretending I don't even know that it's him. And I would have told you…"

And of course, she hadn't given him even a fraction of a chance, meeting him at the door with all her hunger and desperation. "The proper time to tell me that I was *one of your targets* was *before* we had sex for the *first* time." *Before you said I love you.*

"You're not being fair," Drayger said, and Luke wasn't sure he was wrong. But she was too angry for logic now. She'd had a certain timeline in her mind. She thought that she'd been singled out by Drayger because he'd seen something in her, that he knew she could help him, not because he'd been *told to seduce her*. Whatever they were *now*, it hurt unbelievably to think she'd been just part of a mission, that his attraction to her really had been fabricated at first.

And that he hadn't *told* her.

"Get out!" she commanded.

"Alasie…"

"Don't call me that again."

"Can I at least get dressed?"

"*Get out.*"

Drayger went, glancing behind him like he was

expecting Luke to give him a last-minute reprieve. "Alasie Luke…"

That was even worse than Alasie. AL was an *objective*. "*OUT.*"

He did an admirable job of gathering his dignity and his clothing. "Captain," he said on the way out.

Luke slammed the door behind him and leaned on it. She wasn't going to cry and give him the satisfaction of her weakness. She wanted to dismantle something, anything.

Starting with her heart.

# CHAPTER 35

～

Drayger had taken plenty of walks of shame, in various states of mussed and undressed.

He had never been ejected into a hallway completely nude in the view of guards who did an admirable job of not staring, laughing, or even smiling. They were Alasie's guards, and they were probably as stunned by his ejection as he was himself. He gave them a friendly wave and jaunty smile, like it was no big deal that he'd just been kicked out of her rooms as unexpectedly as he'd been invited into them.

He didn't pause to dress himself, though he did adjust his armful of clothing so that he wasn't entirely indecent. Anyone behind him would get a fine show, and Drayger added a playful whistle to cover his slink back to his own rooms.

He could feel Alasie's prickly outrage and hurt in his head, and he had to search past it to feel the comfort and reassurance of the mate bond, which was still somehow convinced that they had a possibly perfect future together.

"Are you sure?" he asked the air as he got to his own

suite and dropped his armload of clothing on the bed. Alasie was furious, and he didn't see a way past this rift.

The Compact didn't conveniently appear and explain what she had in mind.

Since he was already naked anyway, Drayger took a long cold shower that couldn't numb the ache in his chest. Was Luke *right?* Should he have told her about that aspect of his job from the start?

He'd been candid about the rest of it, but the directive to seduce Alasie Luke had seemed like such a minor and inconsequential part that it was barely worth mentioning. It wasn't out of character for him to flirt, it was a natural part of his cover, and he would have pursued the captain without the orders, especially when he realized that she was the one who might be able to free him. It wasn't that he'd *forgotten* he'd been ordered after her, but it *was* the least of the reasons that he had courted her.

Drayger guessed now that Fask had realized that the captain of his guard was too clever to remain oblivious and needed her to be distracted during the final parts of his ploy. Drayger's primary job was to play that distraction while he waited for other orders.

His bed was not the one he'd hoped to sleep in, and he spent a restless night second-guessing every action he'd made and cursing the Compact, because Luke must feel his guilt and use it to feed her fury. She was prickly-hot in his head all night and what rest he got was punctuated by dream-warped memories of every terrible thing he'd ever done.

In the morning, dressed, he went to her office.

The guards there gave him pitiless looks. "She's taking the morning off," one told him.

Drayger was surprised. "That's sorely out of character!"

## CHAPTER 35

"She's done a lot of *out of character* things lately," the other said sharply, then he snapped his mouth shut and refused to say more about where Luke was or how Drayger could find her.

The mate bond wasn't specific enough to act as a compass, only to let him know that she was still mad at him. Drayger wandered the palace until he looped around to the informal dining hall, where the royal breakfast was just breaking up. He had to test his acting skills against the sly looks and smirks that suggested the story of his most recent disgrace had spread through the palace like wildfire.

Drayger kept his chin high. "She'll be back for more soon enough," he said, helping himself to a slice of ham off the table before it could be cleared away. "No one can resist this for very long, and she's had a taste of it now…"

Toren, bless his heart, laughed outright at him, then seemed to remember their conspiracy and turned red and got stammery, and finally bolted away. The crown prince might be learning diplomacy, but he was still as transparent as a child who knew they'd been naughty.

Drayger tucked one of Luke's favorite savory rolls into his pocket and sauntered out.

If Luke wasn't in the palace, she was probably nearby, and Drayger went to the back porch where they sometimes met, though he wasn't surprised she wasn't there. Someone had made a hasty repair of the porch rail he'd destroyed, but it hadn't been painted yet.

It was cold and cloudy, the steel sky threatening snow. The snow on the ground had collapsed a little in the previous day's sun, but there was still plenty of it left. Drayger looked at the marks in the yard for a few moments before recognizing that there was a broad, fresh trail leading out towards the forest. It wasn't a dragon trail, though it was almost wide enough; he couldn't imagine a dragon pushing through on the ground when they could fly.

It was the right size for a polar bear.

Drayger floundered a hundred feet along it, realized that he would never catch up with her at this rate, and shifted. A crouch, and a leap, and he was in the air, powerful wings carrying him up into the lazy breeze above the trees.

Luke's trail was harder to follow through the forest, and when it ended, Drayger thought for a moment that he'd only lost it. Then, what he'd taken for a snowbank moved and looked up at him, and he realized that Luke had stopped and was curled into a furry white ball in a tiny clearing.

It was a challenging landing, with trees crowded too close to get all the way to the ground. Drayger had to fold his wings in to fit, and without that final downbeat, he crashed heavily into the snow beside her.

He shifted as soon as his feet touched, and made a show of bouncing up and brushing off his uniform. The act was thwarted by the fact that the snow was hip deep and he could barely keep his balance in it.

Luke gave a huff of amusement, but didn't offer to rise or shift.

She was an enormous bear, her fur creamy white and luxurious, and her paws were the size of platters. Her bear eyes were as dark and endless as her human eyes, and she had soft-looking ears that were cocked expressively in his direction.

"Alasie." Drayger had to all but swim through the snow to her, keenly aware of his awkwardness. "Dammit, this is not the entrance I usually make."

She still didn't shift as Drayger finally reached her, but she didn't try to get away when he touched her at last. Her fur was coarser than he had expected, and so thick that it felt like it was made of springs. "You're beautiful, you know."

Drayger struggled to stand beside her, but his feet couldn't find purchase in the soft snow. He finally gave up, turned, and sank into her side, half-sitting and half-lying over her front leg. She gave a bear groan that didn't sound displeased and snuffled his hair. He hadn't bothered with a hat.

For a time, they just lay that way, and it began to snow. Big, puffy flakes gathered on the tree branches and covered the signs of Drayger's sloppy landing. Alasie put her heavy head down on her other paw and sighed.

"Look, Alasie, I'm not used to trusting people and I'm not very good at it. I should have told you that I'd been directed to pursue you when this became something real, but I didn't think it was important. And by then, I was already half in love with you and it *wasn't* just business. It's never been *just business* with you."

Alasie blinked a few times, and Drayger could see the vapor from her breath at her nose, but she remained stubbornly still.

"You're beautiful," he said, feeling raw and hoping that she could feel the truth from him. "You're beautiful and smart and competent and everything I'd ever want in a partner, everything I never dreamed I might have. And no, I wouldn't have pursued you if I hadn't been told to, because you are so far out of my league that I couldn't have imagined you at my side."

He breathed out, watching the swirl of steam that he made. "I didn't ask to be your mate, and I don't deserve you, Alasie. I don't deserve the kind of happiness we could have."

She was silent and unhelpful, but Drayger thought he

could feel her unbending in his head as they sat together, understanding and…even forgiving. It was hard enough to sort out his own emotions, and hers were tangled even deeper and more distant. Was their bond beginning to *fade*? As much as he hadn't wanted the connection, the idea of losing it now filled him with regret.

"I didn't know that falling snow had a sound," he said, after they had been quiet for a long while.

It did, though. A swishy sound like softer rainfall, a gentle, muffled patter. A whisper.

There were some bird calls, high in the trees, and every so often a larger clump of snow would fall from a branch.

Otherwise, it was utterly silent, peaceful and perfect.

Luke shifted rather suddenly, and Drayger found himself tipping backwards into her arms. "Whoops, you're a lot smaller this way," he said, as they negotiated the new space. "Not that you aren't magnificent in either form." He turned just enough to wrap his arms around her and pull her down to lie with him.

Luke's polar bear bulk had left a large bowl in the snow and they lay together, sheltered in its curve.

"You're not mad at me anymore," he said in relief. Whatever pain in the ass the mate bond was, it gave him that certainty at least.

"I'm not sure I ever was," Luke said. Her face was very close to his, and Drayger couldn't help but admire the clarity of her warm terra cotta skin, even though he resisted his urge to kiss her. There was a tiny mole near her eyebrow, and a scar by her nose that Drayger wanted the history of. Every little flaw seemed to make her more perfect.

"You felt mad to *me*," Drayger said. "Whew, I'm lucky I got out of that room with all my parts intact because I gotta tell you, I had a moment there I wasn't sure I would."

"I was *insulted*," Luke said quietly. She had snowflakes gathering in her eyelashes and hair already; they melted on her face. "I'd gotten used to the idea that you found me irresistible, and it was a blow to my ego to find out that I was part of your mission."

"Does it help to know that I *do* find you irresistible?" Drayger asked.

She smiled then, that slow, subtle smile that would have been lost on anyone else. "Yeah," she said sheepishly.

He kissed her then, slowly, giving her time to protest if she was going to, and she tipped her head to meet his mouth with hers.

## CHAPTER 36

Luke both hated and loved how the world went away when Drayger kissed her.

For those moments, she could believe that everything was right. Good would triumph over evil, there was never disappointment or betrayal, and the most powerful thing in the world was love. Happy ever afters were not just possible, but inevitable, and justice was uncomplicated.

He was also the sexiest and most distracting thing she'd ever seen, and she wondered how much of her fury with him was at her own weakness.

"I brought you tribute," he said, when they broke apart and sat up. "Oh, rats, it's been a bit smashed."

Luke accepted the crushed dill and cheese roll and offered him half. They inhaled it together, picking crumbs out of the falling snow in their laps.

"What now?" she asked, when they had finished. The snow had slowed, but it still made a silver crown on Drayger's dark head.

"Sex?" Drayger proposed, patting the snow and nearly

losing his balance into it. "It might be a little hard to get purchase on this stuff, but I could manage. You know, I always thought of snow as being something you could pack down, but your devilish Alaskan snow is like slippery sand."

Luke had to laugh, because *how could she not?* and that meant Drayger had to kiss her again, because—she could tell!—he loved making her laugh so much.

"We're not having snow sex," Luke said, pushing him away. "Put your nuts in a snowbank if you must and get back to business. We can speak freely here, for now, and we're running out of time."

Drayger sensibly sobered and Luke couldn't decide which of his moods she loved best. His clownish humor didn't annoy her nearly as much as she thought it should, but it took her breath away when he was suddenly all business.

"I talked to Toren some more about stealing the pages of the Compact," she said, following his lead to seriousness. "He's still on board, if a little freaked out about it. He and Carina are going to do some diplomatic rounds and get the anchors in each of the vaults."

"Is that little twerp capable of pulling that off?" Drayger asked. "Maybe we should have Kenth or Tray do this part."

Luke punched him in the arm. "That's the crown prince of my kingdom you're talking about."

"Sorry, you're right. Is *His Royal Twerpness* capable of…"

Luke shoved him hard into the bank of snow and there was a laughing moment where Drayger couldn't push himself back upright because the snow kept giving way.

"I think he can do it," Luke said, when they were both sitting again, leaning into each other. "Carina can help him, and who's going to suspect that innocent face? But we don't have enough anchors for every vault and odds suggest that not all of the ones we send will get into vaults or activate correctly. How many pages will we need to perform the Renewal? A few are already missing."

Drayger shrugged unhelpfully. "Only the Compact knows."

Luke frowned. "I haven't seen her since we spoke."

"We could have Tania and Rian go to Japan and try to get the pages legitimately. She's a scholar of the Compact, and they stole her thesis. If she could get in and speak directly with the Queen, she might have a good chance of simply convincing her to hand them over."

Luke nodded. "I'll talk to Tania and arrange it if she's on board."

"We don't know for sure that another brother isn't working with Fask," Drayger warned.

"But the other brothers all have mate bonds. The Compact wouldn't have done that if she wasn't sure of their loyalty, would she?"

"Who knows why that old bat does anything," Drayger said. At Luke's flash of outrage, he hastily added, "Probably you're right, but she's said herself that she has been damaged, and who even knows what that entails."

"Speaking of trust…"

"I should have told you I was sending that note," Drayger blurted. "I should have told you that I'd been directed to distract you."

Luke was quiet and she could feel the turmoil in his head.

"If it's any consolation, you were probably the toughest mark I've ever had," he said, elbowing her in the side. "You have no idea how much it damaged my ego that I couldn't seduce you. I haven't failed that badly since I hit puberty and got abs."

She smirked at him. "Your poor, over-inflated ego," she said, reaching to tuck a lock of snow-dusted hair behind Drayger's ear. He caught her hand and kissed her palm. She was so warm that the snowflakes steamed from her skin.

"Is there anything else you need to tell me?" she asked quietly, letting him keep her hand. "Like, why *you* were chosen to kill Carina and Toren?"

"You know my background," Drayger said confidently, holding her hand against his cheek. He needed to shave, there was the slightest stubble there and Luke had to keep herself from scratching at it. "I know that you did due diligence. Your records are probably more thorough than my own family's."

Luke was pleased by his praise. She was more invested in her competence than in her looks. "I'm sure that there are gaps," she said modestly. "Like, how you got a price on your head in Majorca."

She could tell that Drayger would have rather continued kissing her hand and testing the resistance of the snow, but he also seemed to recognize the chance she was giving him. "Our family…is not like your Alaska cousins'. My father relished having illegitimate children that he could pit against each other with promises of land and prestige. Even if none of us ever thought that we have a genuine chance at a crown, there were still riches and power to fight for, and my father encouraged us to squabble and backstab. In some cases, it worked to divide us. In some, it only brought us closer together as we grew up and realized what pawns we were."

Luke wasn't surprised by this. "You retain ties to at least two of your brothers," she observed. She had been frank about the fact that she monitored his communication.

"Forsch and Talgor. They were able to intercept Leinani and Tray when they escaped Amara. I still owe them a favor for that."

"You don't like owing favors," Luke observed.

"Neither do you," Drayger countered.

"Truth."

Luke was quiet, waiting for him to continue, and after a moment of stroking her hand, he did. "I did some dirty work that I'm not particularly proud of. Enforcing the peace, roughing up insurgents, that kind of thing. Being a dragon shifter gives me a certain advantage of strength and speed in back alley reminders of allegiances. My father was not a popular ruler, not kind and beloved like your uncle. We've squashed most of the rebellions and covered up most of the unrest, but the whole Kingdom was ripe for Amara's rhetoric. I...had never actually murdered anyone, until I was sent to put down a violent protest. I was told they were well-armed, and that they would not respond to anything but a show of strength. Forsch and Talgor and I went in spoiling for a fight...and found a bunch of college kids armed with pencils and bookbags. When we got an order to make sure that they were stopped in their march to the capital, Forsch and Talgor refused."

Luke's hand cupped his jaw and her thumb made scratchy circles in his stubble. She waited patiently, and the falling snow seemed to lighten.

"I went on without them, and it was still not a fair fight. I wasn't trying to kill them, only subdue them, but I overestimated their strength, or underestimated mine. It was a complete crush, and several of them died. That wasn't in the news, of course—that would be bad press for the dear leader—but I saw the intelligence reports afterwards."

"You got an award for that action," Luke said without judgment. "A landed title, even."

"It was a military slaughter," Draygor said harshly. "And I was covered in glory for crushing a bunch of unarmed *kids.*"

Luke waited for him to go on, and when he didn't, prodded him. "What did you do next?"

"Whatever I was told," Draygor said. "I was a good little bastard son and I did the jobs I was assigned."

Luke could feel the sharp prickles of his guilt and regret and hoped that he could feel her understanding. She wasn't sure what she would have done in the same place, with the same upbringing, and the same awful choices.

"Until…?"

"Until Carina and Toren. I looked through the scope at them kissing, shining with love for each other and I knew that I couldn't pull that trigger. I could stir up international unrest and frame diplomats with kinky sexual blackmail and kidnap trophy wives for ransom and threaten to remove pinky fingers when payments were late, but I could not end those innocent lives and I hated that I'd gotten to a point in my life where it was even an option and why are you looking at me like that?"

"Because I can't imagine how strong you had to be to get through that and still be *good*," Luke said simply.

"I'm *not* good," Drayger said, feeling raw and hopeful all at once in her head. "I mean, in bed, maybe…"

Luke laughed. "Whatever annoyance this stupid mate bond is, I *know* you now. I know you don't want to hurt people. You want to be a part of something better. *That's* why you really defected to Alaska. Because you'd learned enough about who we were, how we ruled, to have hope.

You realized that there were options other than tyranny and oppression."

"Yes," he said, his voice almost breaking with the relief in his mind. "*Yes.*"

Because of the mate bond, she knew what he craved from her now, and it wasn't sex in the snow, no matter what he said.

"Drayger, I *forgive* you."

Drayger didn't speak, but Luke could feel him go bright with release, like an orgasm in his soul as he clutched her into his arms and buried his face in her hair. "How can you know me, know what I did, and still forgive me?" he asked.

Luke thought, *Because I love you,* but still didn't dare to say it. "I *trust* you. I will always trust that you will do the right thing."

"You *were* really pissed at me earlier," Drayger pointed out, drawing back. "I could tell. The whole *castle* could tell."

"You're not the only one with an ego," Luke said honestly. "My pride was hurt. How dare you not worship me without strings or ulterior motivation from the moment we met?"

"Oh, but I did," Drayger said. "You were the reason I could cut my puppet strings at last. You were my inspiration, you were my escape. If there were people like you in the world, I could finally believe in a world where I could be free and better than my past allowed for. I *do* worship you. I worship your goodness and resolve and everything about you. You are my inspiration, Alasie."

Luke still couldn't say that she loved him, but she could kiss him, so she did.

## CHAPTER 37

Waking up with Luke in his arms was even more perfect than Drayger could have imagined.

She was so soft and warm and strong and long. He had morning wood that he knew she would appreciate, but he didn't want to wake her, so he stayed as still as possible, listening to her steady breathing. It didn't matter that his arm was in an awkward position and it would probably hurt when blood flowed to it again, or that her hair was tickling his nose, or that there was a slight stickiness of sweat between them.

This was where he belonged, curled around her, her ass in his lap, her lean back curved perfectly against his belly, their legs against each other all the way down to the toes.

The whole world could burn, as far as Drayger was concerned, as long as he could cling to this moment of happiness a little longer.

His traitor brain reminded him that he didn't deserve that happiness, and that it was his responsibility to *stop* the world from burning. Drayger gave an involuntary sigh that woke Luke with a shiver and a catch of her breath.

Her whole body went stiff with surprise and Drayger felt her take stock of her unexpected situation and figure out how to react.

"Good morning, beautiful," he said quietly near her ear. He could not quite help grinding his cock against her to remind her of what he had to offer.

"What time is it?" she asked, startled. "Did we set an alarm?"

"Only my friend between your cheeks there," Drayger said.

She turned in his arms and it didn't matter that his arm immediately turned into pins and needles of protest. She was there and she was kissing him and she trusted him, and she *forgave* him. Drayger still wasn't sure why. Luke was the most moral person he'd ever met. How could she not be appalled to learn the ugly truth of him?

Then, just as abruptly, she was crawling over him off the bed. "Dammit, it's after six. I'm already late to drills and I will *never* live this down. Let yourself out!"

She dressed as efficiently as she did everything, ran fingers through her loose hair and twisted it back and up into a bun so swiftly that Drayger couldn't even track what she was doing with it.

Then she was gone and he was stretching out in her sheets wondering if he should masturbate and whether that would distract her from drills. He finally decided that it wouldn't be worth her wrath, and took a cool shower before sauntering out of her suite with a jaunty salute for her guards.

A few hours later, he slid into his seat at the breakfast table by Toren and blew a kiss down the table towards Luke, who ignored him.

## CHAPTER 37

There was nothing they could do about the wild rumors swirling through the palace now, but the unexpected advantage of having a whirlwind suddenly-public romance complete with argument and ejection from Luke's room was that no one seemed to suspect that there was anything more urgent going on in the palace.

It did, exactly as Fask had probably predicted, draw all the attention away from the more drastic and immediate problems. The Renewal was still technically a few weeks away, and it felt very much like the Kingdom was in a lull of inactivity, poised and waiting for the big event. The only topic of any urgency was a coronation, and Toren was still their highest contender. Fask wouldn't hear of Kenth taking the crown, Raval flat out refused to be considered, and Rian and Tray would both point to each other at any hint that one of them might be a possible king.

At the end of it, Toren had agreed to take the crown...and to Luke's surprise, Fask had supported the action. There was even a date set for the ceremony.

"Are you ready, Your Highness?"

Toren looked a little like he was going to be sick, but nodded bravely. Drayger wasn't sure if he was referring to his pending coronation, or his tour of the Kingdoms to plant the portal anchors.

Luke requisitioned all the spells and artifacts from evidence and had Mackenzie and Raval check them against the accounts. The few discrepancies were so minor that they would have gone unnoticed altogether, dismissed as record-keeping errors.

As she had predicted, Fask could not easily stop their travel plans when the proposal was made in public, and he didn't have any reason to suspect that they were anything other than Toren trying to flex his royal muscles a little.

It had taken some cleverness to alter the artifacts to

hide each anchor well enough to defy a cursory inspection by the receiving royalty, and securely enough that the anchor wouldn't fall off and get activated in some unwelcome space. "This is a test of my grade school craft skills," Tania had said, working on a false bottom for a wine goblet that reduced aging and memory loss.

Katy laughed. "As a grade school teacher, I can assure you that most elementary schools do not teach magical deception as a matter of course."

They couldn't really test the anchors, they were just going to have to set them up and hope they worked when the time came.

Drayger didn't particularly like hope as a strategy, and he knew that Luke hated it, but they didn't have any better ideas. There also weren't enough of them for every vault, so some diplomacy was going to have to come into play.

The Compact herself was the most valuable tool in their box of tricks. The protections of the Compact itself, taken for granted for so long, were something only she could get around.

When the meal was cleared away, the mood at the table turned to business. Fask gave the floor to Luke.

"Toren starts his impromptu repatriation tour this afternoon," Luke said efficiently. "I've got a jet lined up at the airport to take him with Carina. You'll be visiting six Kingdoms in four days, so pack accordingly and practice your speeches. I'm sending you with an honor guard. Mackenzie has been extended an official invitation to meet with the prince of New Siberian Islands, who has been confirmed as her father by blood. Kenth and Dalaya will accompany her. I presumed that you three would be comfortable flying as dragons, as it is not that far and our jets are otherwise occupied? It should be a quiet trip with no press, so we don't need to maintain any cover."

Kenth gave a nod and kept a protective hand over Mackenzie's. "They are both accomplished fliers now." *Their* nervousness was easy enough to explain, at least; Mackenzie was going to meet her father for the first time.

"Tania and Rian will be leaving in the morning, on a research invitation."

"It's kind of an apology invitation," Rian said—unnecessarily, in Drayger's opinion. "They felt bad for having stolen Tania's copy of the Compact and destroying her paper."

"And making me doubt my sanity," Tania said, laughing timidly.

The problem with rookie spies is that they felt like they had to over-explain everything. And it was somewhat conspicuous that none of them was looking at Fask. It helped that he was sitting at the head of the table and everyone else had someone across from them to look at instead, but Drayger still found it painfully obvious.

Luke, wisely, did not give any justification for these actions happening *now*, instead of waiting until the Renewal was past, and if Fask looked a little suspicious, Drayger also thought he looked a little relieved. Maybe he was glad to have them all out from underfoot while he positioned everything for whatever his final gambit was.

Drayger wished he didn't have to leave Luke alone to keep tabs on Fask by herself. Not that he didn't trust her, or think she was completely capable, but he wanted to be at her side if there was trouble. His heart hurt for her, knowing how she had cared for her cousin, and how long she had trusted and served him.

"Did you have something to add, Drayger?" Fask asked mildly, making Drayger realize that he was glowering in the prince's direction.

Drayger gave a deep sigh. "I'm afraid you'll have to do

without my sunny company for a few days. There is business with my half-brothers that I need to put to rest." It wasn't entirely a lie. Drayger did plan to go to his brothers for the latest information about the power in the Majorcan palace before he attempted to bluff his way into the vault himself. He didn't add that he also wanted to explain himself to them, and see if he couldn't mend fences with them.

As carefully as the princes and their mates had not been looking at Fask, now they were not looking just as carefully at Luke. Everyone seemed to have something very interesting on their fork or in their lap. Even little Dalaya noticed. "Papa," she said, tugging on Kenth's sleeve. "What's wrong with breakfast?"

"Nothing, kit," Kenth assured her. "Just a lot going on."

"Royal stuff," Dalaya said, nodding sagely.

Everyone laughed at that and she looked quite affronted by their humor.

Fask's phone rang, as they were finishing their meals. "Excuse me," he said politely. "I should take this. The King of Madagascar waits for no prince."

The mood in the room changed abruptly the moment the door closed and everyone stared at Luke and Drayger.

"You all know what to do," Luke said mildly. "I suggest you go pack."

Tray started, "Should we be—"

"You don't have to worry about my personal life," Luke snapped.

Tray raised an eyebrow. "I was going to ask if we should be prepared to escalate our attempts to force if diplomacy doesn't work."

Luke's ears and cheeks went red. "Ah. I really hope it doesn't come to that. Try not to hurt anyone, but do try *very hard* to impress on them how critical all of this is. Keep in mind that we don't know for sure what Fask has been telling them, only what he tells *us* he's telling them. They might not understand how important the Compact really is." She hesitated. "If you see an opportunity to take what we need, I won't tell you take it, but I won't tell you not to take it, either."

She dismissed them all with an impatient gesture and everyone shoved back chairs and left.

"We're going to fly!" Dalaya said eagerly, running ahead of Kenth and Mackenzie. "With wings! I'm a dragon!"

"The worst thing," Drayger said as they left and he was alone at last with Luke, "is that she is not the biggest blabbermouth of this family."

"Fask didn't try to stop us," Luke pointed out. "He didn't object to a single thing on the agenda."

"Strength in numbers?" Drayger suggested. "Witnesses? Maybe he's just really confident in his position of power? Why are you worried?"

"Because this whole thing is absolutely insane, and I hate that you're going to Majorca. You said there was a contract out on you."

There it was! She was worried for *him*, and Drayger melted a little. "That's how my family shows love," he quipped. "It'll be hard to shoot me in public when I show up at their front door with a gift. Liam will wait until later and have me shot in the back."

Luke glowered. "I really don't want you getting shot in the front *or* the back. We could send Toren or Tray to Majorca."

It was adorable how she tried to look angry to cover her concern for him, and it was ridiculous how much he loved that she was trying. "Tray's not going to leave

Leinani, and Toren's dance card is completely full. I'm the best one for this job, and I want to check in with my half-brothers anyway. We still owe them for collecting Tray and Leinani after they escaped."

"And I'll handle Fask," Luke agreed reluctantly.

"And you're going to miss me," Drayger said smugly.

She punched him in the shoulder. "And I'm going to miss you, you ass."

They kissed, chastely at first, and Drayger was keenly aware of the open door. Everyone knew now. Everyone knew that she was his and he was hers and Drayger didn't care if they laughed or mocked the unlikely pairing, no one in the world could ever make him as happy as she did.

"You could go later," Luke suggested, when their kiss refused to stay the kind that should be shared in public. They should probably not make love on the dirty napkins and breakfast crockery.

Drayger was sorely tempted to delay his departure, but gave her a kiss on the forehead and set her to arm's length with effort. "I want to get there during daylight, and I figured it out with time zones. I have to leave now if I don't want to get there in the middle of the night, and I want to start this meeting on the best footing I can. They need their beauty sleep even more than I do."

"Stay safe," Luke said, and Drayger watched her struggle for words as he'd never seen her do before. Would she say it? Would she admit how much he meant to her? Would she confess the love that sizzled between them? Drayger didn't want to say it first and force her hand. He wanted her wild and willing.

"Miss me!" was all he said, and then he turned and left before he lost his will to leave her altogether.

CHAPTER 38

*L*uke wished she were someone else, in someone else's story.

Someone who could tell Drayger how much she loved him without choking on her entire vocabulary. Someone who was not in a Greek tragedy complete with a corrupt ruler and dire consequences. She feared that she was watching the end of an empire, and she was terrified of what might follow it.

"Oh my ancestors, Pickle, will you please just pick a place to pee so we can go back inside?"

Of all of her jobs, the most demanding was walking Pickle three times a day. He had a patch of absorbent artificial turf that served him the rest of the time, but Nathaniel insisted. "At least one of us should get out and get good exercise," he said. A stationary bike had been added to his prison cell, but Luke knew how much Nathaniel must miss being outside.

"I'm working on this," she promised him, every time that they exchanged Pickle's leash. "I *will* get you freed."

Pickle himself had to go through a security sweep at

the top of the stairs, but Nathaniel was not the type to try to smuggle anything in or out. No, it was Luke who somehow found herself in the position of deceit and lies. She had gone through the magical arsenal with Mackenzie and recklessly stolen anything that looked useful, whether it was part of their repatriation facade or to protect what remained of the Compact. One benefit to being a person in charge was that no one questioned anything she did.

Did Fask have that same certainty? Luke caught herself wondering as she waited for Pickle to pick the perfect place. Sometimes they walked to the kennel to greet the other dogs, but more often they went to the edge of the forest.

Considering how much stress Fask must be juggling—even if he hadn't been planning to unseat the structure of magic itself—he was remarkably serene.

Luke caught herself doubting everything with Drayger gone. Maybe they were wrong about Fask's betrayal. Maybe he had a good reason for what he'd done. All they had were bits and pieces that didn't fit together, and she struggled to find a justification for his actions. He had so much power as the oldest prince of Alaska. Even if Toren wore the crown, Fask had a position of trust and control as his adviser. He could have continued to rule Alaska in all but name. Why would he risk all that to rewrite a Compact that protected the entire world? What would he gain?

It bothered Luke that she was still missing some key pieces of this puzzle.

And she *missed* Drayger.

It was astonishing how a single night in her bed had changed that space from her private domain to *theirs*, and how lonely it was without him.

She ached for him like a fainting flower from a Victorian novel. It might not suit her to swoon, but she found herself dawdling over simple tasks and doodling in the margins of her notes. She scowled down at the paper. Fish and abstract swirls bordered her list. At least she hadn't put their names together, or drawn a bunch of hearts and flowers.

She crumpled the list. She didn't need it if she focused, and she was determined to focus. Toren's pending coronation was going to be quick and private—no guests beyond the necessary witnesses, with tight security. She was giving Fask one story about her protections and doing her own thing on the side. She would personally be at Toren's side for the ceremony, and her harpoon was not strictly ceremonial.

Four days.

Four days before Toren was crowned.

Luke firmly told herself that the largest problem she was facing was *not* that she wasn't getting laid, but her bear didn't believe her.

## CHAPTER 39

The most direct route to Majorca was over the pole, and Drayger went under his own power.

It was a stunning flight, over the forests of interior Alaska, the spectacular Brooks Range, then the treeless north slope, stretching to the ocean. Was this where Luke's home was? Drayger didn't fly close enough to identify the villages or landmarks she'd spoken of.

Then there were miles and miles of bright, reflective sea ice, endless and monotonous at this distance, before he came out on the Greenland Sea.

His wings were aching by the time he had passed Scandinavia, and he flew over Germany quite exhausted and wishing that he'd accepted Luke's offer of a jet. Had he become soft while he was pretending to be, lazing about the Alaska palace?

He angled slightly east of Majorca, aiming for the island of Corsica between Italy and France, and he wasn't surprised in the slightest when two dragons rose to meet him as he circled down out of the sky. He had texted his brothers before his departure.

He made it clear by posture that he wasn't interested in a fight, and didn't try to outrun them or attack. They fell into an escort formation, and one took point to lead him down to a stone mountain chalet with a broad, sturdy deck that already looked as if it had been scratched by dragon landings. It was solid underneath him as he backwinged to a landing.

It felt odd to be on feet after so long flying, and even odder to shift them to human feet.

"My goodness that was a flight," he said in Spanish, as he stretched his aching arms. "I haven't been a dragon for such a long time in a while."

The other dragons thumped to a landing on the broad deck behind him and shifted into human form.

"Forsch!" Drayger greeted them. "Talgor! My brothers!"

He wasn't surprised that they didn't welcome him warmly, but he wasn't expecting the outright hostility in their faces, or the fact that they didn't invite him in at all, both of them blocking the door into the house in a gesture of unmistakable protectiveness.

"I suppose this is a social visit?" Forsch asked, crossing his arms.

"Is there another kind of visit with more than one person? We're people, we're being social. It's a social visit. Break open some wine and say hello to your long-lost brother."

"Not long enough," Talgor muttered.

"Admit it," Drayger joked, "you missed me. I was always the one who knew how to have fun."

Neither of them rose to the jibe.

"Are you still burning over the fact that I failed to desert when you did?" Drayger asked, sobering. "I did get out, eventually. You were right, is that what you wanted to hear? You were right and I should have stood down with you and don't think for a minute that it doesn't still haunt me."

"So, you've come to make *amends*?" Forsch sounded skeptical.

"If I could, I would," Drayger said flatly. "But that's not why I'm here."

"Why, then?"

"You know why he's here," Talgor spat. "Why are we wasting time even listening to him?"

"I don't know what you've heard from Fask," Drayger said, "but it's probably at least half lies."

"Fask?" Forsch looked puzzled.

"Oldest prince of Alaska. Kind of a dour guy, chip on his shoulder type, lots of nobility and such."

"We know who Fask is," Forsch said impatiently. "What does that have to with us?"

"He's trying to prevent the Renewal. Or corrupt it, really, so that he gets all the power. Classic, actually. All he needs is a handlebar mustache. Are you sure we can't talk about this over a carafe of wine inside, out of the wind?"

"I would rather pour an entire cask into the dry earth," Talgor said furiously.

"We don't know," Forsch cautioned Talgor. "We aren't *sure*."

"*I'm* sure," Talgor said passionately. "I've never been more sure. He comes sailing in, *now*, of all times, and it's not because he has a sudden need for *confession*."

"I need to talk to you about the Renewal," Drayger said, still not sure why Talgor was so worked up. "I need your *help*."

"You want us to make your job easier?" Talgor scoffed. "You've always overestimated your own charm, but I'm not going to lay down and let you—"

"We don't *know*," Forsch said forcefully, catching Talgor's arm before he could finish the sentence. "He might not *know*."

Talgor's look was agony and anger, and Drayger had a sudden sizzle of understanding. "You have a mate," he said in astonishment. Only finding a mate could have fired Talgor up like that. Drayer knew, because he *knew* that fire. He knew how finding a mate put everything suddenly into sharp emotional focus, how he'd burn the world to save her. He'd certainly turn against his own half-brother to protect her. Especially if…

"You think I'm here to kill her!"

"I *know* you are," Talgor said.

Drayger's dragon gave a flare of warning as Talgor pulled an etched gun from a holster under his jacket and fired a round of sizzling power at Drayger. He tried to leap out its way into the air as a dragon, but instead, he was tangled suddenly in a net of agony, pulled inexorably back into his human form, and pinned to the ground.

"Oh," said Forsch mournfully. "You really shouldn't have done that."

Drayger wasn't sure which one of them he was talking to as his vision went dark.

## CHAPTER 40

Luke liked work that was immediate, with objectives that could be achieved with effort and persistence. The more physical the task, the better. She could drill rookie guards until they were begging for mercy, drenched in sweat, and make them *like* it. She could out-shovel any team of hers after a major snowfall. She could outlast her opponents in any test of endurance and pain, and frequently came away with medals in ear pull competitions. She had earned her stars with patience and hard work.

*Handling Fask* was the exact opposite of all her skill sets and comfort levels.

She had to lie and pretend that nothing at all was wrong. She had to let Fask think he was leading everyone down the garden path and smile at him and fake the trust and affection she had once actually felt, never giving him a hint of her grief or uncertainty.

She was grateful that Fask seemed busy, making diplomatic rounds with other rulers. He claimed that he was trying to persuade them to join the Renewal, insisting that they were reluctant, even though Luke deeply suspected that he was doing exactly the opposite. But he still seemed weirdly unconcerned about the jaunt that his brothers were taking through the Small Kingdoms.

Shouldn't he be worried that they were going to uncover his duplicity? Had he been honest about what he was telling the other royals? Toren would be back tomorrow, and he would have spoken with six monarchs. What were the chances that *none* of them had exposed Fask's double-dealing?

Luke hated having doubts.

She was heading down to the sublevel to walk Pickle, which had become a familiar routine, when the alarms blared the sound of long-distance aerial wards being activated.

Luke's first heady hope was that Drayger had returned as she turned on the steps and ran for the back entrance. He'd only been gone four days, and Luke was dismayed by how *long* four days had felt without him.

But three dragons landed in the snow-covered yard and Luke told herself firmly that it was unreasonable to be disappointed that one of them wasn't Drayger. There had been no word from him since he'd left for Majorca, but that didn't mean there was trouble. Their mate bond seemed muted by the distance between them, and Luke tried not to fret.

Kenth's landing was confident, sending a cloud of snow around him as he crashed to the earth. Mackenzie was more careful, back-winging until her feet hit the ground, snow swirling around her. Dalaya cannonballed into a snowbank and emerged as a joyous little girl.

"I got candy!" she said. She was wearing a Russian headdress and had a fox fur scarf around her neck. She bolted for the porch where Luke waited beside Mrs. James.

## CHAPTER 40

Mrs. James scooped Dalaya into her arms. "You must tell me all about your adventures!"

"I want to see my room!"

Kenth, taking the steps up the porch more sedately with Mackenzie at his side, nodded his approval. "If you wouldn't mind settling her in, Mrs. James."

"We have a lot to catch up on!" Mrs. James said fondly. "I found you some more stuffed friends to meet, and we redid your play kitchen while you were gone."

"She spoils her," Kenth observed, when they were out of earshot. "Dalaya isn't used to having so much stuff."

"It probably won't harm her," Luke said mildly. "Did you get the *answers* you were hoping for?"

Mackenzie's flush wasn't from the cold. "I met my father," she said, her voice breaking. "I met him, and he was kind to me and it was a little awkward, of course, but I have a *father.* He even told me a little about my mother. I'm not legitimate, of course, but I am *acknowledged*, and I didn't realize how much that would mean to me. They fed us caramel cakes!"

Clearly, she was very emotional about their reunion. Kenth had an arm tight around her shoulders and Luke felt bad for persisting quietly, "And the Compact?"

Mackenzie's glowing face fell. "We failed," she said. "I tried to convince my father why we needed the pages, and explain about Fask and the Compact and the Renewal, but I don't know if he believed me and he said that he couldn't help even if he did. He's just a second son. We made the trip for nothing."

"Clearly not for *nothing*," Luke pointed out, trying to squash her disappointment. "You were able to reunite with your father, and that must mean a lot." How many pages would they need to do a successful Renewal? Would

Drayger get the pages from Majorca? Tania and Rian were still in Japan. How successful would Toren be?

"Definitely not for nothing," Kenth said, pulling away from Mackenzie with an unexpected grin and reaching into his uniform coat.

Luke knew that grin. That was his prank grin. His *I'm about to unleash merry hell* grin.

"What do you mean?" Mackenzie asked suspiciously.

"I might have taken advantage of you occupying all of their attention there at the end of our visit to take Dalaya on a little tour of the castle. A tour that included the vault."

Mackenzie stared. "How could you get into their vault?"

"Are those the pages?" Luke asked in wonder.

They were larger than letter paper and Luke winced to see that the thick paper was folded roughly in half. It was like Kenth to fold priceless magical documents.

"I had Dalaya steal them," Kenth said without remorse. "I promised her ice cream and a dollhouse."

Mackenzie groaned. "That's what she meant when she said she walked through walls and got the menus for her game with you. I thought it was just pretend."

"I had her draw a door on the wall of our suite," Kenth explained, "and told her where it should go. It worked like a charm."

"And the Compact didn't stop you," Luke said, reverently taking the spell and smoothing the paper flat. Tiny print covered every inch of the document, and it was the same dark ink and creamy background as the pages in their own vault.

"I don't know if she's lost more of her power than we realized, or if we had her permission," Kenth said with a shrug. "But we got the pages. I doubt they even know they are gone. Dalaya's spells fade quickly and the door was gone in hours. It didn't trip any alarms."

Is this what it had come to, stealing pages of the Compact with the very chaos magic that it had been designed to stop?

Mackenzie was sputtering in surprise. "You stole my uncle's property? You used Dalaya's chaos magic? You didn't *tell* me? It's…it's…"

"Completely immoral and a *terrible* example to my daughter," Kenth said without a shred of remorse. "It's a good thing that you are in her life as a beacon of honesty and upright citizenship."

Mackenzie looked like she wasn't sure if she was being teased while Luke smothered a laugh and tried not to crinkle the Compact any further.

"Who else is back?" Kenth wanted to know. "Have any of the others been successful?"

"Tania and Rian are still negotiating with Japan. Apparently, they were really impressed by her thesis, and she is hopeful that she will persuade them to join us. Toren will be back tomorrow. Leinani said they would be back for his coronation." And no word from Drayger.

"And no word from Drayger."

Luke hadn't planned to say it out loud, so she was surprised when Kenth did.

"You really love him, don't you." Mackenzie didn't say a lot, but when she did, it was worth listening to.

Luke set her jaw so that she wouldn't sigh dramatically or flinch or otherwise give herself away, picturing the tattoos on her chin as iron bars that protected her.

Kenth laughed. "Good luck getting *Captain Cold* to admit something like that."

Luke had heard the name before, but she'd never wished quite so much that it wasn't true.

# CHAPTER 41

Drayger didn't particularly enjoy prison under the best of conditions, and Talgor and Forsch's cells were not nearly as nice as the Alaskan ones. There was no carpeting, no entertainment, no fully stocked bar, no exercise bike. It was a concrete and iron cube, with a toilet, a bed, and a desk with a chair…but nothing on or in the desk. There was one flat pillow and a thin blanket.

The spell that Talgor had hit him with seemed to have muted his dragon's ability to shift and Drayger had a sinking feeling that they were going to have to decide what to do with him before it wore off.

"Ah!" he greeted Forsch at the sound of a door opening. "It's room service!"

Drayger hoped that it was a good sign that they were feeding him. They didn't want to kill him, they were only afraid that they would have to, to protect Talgor's mate.

Drayger wouldn't have done any less to protect Luke, if he were in their shoes.

"We found a brooch in your pocket," Forsch said, passing a tray of bread, cheese, and olives to Drayger. He'd even brought a child's tumbler of wine. "It was etched all over with castings. And when we took the back off, we found a scrap of paper with another spell on it. Was that how you were going to kill her?"

"Chardonnay? Is this from Talgor's grapes?"

Drayger hadn't been terribly surprised that Talgor had turned to agriculture. He'd always had a knack for growing things. Drayger was as good at killing plants as he was at terrorizing people.

"Yes," Forsch said shortly. "We have an arrangement with a winery in Italy. Are you going to answer the question?"

"I wasn't here to kill her. I didn't even know about her. What would I have against her?"

"You never took your jobs personally," Forsch said.

Drayger didn't correct him.

"You'd get your title back, heaps of money, a worthy hoard, our brother's favor. Why wouldn't you? Why else would you come here?"

Drayger leaned his head against the cold iron bars. "I'm here because Fask has it in his pointy little head that he can do better than the Compact, putting the full power of magic in his own hands instead of in nobody's hands at all. I don't know what he's been telling you, but the Compact is much more powerful and complex than we realized. It keeps magic itself from running rampant, and if the Renewal doesn't happen, the world will burn."

To Drayger's surprise, Forsch was nodding impatiently. "You already knew that?" Had Fask actually been honest with the other kingdoms?

"The Compact told us," Forsch said. "Our dragons confirmed it. We thought she was just another vineyard spirit until she explained it to us."

Drayger felt foolish for thinking that they'd been special

for the Compact's attention in Alaska. Of course she could help other countries. It was in her best interest to spread out her influence. Did other countries have secret mates waiting to be found for a proper Renewal?

It would have been nice if the Compact had been more forthright about that before she stopped showing up. But forthright wasn't really her thing.

"Liam doesn't have a mate, does he." Drayger didn't make it a question.

"He says he does, but…" Forsch spread his hands.

"Honesty is not one of our dear brother's virtues," Drayger said. Then he guessed, "But you do?"

Forsch's face shuttered, but not before Drayger confirmed his suspicion.

"I don't blame you for not being public about it." Drayger debated telling him about Luke. But if Liam was putting out hits on the mates of bastard brothers, he would put her at risk by letting that little nugget of information out. No, that was definitely something he should keep close to his chest.

In some ways, it was a relief to find out that the Compact was calling multiple mates from Majorca, too— he had no desire to rule, and he wouldn't have wanted to make Luke choose between her land and his.

"Eat your food," Forsch said. "We've got some time to decide what to do with you."

He meant it threateningly, but the teeth were gone from the statement. Drayger was hopeful that his story would sway them.

"Lovely to see you!" he called up after his retreating brother. "We should do this again some time!"

*D*rayger woke to the sound of footsteps on the stairs. Prison was as bad as Alaskan winter—because of the perpetual darkness, he had no idea what time of day it was, or how long he'd been there. A few days at least, maybe a week? Most of his meals had been delivered by uncommunicative servants. Toren was probably already crowned by now. Would Luke organize a rescue if he was too late to return? Distance and time had muted their mate bond.

"Have you come to gloat?" he asked, before he sat up and saw his visitor. "You're much better-looking than my brothers."

A slight woman stood, poorly lit in the puddle of light from dim overhead lights. Red hair, Drayger thought. Probably freckles. She stood sensibly far away from the prison bars.

"I'm Mirrim. I wanted to see the man who was sent to kill me."

"I wasn't going to kill you. I didn't even know about you!"

"I'm sure that an assassin would also say that. To get me to let down my guard." Mirrim looked critically at him. "I expected someone…more impressive. Your brothers made it sound like you were some kind of horrible brute."

"Aw, it's nice of them to say that." Drayger had deliberately remained seated so he wouldn't look aggressive or intimidating.

"If you didn't come here to kill me, why *are* you here?"

"To mooch wine and play Pinochle?" Drayger suggested. "Like I told Forsch, I'm here to try to stop Fask from preventing the Renewal and taking control of the magic for himself. He's power-hungry and possibly insane. He killed his own father."

"Do you have proof?" Mirrim asked shrewdly.

"None of our evidence is definitive, but the Compact herself set us on this mission."

"You could just be saying that." Mirrim shrugged. "Alaska and Majorca have always been at odds. Maybe you're working for Liam to *discredit* the true prince of Alaska."

Drayger stood up and came to the bars. Mirrim took a step back. "I'd say you should ask the Compact, but she's a little on the obscure and unhelpful side of things."

"What were you planning to do with the brooch you brought? Was it meant as a gift? What does the spell do?"

"I planned to give the bauble to Liam to buy my way back into his favor; I'd tell him that I stole it from Alaska, and that I don't need jewelry that makes me look beautiful. That spell inside of it was meant to anchor a portal into their vault." Drayger thought that being forthright was probably his best bet at this point. Mirrim seemed more interested in listening to him than his brothers were. Should he tell her about Luke? It was absurd how much he wanted to tell everyone that they were mates, to make his claim on her properly public.

Mirrim gave him a critical look. "I don't know," she said drolly, "you could probably use an illusion spell to make you look better. I never did care for that kind of pretty playboy pout."

Drayger gave a shout of laughter. "Talgor deserves you," he said frankly.

"Mirrim! Mirrim!!" Talgor burst through the door at the bottom of the stairs like a firestorm, and Drayger was glad that there were bars between them at his half-brother's look of rage. "If you've hurt her…"

"Still behind bars," Drayger reminded him.

Help came from an unexpected angle. "We have to let him out," Mirrim said firmly. "He's not here to kill me."

"Did he tell you that?" Talgor said with a look of supreme distrust. "I warned you about him."

"I'm wounded," Drayger said. "Not surprised, but definitely wounded."

"I can make up my own mind about people," Mirrim said. "I did some research before I came down here, and it's surprising how many of the people he's worked with are willing to vouch for him. Some of them even called him a friend."

Drayger was surprised by the realization that he had friends, and he wasn't entirely sure what to do with that information.

"He had a chance to kill the prince of Alaska and his mate and refused to take it," Mirrim said. "He's considered unreliable on the black service market."

"How'd you find that out?" Drayger asked in astonishment. This Mirrim character certainly had unexpected depths.

"Girls can be competent, too," Mirrim murmured.

Talgor was staring suspiciously through the bars at Drayger. "I don't trust you," he said flatly.

"I certainly wouldn't trust myself," Drayger agreed. Then he sighed. "I have a mate, too and I know what I'd do to keep her safe."

Talgor was silent, chewing this new information.

"Mirrim?" There were more steps on the stairs and a robust Spanish woman with arms like a swimmer came down, side-by-side with Forsch. The two of them together barely fit in the stairwell. "I wanted to come see the prisoner as well."

"What a charming family reunion," Drayger greeted

them. "You must be Forsch's mate! How lovely to meet you!"

"You told him about Chloe?" Talgor frowned at Forsch.

"What's he going to do from in there?" Forsch challenged.

Drayger offered his hand to Chloe through the bars of the prison and she graciously let him draw her fingers close and kiss them.

"Charmed," she said, in a way that suggested she really wasn't. "So you have your own mate?"

"I'm sorry she couldn't attend this little soiree," Drayger drawled. "All the best parties are in prison."

"Who is your supposed mate?" Talgor wanted to know. "Why didn't you mention her before?"

"Probably the same reasons you two didn't post bans," Drayger said dryly. He hesitated only a moment before adding, "Captain Alasie Luke."

Forsch gave a shout of laughter and Talgor sputtered in disbelief. "You're trying to convince us that *Captain Cold Luke* is your mate?" he chortled.

"It's a lie only our brother would attempt," Forsch agreed.

Mirrim and Chloe didn't laugh as outrageously as their mates, but they looked distinctly dubious. "It's unlikely," Mirrim said. "She seems like someone with good taste."

"But would he lie about something so obviously false?" Chloe wanted to know. "If he was truly trying to deceive us, why not pick a less well-known name?"

"It's just impossible enough that it might be true," Forsch said.

"I'm *right here*, you guys," Drayger said, feigning insult. "It's not that impossible."

"Pretty impossible," Talgor said flippantly.

Despite their laughter and protest, there was a lightness to their disbelief that set Drayger at ease. They might not believe all of his story, but they were listening now, and seemed willing to accept that he wasn't there to kill one of them.

"What did you want from the vault?" Mirrim asked. "What did you need to do that much work to liberate?"

Now that he was on a track of truth, Drayger figured he might as well continue along it. "I planned to steal the pages of the Compact from Liam, so that we could do our own Renewal free of Fask's influence."

He was surprised by the quality of the silence that met his statement as his brothers exchanged long, wordless looks with their mates.

"You can't steal it," Forsch finally said.

Drayger hadn't come this far and spent who-knows-how-long in their very uncomfortable prison to give up now, but before he could launch into a persuasive speech about how this was something he had to do, Talgor gave a shout of laughter.

"We already did!"

## CHAPTER 42

Toren's coronation went exactly to plan…except that Drayger wasn't back, and wasn't answering his text messages, and Luke was sick with worry. If she was short-tempered and scowling through the ceremony, no one dared to tell her that they suspected it was anything but her concern for the new king's safety. They saved the big media blast and public ceremony for after the Renewal. Or whatever Fask managed to subvert the Renewal to be.

Luke spent her time working feverishly on a dozen contingency plans, and she tried to squash her hope when the aerial wards alarmed a few days later. Everyone *else* was back. They weren't expecting any diplomatic visitors.

She didn't rush. The wards gave her plenty of time to saunter easily to the back porch, where she stood at perfect attention, feeling her stomach flutter in ridiculous anticipation. She watched the little ripple of light and space that resolved into a dragon if she thought about it hard enough.

She was absolutely not going to run to meet him.

This was not the moment out of a movie, the sweet reunion of lovers to a swell of dramatic music, and Luke was no insipid Hallmark heroine. She wasn't weak-kneed at the return of a man that until just a few scant weeks ago meant nothing to her beyond being a persistent thorn in her side.

And she was certainly not going to get all swoony because Drayger managed to look like a shirtless Viking hero after he'd landed and shifted to plow, half-dressed, through the snow that was still left in the backyard. It was late enough in the season now that bare batches of lawn were showing, but early enough that plenty of snow was left in shadowed places.

Drayger was wearing a long, open, sleeveless Spanish vest with no shirt beneath it. He trotted up the steps, stomping the snow from his feet, and came directly for Luke, catching her gaze and refusing to let it go or slow until he was standing right in front of her taking her face in his hands to kiss her passionately.

It was not one of his casual cultural cheek-pecks. This was a claim of her mouth with his, a bold, ferocious kiss that forced her lips apart and made her melt to the core.

Luke completely forgot to push him away or to twist out of his embrace, too swept up in the taste and feel of him again at last. Somehow, her arms were around his neck and at his waist, and she was pulling him as close as he was pulling her.

The sound of applause finally had her drawing back. Her guards at the doors were clapping unabashedly and Drayger took the slight space she gave him and executed a graceful bow and pretended to tip a hat.

"Remind me to demote them," Luke growled. So much for her attempt to retain any kind of dignity. "Why aren't you wearing a shirt?" she asked crossly. Her lips felt bruised

"I spilled wine on it," Drayger said, shrugging carelessly. "Ruined beyond saving."

"Of course you did."

"You missed me," Drayger said, trying to tuck her arm into his elbow. "Come and show me how much."

"You are impossible," Luke said fondly. She batted off his hands and marched ahead of him into the castle past her deeply amused guards.

They barely made it out of sight before he'd caught up with her and dragged her back by a hand to press her up against a wall and kiss her again, even deeper.

"I missed *you*," he said, nibbling her earlobe. Damn the mate bond for letting him know how much she loved that particular trick. Then he was kissing down the side of her neck and she was sighing and tipping her head to the side because his mouth on her skin was the most wonderful sensation she'd ever felt.

"I…" Luke couldn't bring herself to admit how much she'd missed him. Would he know? Even at this proximity, the mate bond was weaker now, and muddled with all her other immediate emotions.

"I got the Compact pages," he breathed. "They're in the back of my pants and they are starting to slip..."

"You would stop at nothing to get me in there," Luke said with a hoarse chuckle. She slid a hand down his back and found that there was indeed a thick package over his ass, the size and stiffness of pages of the Compact, once again folded.

"Someone normal might have brought a briefcase or a bag," Luke suggested.

"I wasn't sure if Fask would be greeting me," Drayger said. "I figured he wouldn't want to pat me down, but you might…" He seemed to think that her wandering exploration of his ass excused him to do the same to hers. "I *missed* you."

The package pressing against her now was definitely not the Compact.

"My rooms..." Luke said.

"Mine are closer," he suggested.

Luke had made it clear from his first day in the castle that she reserved the right to search his guest rooms at any time, for any reason at all, and she had, several times.

But it was much different being there now, without even a charade of authority, and Drayger didn't turn on the lights as he opened the door and drew her in. Without asking permission, he abruptly swept her up off her feet into his arms as he kicked the door closed behind him.

Luke was too startled to struggle, and let him carry her straight to his bedroom. In the dark, they undressed, kissing and caressing and clasping each other in wordless desire.

They paused to put the priceless pages of the Compact in a dresser drawer, then Drayger's pants were discarded on the floor with far less care and Luke was shimmying from her own clothing with his determined help.

Every touch was electric, every kiss was magic, and Luke couldn't get enough of him. They were so matched in strength and desire, two instruments perfectly in tune, and he played her like a master.

It was frantic, hungry lovemaking at first, desperate coupling and kissing and release, then a swift meal, followed by hours of sleepy cuddling and slow, stroking games. Even sated, she could not get enough of the feel of his skin over muscles, the softness of his hair and the roughness of his stubble. Every time she thought she might finally drowse off, thoroughly satisfied, he was teasing her again with his fingers and tongue, making her nipples hard and tantalizing all her most sensitive places until she was eager for more.

Sometimes he held her down, sometimes she pinned him and took her way with him, sometimes they were side-by-side, experimenting with every position and exchange of power and pleasure.

They got very little sleep, but Luke had no regrets until morning, when her eyes were dry and she was afraid she would be sore sitting for any length.

"It's like I just got out of prison," Drayger said, sitting up in her bed with his hands clasped behind his head to watch Luke as she dressed for drills. "Oh wait, I did!"

He had told her about his travails with his half-brothers, and their secret mates.

"I don't know if they'll brave bringing their mates to the Renewal," he admitted now. "No matter what the Compact herself told them to do. And I don't blame Forsch and Talgor for wanting to protect them. But they gave us the Majorcan pages of the Compact to use ourselves."

"I would have loved to be a fly on the wall for that heist," Luke admitted. "It's probably a good story."

"What now?" Drayger asked more seriously, sliding his sexy legs out from under the covers and coming over to help Luke button her collar.

"I don't need help," she protested.

"I know," Drayger said, doing it anyway. It was very distracting having him so close and so naked, even after a whole night of having him to herself.

"Do we have enough pages to do the Renewal now?" Luke asked thoughtfully, forcing her thoughts back to business.

"According to my brother's mate Mirrim, the Compact says that she's gathering the true mates from around the world," Drayger said. "It's not just Alaska getting weird about it. I've got some private contacts to add to our list. Not all of them are being formally acknowledged by the kingdoms. And it sounds like some of the players who claim to be mates might not be. My half-brother Liam, for one."

"The Renewal is not supposed to happen for a few days yet," Luke said. "Do we just wait until that date, or do we push forward faster to make sure it happens before Fask and the false mates can sabotage it? I think we've gotten what we can, besides Alaska's pages."

"The Compact made it sound urgent when we spoke to her," Drayger reminded her. "Where are you keeping the other pages?"

"In my office," Luke said briefly, reminding herself to stick to the plan she'd made while he was away. "A file drawer on the right."

"The Compact made it sound urgent," Drayger said. "She said to do it right away. I think that means we don't wait."

"It would be helpful if she were more specific about things," Luke said crossly. "I don't like answers like *soon* and *maybe*."

"Let's get the Scooby Gang together this afternoon and see what happens," Drayger proposed, and because he was naked, Luke might have agreed to anything he suggested.

"I'll contact the other royals I'm sure of this morning so they have time to get there," she agreed reluctantly. "And whatever happens...*follow my lead*." Did she lean into the words a little too hard?

Drayger was kissing her neck. "Anywhere you go," he promised.

## CHAPTER 43

Drayger took the chair behind her desk before Luke could get there, and he patted his lap invitingly. "You can sit with me," he offered.

Luke gave him a quelling look and remained standing as the rest of the princes and their mates trickled in for the meeting.

She stood at easy attention as she locked the door and caught everyone up.

"We're really doing this," Toren said in awe. "We got all the pages."

"All the ones that were left," Tania pointed out. "Wildfire took out South Madagascar's. And Rapa Nui's is under feet of rubble after an earthquake triggered a landslide."

"Does that seem weird to anyone else?" Rian asked thoughtfully. "Last I heard, Madagascar had a robust public water system and perfectly adequate fire suppression technology and the earthquake at Rapa Nui was very oddly specific."

"It is in the ring of fire," Tania said. "It's not uncommon to have seismic activity there."

"Seismic activity that just happens to bury the vault under twenty feet of rock and damage *nothing else?*" Rian and Tania loved to debate, and their affection never seemed dampened by disagreement.

Tania and Raval both agreed that there were *probably* enough pages remaining to successfully execute the Renewal.

"The redundancies in the spell are pretty thorough," Raval said with a shrug. "But I wouldn't want to do it with anything less."

"Are we sure it's the right time to do it?" Tray asked. "Maybe we should be waiting three days for the scheduled time?"

Luke nodded. "Lacking clear direction from the Compact, I think we base this on her instructions to *hurry*. It's possible that waiting would let Fask and whoever he's working with get the edge up on us. We have the advantage now, and the others are already arriving in Mo'orea."

Forsch and Talgor hadn't responded to Drayger's coded text letting them know that they were executing the Renewal early and Drayger wasn't expecting them to attend.

"All we need are Alaska's pages and a portal to Mo'orea," Luke said briskly, like it was no big deal at all.

Drayger was watching Luke's face and he wondered if she didn't look a little…wary. Like she was still expecting another shoe to drop. That was very much in character for her. She liked to anticipate every eventuality, and there was still a lot that could go wrong.

"I'm going to the vault to get the pages," Luke announced. "The Compact said her protections were down, so this is our opportunity."

She paused at the door and turned back. "Whatever happens next, I'm proud to serve Alaska and the Small

Kingdoms. I believe we're doing the right thing for the world. I have faith in everyone in this room and I am glad to call you family and friends." If her gaze lingered slightly on Drayger, he wasn't sure if she was implying something more. "We are better and stronger together than we are alone."

Then she turned on her heel and left.

"That's why she helps write my speeches," Toren said, when she was gone.

"I can't believe we're doing this," Tania said nervously.

"I know!" Carina was clutching a throw pillow to her chest.

"Maybe we should stay here," Tray suggested to Leinani. "Alaska has some extra mates, and your brother will be there. Maybe they just don't need all of us for the ceremony."

Leinani fixed him with a gimlet eye. "You are not suggesting that we miss helping with what might be the most important magical act of our century because I am knocked up."

"I just…you…it might be dangerous?" Tray seemed to recognize that he was on very shaky ground indeed and he took Leinani's hands earnestly in his own. "I love you, Leinani, and if anything happened to you…"

She softened. "Then trust me," she told him. "Trust me to know my own limits and be a part of the team. I will tell you if I feel it's an unnecessary risk."

Raval turned to Katy. "Will you tell me if it's an unnecessary risk?" he blurted.

"It's not," she assured him. "It's all a very necessary risk."

Drayger's pocket gave a little buzz. Did Luke need him? Talgor or Forch, agreeing at the last moment to take part? But the message list showed nothing new until

Drayger excused himself out into the hall and tipped the phone back with the magic passcode.

He read the message twice before he could parse it, and when he did, his heart sunk somewhere down to his toes.

## CHAPTER 44

Just as the Compact had promised, all of the protections at the vault were down. The heavy door opened to simple shifter strength and Luke was standing in that sacred space wishing it had never come to this.

The vault was lit with electric lights, and a lightswitch illuminated a trove of treasures. There were sculptures and chests of gold, lit cabinets showcasing jewels and artwork. It was a priceless hoard, the equal of many small countries and even some large ones.

In the center was an ornate table, and here was the Compact itself, with a selection of the most valuable and magical items in the hoard.

*Her*self? When did the spell, learning from itself, take sentience and identity? How had it chosen a feminine aspect? Was there something written into the Compact itself that implied gender? Luke had more questions than answers.

Alaska's share of the pages were displayed behind glass, and Luke knew that the magical wards were still in place by the slight sheen in the air around the pages of the Compact, though they had faded. No spells lasted forever.

Not even the Compact.

"It's a relic of a time long gone," a familiar voice said behind her.

She had left the vault door open, but he would have been able to get in anyway.

"Fask."

"Captain Luke."

She turned to face Fask with her best blank face. It wasn't that she thought he was still deceived, but she didn't want to give him any clues that she didn't have to.

"You're here for the Compact," he said mildly.

"So are you," Luke said mildly. "But I haven't been able to figure out a few things about your plan."

"You must know that you can't stop me," Fask said, drawing a finger along the edge of the center table as if he were checking for dust.

"You must know that I have to try," Luke said, just as mildly. Maybe she could distract him long enough to make a mistake. "Why did you kill your father?"

"His death solved several problems," Fask said, as if they were talking about the weather. "He was starting to ask questions and draw conclusions, and I needed his dragon. He was old. His end was near anyway. All I really did was hasten it."

*Power*, Luke thought mournfully. He wanted power, and he would stop at nothing to get it. Even killing his own father.

"And how did you lose your dragon?"

Fask gave her a narrow-eyed look, as if he suspected that she was leading him on. Luke tried her best to look helpless and innocent.

"How long have you been free of the memory spell?" he countered.

Luke hesitated in answering, trying to decide what answer would serve her best. "Not long," she said vaguely. "It was kind of slow and hard to pinpoint." That was a bald-faced lie. It had vanished the moment Drayger had kissed her.

But Fask accepted the answer, looking pleased. "Long enough for you to gather the others and enough of the Compact's pages to try to cast the Renewal yourself."

"You have to know that I'm not going to let you do a power grab of that magnitude. If we don't have a proper Renewal, there will be chaos, that magic might burn up our world. If you had a dragon, you could ask it. They worry that it will be the end of everything if the Compact fails."

"They don't *know* that," Fask scoffed. "They like to think that they are infallible and morally superior, but they don't know the future any more than we do. The only reason they could see *this* far ahead is because Raval and Katy went back and took all that knowledge with them."

"You didn't answer my earlier question," Luke realized. "How *did* you lose your dragon?"

Fask's expression was so cold and heartless that Luke wasn't sure how she had ever thought of him as family, let alone a *friend*. There was nothing left of the boy she'd known as a youth, only a shell of a man who had consumed himself with greed and selfishness.

"I threw him out," Fask said impatiently. "I didn't need his grief and goody-two-shoes. I didn't need him at all."

"But you needed his strength," Luke observed.

"I could get that *without* the patronization," Fask spat. "This is how dragons and men were supposed to merge. Not with children, but with full-grown people who could *control* them. We don't need their condescension. It is past time we were out from under their thumbs!"

Luke wondered if he realized how much like Amara he sounded. "Does your dragon still live, haunting the castle like a spirit?" *Or the Compact...?*

Fask looked ugly-smug. "He could not live without me."

Luke could not imagine the will it would take to expunge her polar bear, or how desperate she would have to be to try it. Had the act of doing it broken Fask's mind? Or was the fact that he could do it proof of his derangement? What would it be like without her bear in her soul?

Her bear hated the idea as much as she did. *We are meant to be together like this. This is how we are whole.*

But there was nothing whole about Fask now. He was a gaping hole of greed and egomania. He genuinely thought that *only he* should have the tools to control magic.

"It was you that tried to get to Alaska's pages a few weeks ago," Luke said. "You used a memory spell on the guards at the entrance and portalled out when you triggered the protections I set up."

"That was unexpected," Fask admitted. "I thought you would go along with my command to stand down the security, not step it up. I'm going to need you to release that spell."

"I can't," Luke said frankly. "I wasn't sure if you'd be able to control me, so I made it extremely specific to open."

To her surprise, Fask didn't press her for the key to countering the spell. "I don't *really* need them," he said with a shrug. "I already planned to destroy the rest of the pages and those alone won't be enough for the Renewal to go through. Drayger will be here soon enough, like a good little lapdog, to give me the rest of the remaining Compact."

Luke could not quite suppress the sizzle of alarm as she recognized the ring on his finger from their inventory of Amara's artifacts. It was a stun device, capable of rendering a human or a shifter immobile. She reminded herself she had *expected* this. And if he didn't touch her with it, he couldn't stun her.

"What makes you think you'll be able to do a new Compact in your own favor?" Luke asked desperately. "You're not a magician. You don't have the skill for something this major." Not by himself. There was still something she was missing, she thought in frustration.

Fask didn't answer. They were circling each other now and Luke was trying to stay subtly just out of his reach. She didn't want him to think her capture was too *easy*.

"The Compact prevented you from directly damaging pages from other Small Kingdoms, didn't it? But your alliance with Amara let you get your hands on some of their other artifacts."

"She was a tool that outlived her usefulness," Fask said casually. "She stopped being rational and doing as she was told."

"That happens when you try to use unhinged cultists for your dirty work," Luke said wryly.

She dodged around a statue. Fask was still trying to close the distance between them and his chase had moved from artful to obvious.

"Were you behind the loss of the pages in Rapa Nui and Madagascar? How did you pull those off?"

Fask lunged for her and Luke dodged out of his reach.

"Is there someone else?" Luke taunted. "Someone pulling *your* strings, perhaps? Someone with the magic to make promises like a Compact that obeys you?"

The flash of outrage in Fask's face suggested that Luke was close to the mark, but not on it.

How long had she been in the vault now? Drayger should *be* here by now.

Luke fabricated a trip over the leg of a statue and let Fask close the distance between them, reaching his ringed hand out first. She felt the spell release over her, stinging and subduing her like she'd just been tased.

It could be worse, she thought, fighting the numbness in every limb as she fell without catching herself.

## CHAPTER 45

When Drayger had idly wished that he had a chance to prove his loyalty to Luke, he hadn't ever realized it might come with a choice like this.

And it wasn't a choice at all.

*Bring the Compact pages to the Vault. AL's continued wellbeing depends on it.*

The other shoe had dropped at last, and Fask was giving his leash one last yank.

"I got a text from Captain Hotpants," Drayger lied, coming back into Luke's office hoping that habit and practice would keep him from looking as panicked as he was. "She's got the Alaska pages ready to go, our allies are in place, and she wants to get this all done with before something can go wrong." *And oh, how it **had**.* "She wants to meet us in the throne room so that Mackenzie can portal us all to Mo'orea."

He went, oh so casually, back to her desk and hoped that none of them would remember that there was no phone service to the lower level, so the message could not have been from her. Not by non-magical means, at least.

The desk drawer was locked, but it was a mechanical lock, not magical. Drayger wouldn't have any trouble breaking it, but he couldn't do it in front of the others without exposing his hand.

"Get anything you might need and we'll meet you in the throne room in ten minutes," he fabricated, leaning back in Luke's chair like he didn't have a care in the world. "Then we'll all go save the world together already."

Except that he was willing to let the world burn because he couldn't see a way to save both it *and* the love of his life.

The others, suspecting nothing, took the hint he was offering and trickled out of their last little revolutionary meeting.

"This is it," Toren said. "Sedition."

"It's not really sedition," Carina said comfortingly. "You're the king now."

"Sedition only has to be against *authority*," Raval said thoughtfully. "Technically it could be if we're talking about Fask's authority."

Toren groaned and Katy dragged Raval out, saying, "I want to have better supplies in my purse this time. Just in case we get stuck without toilet paper for a few months again. Can you carry a suitcase for me?"

Drayger didn't want to hurry them out and had to force himself to stay casual, but finally, he was alone in the office. He rose and shut the door behind the last prince.

The wood around the desk drawer lock shattered when he gave it a hard enough pull and he could scoop up the priceless papers. Even just five hundred of the pages was a hefty armful and Drayger cast around to find that Luke had already requisitioned a duffel bag to transport them in. She thought of *everything*, Drayger thought with aching awe.

Drayger's dragon was a swirl of concern in his head. Their mate was being held hostage, which was outrageous enough, but there was something else, too. *The magic is wrong*, it protested, but Drayger couldn't pin down what it was that was so wrong. Sometimes, when it tried to describe magic, it applied senses that Drayger had to patiently explain humans simply didn't have. *It smells confusing*, it said, but couldn't say how.

The guards outside Luke's door didn't give him a second glance. *No big deal*, he tried to project. *Just taking a duffel bag stuffed with the most valuable document in history to our rendezvous. Not selling them for my soul or anything.*

Maybe Luke would have a brilliant idea when he went to trade her for the Compact.

Maybe he could put his hand around Fask's throat and squeeze the life out of him for daring to threaten her.

The further he went, the angrier he got, until he was surprised that the air wasn't steaming off of him. He kept his stride unremarkable at first, but couldn't keep himself from speeding faster and faster. Had Fask hurt her? He couldn't get any clues from the faded mate bond. If she was suffering…

The guards at the top of the stairs to the sublevel were noticeably absent, as were the magical protections, and Drayger rushed down the steps two at a time, skidding down the sloping hallway for the ajar vault door.

His brain felt like it was on overdrive, trying to find a solution that didn't end the world or the woman he loved, and always looping back to his helpless anger. He thought he'd slipped his control collar, but it was tighter around his neck than ever.

Drayger forced himself to stalk the last few steps, not go skidding frantically into the vault. He felt like the Compact weighed a hundred pounds. Was it guilt, or just the heavy realization that Luke would *want* to sacrifice her own life to stop Fask. She would never forgive him for giving the traitor the Compact.

"You rang?" he said, standing in the doorway. Fask was standing with Alasie at his side, her eyes downcast. Had Fask put her under another memory spell? Or some other kind of obedience enchantment? Amara had certainly had plenty of those to choose from.

Fask had a blade at Luke's throat.

The mate bond by now was so faint that he couldn't separate his own worry and love from whatever she was feeling.

Fask gave him a smirk and Drayger had to suppress his urge to close the space between them and punch him in his smug royal face. How dare he hold Luke hostage!

She looked up then, and Drayger had a stab of hope at the sparkle in her eyes. Her face was impressively blank, but there was something there that said she hadn't given up yet, and if she hadn't…

"I haven't decided whether I should give you these or not," Drayger drawled, holding up the duffel bag. "Maybe my prices have gone up."

There was nothing he valued in the world more than Luke, but maybe Fask didn't realize that.

"She's your mate, isn't she?" If Fask was fooled by Drayger's bluff, he didn't give a sign of it. "I gave you an impossible task. I knew she wouldn't fall for you without magic."

"Insulting me is no way to get what you want!" Drayger protested, even if he didn't exactly disagree with Fask. Without the mate bond, he would never have dared to hope that he had a real chance with her. But he also knew that the magic of the Compact wasn't a love spell. It hadn't forced them to feel any way they wouldn't already.

All it did was connect them, and allow them to grow into the amazing potential of their bond.

Fask was still waiting for his answer.

"If you know that she's my mate, you know that I'll do anything for her," Drayger conceded. "But what's the point of trading for her if you're going to rewrite the Renewal and subjugate all of us?"

"You'll have an advisor role at my side in the new world order," Fask promised. "And you'll have Captain Luke."

Drayger had to admit that Fask appeared to have all the cards in this game. If Luke was bothered that they were talking about her as if she wasn't there, she gave no indication. She was looking down again, like she'd been stunned and subdued.

"Fask, you fool." Drayger was honest by desperation. "You aren't enough of a magician to bend the Renewal to your own will, and ending the Compact altogether will unleash chaos magic. Without rules, can you imagine the world?"

"The world is already broken," Fask said. "I would only make it better."

"You're an egomaniac," Drayger said. "Putting the power into your own hands would not be an improvement. You don't have the skill or the diplomacy to pull it off."

"But I have your mate." Fask gave the blade at Luke's throat a little wriggle and Drayger had to squash his flash of fury and fear.

"Give him the pages," Luke begged. "He'll *kill* me!"

She was an *awful* actress, Drayger realized. She had been staying quiet not because Fask was controlling her, but because she knew that she would show her hand if she spoke too much. She'd managed to fool Fask about being under his memory spell by staying quiet and grim, which was in character for her. It was not at all in her comfort zone to act desperate, and there must be a reason she was doing it.

Whatever else he did in this world, he trusted Luke. *Follow my lead*, she'd said in her bedroom, when he'd been distracted kissing her neck. She genuinely wanted him to give the pages they had collected to Fask. He wished that the mate bond was stronger still, or more specific so he could get more of an impression of her plan. Telepathy would be really convenient about now, but the only voice in his head was his own dragon, who was as confused as he was.

"Don't hurt her," he pleaded. He was much more convincing than she was, and Fask looked smug as Drayger, feigning desperation, slid the duffel bag across the floor with one foot.

Fask dragged Luke with him to kneel at the duffel bag and had her open it. That was when Drayger was sure about her deception, because even if Fask had dragon strength, Luke was a skilled fighter who could easily have broken his grip and turned the blade on him using that moment of split attention.

Her struggle was as fake as her fainting plea and it would have convinced no one if Fask hadn't been focused on the thick papers that she too-reluctantly showed him.

The prince tsked at the state of the priceless document. "I can't believe you folded the pages. Rian let you treat these so shabbily? He doesn't even dog-ear paperbacks."

"I didn't exactly have time to arrange archival-quality transport," Drayger protested. "Do we have a deal or not?"

"You've got the pages, please don't kill me!" Luke wailed, laying it on entirely too thick. She was worse than any of the princes, and she snapped her mouth shut at a warning look from Drayger. He still wasn't sure why Luke would want Fask to have the pages, but he utterly trusted her. Maybe the Compact had told her about protections they had and she knew they weren't at risk.

"I am an honorable man," Fask said, touching the pages reverently, "and you served me very well for many years. Thank you for all the work you went to to get these." He lowered the blade from Luke's throat and shoved her off-balance towards Drayger as he reached into his pocket and retrieved a very ordinary-looking lighter.

"What are you doing?" Drayger demanded of him, catching Luke in her forced forward stumble and setting her onto her feet. She kept her face low, like she was afraid to meet his eyes and betray whatever plan she had set in motion.

"I'm ending an era," Fask said. He had a small bottle that smelled of fuel and he upended it into the duffel.

It took all of Drayger's trust not to try to stop him as he stooped and lit a corner of the pages on fire. This was the Compact. The most complicated spell in the world. The source of all the rules of magic. His dragon howled in protest.

The flames flickered and sputtered for a moment, then merrily burned, higher and higher until the entire stack was engulfed. The duffel bag smoked and smoldered, and it was only a few moments before there was nothing but ash collapsing in the cavernous bag.

"It's done," Fask said in satisfaction. Then louder, like he was expecting an audience, "It's *done*!"

*The Compact is not gone*, Drayger's dragon said in confusion.

Fask was just as confused. "Why are the vault protections still in place?" He glanced at the protected Alaska pages. "That can't be enough to keep the spell intact."

Luke looked up with one of her rare smiles, sly and triumphant. "Because that wasn't the Compact."

## CHAPTER 46

Luke hadn't been *positive* that Fask was going to try to destroy the Compact, but she was glad now that she'd been ready for the attempt.

Drayger gave a whoop of triumph at her reveal. "I *knew* that there was a reason I loved you," he said. "Besides your sexy uniform and sweet ass."

As Fask gave a cry of frustration and disbelief, the two of them turned on him in perfect synchronicity, as if they'd planned the entire thing.

Drayger shifted as he pounced, and Fask might have had dragon shifter strength, but he could not hold his own against an actual dragon in a frail human form. Drayger pinned him down and Alasie dashed in fearlessly to snap magical manacles on Fask's wrists.

"We haven't tried that yet," Drayger said suggestively, when Luke had Fask safely restrained and Drayger could shift back. "Maybe we should branch out!"

"Focus, Majorca," Luke chided him, even though the idea excited her. "This isn't about your pants."

"When did you switch the pages? How did you know?" Drayger gave Fask a brisk, efficient search for weapons. "They almost fooled my dragon."

Fask was steaming but not exactly struggling. Luke wasn't going to let the prince out of her sight for a moment.

"I knew that Fask had been giving the other royals a very different story than he was giving us, and that he must realize we would see through his deception—as the memory suppression spells wore off, if not before. So there must have been a reason that he didn't try to stop us from going, and the only reason I could think of was that he wanted *us* to get all the pages of the Compact for him. It's a good thing neither of you flipped past the top two pages, because those were the only ones the royal caster could finish, along with a standard convincing spell."

"And you let him capture you because…?"

"I needed evidence," Luke said simply. "Solid evidence, not magical suspicion or hearsay. Something like a recording of him confessing his crimes and deliberately acting against Alaska and the Small Kingdoms' best interests." She rolled up a sleeve and revealed a tiny microphone at her wrist.

Only one thing clearly bothered him still. "You didn't think I could be a part of your deception?"

Did he think she didn't truly *trust* him by now?

"I wanted to tell you, but I wasn't positive that he wouldn't have some kind of mind control he could use on you," Luke said frankly. "It's the same reason that I spelled the protections on Alaska's pages against myself."

"What unlocks those pages?" Drayger asked. "Besides waiting for the spell to fade out, which we don't exactly have time to do?"

"Mates," Luke said simply. "If the Compact insists on mates for the Renewal, there's probably a good reason. So I had the royal caster write it so that any mated pair can open it, but only together."

"Then…?"

Luke took his hand and they backed to the table, keeping Fask in their sights. "Open," she said.

"Open sesame?" Drayger said drolly.

The shimmering shield dropped at his first word.

As Luke had been half-braced for, Fask made a bid for freedom as they were gathering up Alaska's pages, barrelling into the table and scattering treasure in all directions. Drayger was as ready for it as she was, and pounced immediately.

Luke wasn't sure of the purpose of the attempt. He was shackled, and surely he must know that Drayger and Luke weren't going to let him escape now. Was it a final desperate act? It did nothing but cause commotion and chaos for a moment before he was subdued all over again.

"What do we do with him now?" Drayger asked, when they had hauled him back to his feet. Luke allowed herself a moment to marvel that he had always treated her authority with respect. Oh, he would tease her and try to torment her into losing her temper, but here, with no audience, he genuinely looked to her for direction, with no trace of macho ego or irony.

"He can unlock the doors to the prisons," Luke said thoughtfully. "I don't trust any other way to hold him. He comes with us, until we find something better to do with him."

"You heard the lady," Drayger said, prodding Fask. "You're our problem for now."

Fask came quietly between them, like the last fight had

gone out of him, but Luke wasn't convinced. She was careful to keep him in her sights, walking a half-step behind. It pained her to remember how he had sometimes chided her to walk beside him as an equal.

What were they now? Traitor and Captain? He was still her cousin.

"Drayger," she said quietly, too aware of Fask's listening ears. "I'm sorry I didn't tell you everything. I came up with this plan while you were away and I thought it would work best if I didn't bring you into it."

"I forgive you," Drayger said expansively. "You were right to be worried about mind control and blackmail." He never took his eyes off of Fask, and neither did Luke.

Drayger led them up to the throne room, where the other brothers were waiting impatiently.

"We were about to send a search—"

Toren's playful quip died at his lips as he saw Fask in glowing shackles at Drayger's side.

There was a moment of tense silence as every one of the brothers must be asking themselves where their loyalties lay. This was not the first time they had been confronted with Fask, or with Fask's betrayal, but it was the first time they had acknowledged it *to* him, even though it was clear now that he was already aware that they knew the truth.

"Well, isn't this a charming family reunion," Drayger joked. "The last time I did one of these, I was the one wearing manacles."

Luke appreciated his effort at humor, even if it fell ironically flat.

Rian cleared his throat uncomfortably. "Did you...did you get the Alaska pages?" he asked.

Luke raised them, never removing her gaze from Fask.

## CHAPTER 46

"Where are the rest of the pages?" Kenth wanted to know, looking at Drayger suspiciously.

Drayger pointed at Luke. "I have no idea. I tried to steal them to trade for Alasie, and Fask tried to burn them, but only the good Captain knows where they really are."

Alasie didn't correct his use of her name in front of others and was surprised to find that she didn't actually mind it. She *was* Alasie. "They're in a box under my bed."

"Really?" This got a murmur of surprise from everyone.

"Sometimes the old ways are the best ways," she said dryly. "No one was going to look for them there and I didn't want them far away from me."

Drayger's face split into a smile. "You mean that you and I—?"

"Focus, Majorca," Alasie snapped.

"We had sex on the Compact," Drayger felt obligated to explain, in case anyone in the room had missed it.

Alasie wanted to be mad at him for being painfully inappropriate, but she couldn't be. "Go get them," she told him, scowling for effect.

"Sex on the Compact!" he called merrily over his shoulder as he sauntered from the room like they hadn't just detained the acting king of Alaska and precipitated a complete and uncomfortable change of command.

Did everyone look just a little more relaxed for Drayger's crude clowning? Alasie certainly felt like *something* was right in the world for a short moment.

"What do we do now?" Toren asked in a small voice.

It was Fask who answered. "You doom the world by renewing a bad contract we should never be bound by."

Maybe she should have gagged him. "We do the Renewal," Alasie said. "We should have enough of the pages now to do it successfully, and that will keep things from flying more out of control than they already have. Mackenzie, can you portal us to Mo'orea now? Is there anything you need?"

Mackenzie looked alarmed at the spotlight turning to her, but nodded bravely. "It will take a lot of energy. I'm not sure I'll be able to do much else, but I can get us all there."

Drayger returned with the pages of the Compact in a pillowcase. "We had sex on the Compact," he reminded Tray, who gave him an indulgent fistbump.

Alasie ignored him, and nodded at Mackenzie to start.

As a user of chaos magic, the lost princess had found that she didn't need the structure of a written spell or an anchor, but she had to concentrate and everyone hushed to let her work.

Alasie kept her attention focused, laser-like, on Fask because she didn't trust his current lofty silence, but saw all the other mates draw close to each other. It wasn't a conscious motion, she thought, just a natural attraction, like plants tipping leaves to light. Drayger was at her side again, and Alasie was struck by how much she liked having him there, like he was protecting her.

She forced herself to keep watching Fask as Mackenzie drew in her breath and traced a circle in the air, as wide in every direction as she could reach and down to the floor. It burst open to a dark space that came with a draft of humid, cool air that smelled like saltwater and flowers.

"Mo'orea," Leinani breathed happily, inhaling.

The called mates from the other kingdoms were all waiting in the cave at the other side and there were subdued greetings and a murmur of conversation. "Are we taking him with us?" Drayger asked, when only he and Fask and Alasie were left on the Alaska side of the portal.

"I don't see what else we can do," Alasie said. "I'm not leaving him here alone."

She prodded Fask forward with a hand on his arm and followed him into the sizzling portal, with Drayger at her side where he belonged.

## CHAPTER 47

*D*rayger had to let his eyes adjust when he stepped through. The cave had electric lights all over the ceiling, but it was still not bright compared to the rays of sun streaming low through the windows in Alaska.

He was braced for Fask to make some kind of break for freedom as they passed the threshold of the portal, but the prince was surprisingly docile and quiet, and Drayger was more suspicious than ever. If the other royal parties were surprised by his attendance in the equivalent of magical chains, they were diplomatic enough not to mention it, and everyone ignored the elephant that he was in the stone room.

Mackenzie wearily said, "Alto," and the portal collapsed into itself, cutting off the last of the sunlight. Kenth held her up by the shoulders, murmuring comfortingly to her.

Drayger focused on Fask, ready to pounce if he so much as moved, and when he could see clearly again, immediately noticed that Alasie was doing exactly the same.

She was so *competent*, Drayger thought with approval. It was one of the sexiest things about her, and that said a lot.

He forced himself to keep his attention on Fask, letting Toren and the other brothers do the politicking that Drayger hated anyway.

"Nani!" A huge figure swept Leinani into a bear hug and Drayger knew that he must be her brother. His mate was a stately Black woman with short, tight braids all along her scalp. Introductions were made all around.

Only half of the Kingdoms were represented, but Alaska had five—six if Drayger counted himself. He still wasn't sure if he and Alasie were meant to represent Alaska or Majorca. Maybe the Kingdoms didn't actually matter.

To his surprise, Talgor and Forsch were already there with their mates and Drayger gave them swift, distracted greetings before returning his complete attention to Fask.

"So this is the prince who wanted to sabotage the Compact," Talgor said mildly. "I always wanted to spit in an Alaskan prince's face."

"Be nice," Mirrim chided him.

Fask ignored them, fixing his gaze across the cave with a disdainful look.

There was a small wooden table in the middle of the cave, already piled with the pages of the Compact that the others had brought. Toren added Alaska's pages, and the pages that they'd stolen from the Kingdoms who were not attending.

"I hope these don't have to be in order," Tania said, standing to the side leaning on her cane. "That's a lot of pages to sort."

She fell into a conversation with a tiny older woman wearing glasses who was with the elderly King of the Falkland Islands; not all of the delegates were as young as the

## CHAPTER 47

Alaskan princes, and one or two were even younger and looked completely lost.

Drayger scanned the people, wishing he didn't have to babysit Fask so he could do some serious analysis of the attendees.

None of them was truly confident of their place there, he could see that much at a glance, but all of them were full of resolve. This wasn't the ceremony that any of them had anticipated, but they all understood that it needed to be seen through and were willing to do whatever was needed.

"What else do we need for a Renewal?" one of the other princes asked.

"It feels like something is missing," another said.

"Besides half the Kingdoms?" Forsch asked wryly.

"You are missing *usssssss*," a disembodied voice boomed through stone walls, and then, suddenly, there was a ring of spirits around the table in the center of the cavern. They looked, at a glance, mostly human, but each of them was wreathed in the aspect of their element. A man seemed made of stone, his skin moving like little pebble landslides as he walked. A woman had trees for hair and leaves over her body like feathers. One man seemed to be smoldering, shrouded in smoke, and another was actively wearing flames.

And there was Angel, standing soaking wet like she'd just come up out of the water, her hair wild around her.

Drayger had a split-second to pinpoint the source of his alarm. It wasn't just that the spirits had appeared very suddenly, but that they had very effectively cut the mates off from access to the Compact, which looked very vulnerable now on the low wooden table.

"Something is wrong," he started to tell Alasie as Angel came face to face with Fask.

"You failed to destroy the Compact as you were charged, so we must take matters into our own hands." Angel's voice was dripping with disdain.

"Fask was working for you?" Alasie said in astonishment. "To *end* the Compact? *Why?*"

"Freedom!" a plant-woman cried. "Angel has promised us freedom!"

"Freedom that Fask was supposed to get us," Angel said, frowning. "He said he could do it, but failed." Whatever alliance Fask and Angel had, it did not seem to be based on any kind of affection.

Drayger was watching Fask close enough to see his jaw grind, but he didn't answer her.

"If you end the Compact, there will be no restrictions on magic!" Drayger protested. "That would be very bad for the world. You would be free, but there would be no world for you to rule."

"Dragons lie," Angel hissed. "Dragons deceive."

"We want our freedom," the stone-man at her elbow growled.

"You were bound to the world so that you would persist!" Katy cried. "It was the best solution we could all find."

That made her the focus of their unearthly attention for a moment, and Alasie could tell that it was not a comfortable attention.

"We are stronger now than we were then," Angel snarled. "And we have been cheated of our rightful place in this world for too long."

"Would you take your freedom at the price of all the life on it?" Raval demanded. "You thought this was an equitable trade once."

"That was long ago, for us," a plant-woman jeered. "Long enough for us to see the mistake of our choice."

## CHAPTER 47

Angel, who seemed to be the leader of the spirits, turned away. Her hair managed to float around her while, at the same time, it seemed heavy with water. "Do it!" she commanded, and two of the fire spirits put their hands to the loose pages of the Compact.

This time Drayger knew that they were the true pages of the Compact by the unearthly scream of agony that filled the cave. The pages did not want to burn, and they resisted, squirming and curling, but ultimately succumbed to the flames being focussed into them.

Drayger gave a roar of protest and flung himself at the spirits standing between him and the Compact, trying to shift.

It was too late.

The pages fell into ash, the letters burning away last of all. Black flakes and a broken, charred table were all that remained.

The Compact was *gone*.

Drayger felt his dragon shudder inside of him as his attempt to shift failed and the stone-man flung him back into Alasie. The ground beneath him shook and shuddered as magic washed over him. He felt like something had passed through him, and his dragon swirled in dismay and concern. The lights overhead rattled in their fixtures and flickered.

How far did the impact wave go? He could still hear the roar of the unsettled earth beneath his feet, and wouldn't have been surprised if it had swept around the entire world away from them.

"At last!" Angel said in triumph. "We are free! We are unfettered! This world is ours, now!"

Alasie gave a surprised cry as Fask used the chaos to shake off her grip, rip apart the sputtering magical shackles, and lunge forward with a familiar knife in his hand.

Drayger cursed, recognizing the dragon-slaying dagger from the vault. Fask must have slipped it into his pocket when he crashed into the table in the vault. He knew that scuffle had not been idle, but he hadn't thought to search the prince again.

Angel wasn't the slightest bit concerned. "You fool!" she mocked him, not moving to block him. "That is a dragon-killing knife. And I am not a dragon!"

Then she gave a wail of dismay when Fask thrust forward and slipped the blade into the base of her throat. "You are not a dragon," Fask said coldly. "But you are *mortal* now."

Drayger moved forward to recapture Fask, but Alasie grabbed him by the arm. "It would kill *you* and if it didn't, I would," she reminded him fiercely. Drayger reluctantly held back as Alasie tackled Fask and pinned his arms before he could take a second stab at Angel.

Angel backed away from them in horror, holding her hand to her bleeding neck. "We persist!" she wailed and gurgled. "We persist!"

"Not without the Compact, you don't." Fask struggled against Alasie's hold. "*You killed my mother!*" Fask used Alasie's shock to free himself and charged the spirit with single-minded fury.

Angel had nowhere left to retreat, her back up against stone. "You told me to do that!" she protested.

"To Kenth," Fask roared. "Not to my *mother*!"

All the final answers fell into place. Fask's motivation for destroying the Compact had never been for power or glory. He wanted the Compact out of the way for *revenge*. The spirit's invulnerability had hinged on the treaty's protection. The spirits' *persistence* was part of the core magic. And now that it was gone, they were vulnerable, as they had never been before. Fask had convinced Angel that destroying the Compact would free her, but his true purpose had been to *kill* her.

Angel reached one bloody hand towards the swirl of watching spirits, the other holding her throat. "Save me!" she begged.

Drayger had watched political tides change before. His father had always enjoyed pitting his progeny—legitimate or not—against one another, and played games of favor with other governments like a cat playing with prey.

He was not sure he had ever seen anything as swift and vicious as the turn of the spirits against Angel as they realized that she had just quite effectively locked them into mortality.

"All we desired was to persist," a woman with trees for hair snarled. "You did not tell us this would happen!"

"We are no longer invulnerable!" a man made of stone was staring at his hands in dismay.

"You have *betrayed* us!" a man with fire licking at his shoulders roared.

Fask took a wild swing with his knife and Alasie intercepted him.

"Stay back!" she insisted, grappling with Fask.

It was the hardest thing that Drayger had ever done, watching her fight a furious Fask, knowing that the slightest swipe of the blade the mad prince held would still kill any dragon. Drayger wanted desperately to wade in to protect her anyway, but he *had* to respect Luke's ability to defend herself. He wouldn't do her any favors getting himself poisoned.

Logic didn't make it any easier to stay back.

*Can we shift?* he asked his dragon.

*I don't know!* his dragon wailed. *The rules are wrong!*

Angel sagged down against the stone wall, blood welling around the hand she held to her throat. Drayger didn't know how much blood a spirit had—he doubted that they knew either, and wondered if one had ever bled before. The other spirits had drawn back in horror and were watching without offering to help her.

"I don't want to hurt you!" Alasie cried, slapping away another of Fask's savage swings. Every time that she tried to get close enough to restrain him, he slashed with the blade and she was unarmed and wearing no armor under her dress uniform. It already had several gashes, and Drayger worried that the darkened edges were blood. The mate bond was too weak now to let him feel if she'd been hurt, but he hurt *for* her and worried helplessly.

Alasie was clearly the superior warrior, but Fask wasn't untrained, and he had dragon strength and swiftness, fueled by his madness and demented anger. He had stopped trying to get away from Alasie to punish Angel and was fighting her in earnest now, and she was hampered by her desire not to hurt him.

Fask slashed her in the neck, just above the collar of her uniform. One of her stars snapped free and went flying.

It was a glancing blow, not fatal, but it bled dramatically. Alasie used Fask's moment of triumph to smash her doubled fist down on the wrist holding the knife and knock it skittering across the floor. The dragon shifters flinched back from it and Drayger lost his resolve to leave Alasie to her fight and charged in to grapple Fask from behind.

Alasie didn't have time to tell him to get back before Carina gave a cry of warning.

Angel had crawled across the floor while all the attention was on Fask and Alasie and reached the evil dagger. She used the last of her life to scoop it up, and stand to drive the blade into Fask's side before Drayger could realize what she was doing and try to stop her.

## CHAPTER 47

Fask wasn't a dragon any longer, but he had a dragon's power in him and the blade recognized that energy and thirsted for it. The lettering all along the hilt flared into flame and burned into Angel's hand as she cried out in a wet, slurred voice. "I'll take you with me, traitor!"

Drayger flinched and let go of Fask instinctively to protect his own dragon, not sure for the moment that the blade would stop at the fallen prince. He looked back just in time to see the essence of dragon seem to burn straight up out of Fask. The Alaskan prince collapsed onto Angel, who gave a gargle of pain and triumph. Violet flames wreathed them both and died away, leaving only a tangle of charred flesh and a spreading puddle that might have been water…or blood.

Kenth knelt just beyond the pool, touching Fask's remains with conflicted reverence. "It was a boyish prank. He just wanted to…embarrass me and it went terribly wrong." His voice was strangled with pain and guilt.

Alasie, her shoulders fallen in dismay, went to stand by Kenth and squeeze his shoulder. The other brothers made a loose, stunned semi-circle around the gruesome carcasses. "It wasn't your fault."

Kenth looked up at her with disbelief. "I could have stopped all of this."

"You couldn't have known," Alasie said firmly. "No one could know that he would go to such lengths."

"You guys…?" Mackenzie's voice was thin and worried.

"He taught me how to skate," Toren said. "*Step out strong*, he used to say."

"I never wanted this," Kenth said mournfully. "He didn't deserve *this*."

"Guys??" Mackenzie's voice was more urgent now.

"This is important. Magic is totally wild right now and I don't know what it's going to do. I don't think it's good…"

Drayger realized that the sense of building pressure was not only in his heart. His dragon was frankly alarmed, as his companion had never been before.

*There is too much magic!* it keened. *The bridge is unguarded and the world will burn!*

Sometimes, communication with a dragon was simple and uncomplicated. *Do this, don't do that, watch out, that's nice,* or *don't be a dumbass.*

This was like trying to make sense of a joke that had been translated between several languages and spit out by a machine that didn't understand it.

*There is a bridge?* Drayger queried, puzzled by the images he was shown.

*This world has one kind of magic,* his dragon struggled to explain. *The worlds to either side have very different kinds, like opposite poles in a strong battery. The Compact is what keeps the current from shorting out and burning everything in the circuit. The poles have been building for many centuries now.*

It wasn't entirely in words, but in concepts and feelings, and Drayger suspected that there was a lot lost in the translation, but he had enough to know that whatever they were going to do, they needed to do it soon.

"I hate to break up this touching family tragedy," Drayger said harshly, "but if we want anything to renew, we've got to do it sooner than later."

He suspected that the other dragons were leaning on their humans just as strongly, because all of the mates with dragon counterparts looked ashen and alarmed.

CHAPTER 48

$\mathscr{A}$lasie might not have a dragon to tell her that something was desperately wrong with the world, but she trusted her gut and her polar bear, and both of them were sure that *everything was wrong*. It was like standing in front of a funhouse mirror—everything seemed just a little distorted.

She glanced around the room.

"We've got to get magic back under control!" Mackenzie wept.

"We have to make a new Compact?" Tania guessed. "But how are we supposed to do that?"

Toren, looking ash-faced, faced the fae. "Can you help us make a new Compact?" he asked. "You were there."

"It was long ago for us," the flame-man said. "The details are faded to time."

They were so…chilly, Alasie thought. The most alien part of them was that there was no warmth or affection between them. Passion, perhaps, but none of them seemed to have any true tenderness with each other. Not one of them gave Angel's burnt body a second glance now, or seemed affected by her loss. They had been more shaken by the possibility of their own deaths than grieved by hers.

She decided that *Captain Cold Luke* was probably not in the best position to judge such things…and then remembered that she still hadn't told Drayger that she loved him. Not out loud.

"Will you help us try?" Toren begged. "The world needs you!"

The fae silently communicated for a moment, then agreed. Their faces were stony, but their elements were agitated—fire sparking, hair waving, leaves trembling. Alasie thought they were concerned.

"We will *persist*," the plant-woman said in agreement. "But we will not be bound!"

"And because we agree does not make us friends," the stone-man warned, his voice like gravel.

"How do we start?" Alasie asked Raval and Katy. "What was first?"

Raval frowned and Katy looked around at the cave. "The kids were in a loose circle with the cave, each with a dragon. I remember thinking that it wasn't a perfect circle, and maybe that was okay, because what's really perfect in this world? I remember thinking a lot about the six virtues of the Small Kingdoms."

Raval gave her an intense look. "I remember thinking about how much I loved you."

Katy kissed him in delight. "I remember that, too."

"End of the world, guys," Kenth reminded them. "Smooch later."

"The Compact said to remember one thing," Alasie said, still not sure what that one thing was.

"The six virtues," Tania said thoughtfully. "Let's start there. Magic loves ritual, let's give it some ritual. Pick your strongest virtue and go to that alcove. Who embodies Courage?"

"Carina," Toren volunteered at once. "I've never known someone so brave."

Carina looked flustered and flattered as Toren took her by the hand and took her to that stone alcove. "Well, then Mackenzie is truth. She saw through Amara's deceptions and found out the truth about the Compact."

Mackenzie looked like she wanted to hide behind Kenth, but stepped up to the alcove where Truth was written in stone.

"Luke is strength," Drayger proposed. "No, patience. She's put up with a lot of crap from me." Alasie reconsidered the punch she was about to deliver to his shoulder and Drayger noticed. "See? Patient."

"*Tania* is strength," Rian volunteered.

Tania looked ruefully at her cane but didn't argue.

Everyone agreed that Katy was kindness, and Leinani eyed the word 'Loyalty' above the final unclaimed space. "My *test* was certainly loyalty," she said quietly, Tray's hand in hers. "Did I pass?"

"You passed," Tray insisted. He leaned over and kissed her on the forehead.

The rest of the mates each chose an alcove and the pressure in the air seemed to swell in the space. Was that a good sign? Was the magic ready to direct?

"Now what?" Alasie asked. "What did they say the first time?"

Katy wrinkled her forehead. "Um, 'I take you to be my own'," she remembered. "And then, 'for peace and the future', or something. I should have taken notes."

Raval added, "I bond with you in this time and the next. But we're not bonding with dragons, so it doesn't apply."

"It shouldn't have to be the exact words," Mackenzie volunteered anxiously. "Chaos magic is from emotion and intention. You should each focus on the virtues and the new Compact will build from those principles. We have to *hurry*!"

Even without a dragon inside her, Alasie could feel the tension in the air. Her bear was uneasy and her entire body felt like it was too close to a hot fire. She wanted to draw back, but there was nowhere to go.

"What do we *do?*" Carina wailed.

"You have to concentrate," Mackenzie explained. "Whatever we think about now will come into being, so think about rules that will protect everyone and keep magic *safe*."

"We will persist!" the flame-man insisted.

"We have to come up with new rules? Can't we just use the old rules?" Toren whined.

"Do you remember the old rules word for word?" Kenth demanded.

"We could get a copy?"

"It's not about the specific wording," Mackenzie insisted. "It's about the *purpose*. You have to think about the most important things the Compact does. You could write the same words, but it would come out a little differently every time because of how it was made."

"This is like one of those woo woo things trying to sell you the latest vitamin supplement," Tray complained. "'Think happy thoughts.'"

"Whatever we think of as the Compact is created, that's what's going to make it," Tania said in awe.

"Think *really* happy thoughts," Toren joked.

"We should focus!" That was Leinani's brother.

Alasie closed her eyes. Loyalty. Patience. Truth. Strength. Kindness. Courage. If you could distill a directive into six concepts, those seemed like good ones to build from.

But the Compact had said she only needed to remember *one* thing.

She could feel the magic swirling in the cave, trying to coalesce. Mackenzie was swaying in place, her face white, and Alasie could feel all the hairs on her polar bear standing on end. It was like walking through a room full of staticky balloons.

Was it going to work? Or would the magic wipe them away? There was *so much* of it, and none of them had the strength of the first dragons. Even the fae seemed afraid of this unleashed power. It needed a focus, a place to go, and Alasie was desperately worried they would do it *wrong*.

What if they made a Compact that was cruel or unfair?

The Compact said they only needed to remember *one* thing.

Alasie felt like a dog on a bone. What was the *one thing*?? Was there a single virtue they should all be focused on? Which *one?*

Drayger had taken her hand at some point, and it was so natural and perfect that Alasie hadn't noticed. Her mate. She wanted to sigh with happiness, then caught herself wondering again what role the mates played? Why would the Compact be so predicated on mates to do the Renewals at all? What was it that made mates special?

The answer made her suck in her breath, and Alasie could feel the magic swirl and burn around her, like she'd caught its interest. "Drayger," she said, tugging on his hand. "Drayger!"

Drayger cracked one eye open at her. "We're supposed to be meditating on our virtues," he reminded her. "Though it's hard to pick a virtue other than sexy."

"Drayger," she whispered, "I love you."

Both of Drayger's eyes flew open and he turned to Alasie with a look of such tenderness and joy that Alasie wished she'd said it weeks before. It wasn't so hard, after all, just the truth, and saying it was actually a relief.

"That's it," Alasie said, and she felt her face split into a broad smile as the magic all around them seemed to dance into patterns across the cavern. "That's the *key*." She raised her voice. "That's why the Compact called mates, so that a Renewal would always be done with *love*. Love is what the Compact wanted us to remember."

There was a murmur from the stone walls, and the magic grew so bright and strong that Alasie feared it would sear them all to nothing, that her revelation had come too late, and even a new Compact could not save them now.

Then it sucked away from her like a retreating wave before a tsunami and there was an explosion that wasn't quite of sound or light that sent Alasie staggering back, unable to feel Drayger's hand in hers any more. The air was so thick that she couldn't even draw a breath.

The terrible pressure released abruptly, and Alasie opened her eyes and then wasn't sure she had.

It was pitch black. She could feel Drayger's hand in hers, clinging desperately, and stone against the knees she'd unknowingly fallen to.

"Is there a new Compact?" Toren's voice asked plaintively from the blackness.

"No one can see anything," Tray answered dryly.

"I can see something!" Katy exclaimed, and Alasie realized that her own eyes were starting to adjust.

All of the lights in the cavern had exploded, and shards of glass were scattered across the ground like diamonds. The only light was faint moonlight from the entrance to the cave. There was no giant tome of parchment or glowing scroll in the broken and charred remains of the table.

Had they failed?

Alasie got to her feet, drawing Drayger with her, as the other mates did the same.

"Where's the Compact?"

"What happened?"

"I don't want to have to do that again, please."

"Ouch!"

The broken glass was a hazard as they navigated the dark cave, but the keenest hurt was fearing that all of their efforts had been for nothing.

Was the magic wild around the world now? Was it off sowing chaos somewhere else? The terrible pressure of it had diminished, but where had it *gone?*

Drayger's hand was still in hers, and it steadied Alasie. Maybe they could try again…

"Hey!" Tray was standing near the center of the cave and he bent to pick something out of the burnt fragments of the table. "This wasn't here before!"

"What is it?" Leinani asked.

"A flash drive," Tray said, turning it over in his hands.

"Well of course," Drayger said drolly. "Ink on dragon-skin is so last century."

"Is that the new Compact?"

"A flash drive?"

"Why not? It's modern technology."

"Is it read-only?" Raval asked, and Alasie was dead sure that he was serious.

# CHAPTER 49

*She loved him.*
　　Drayger had known that Alasie cared for him, but he wasn't sure if she would ever admit that she loved him and now that she had, Drayger wasn't sure if it *mattered* if the world burned down or not.

*She loved him.*

He was thinking of nothing else when the magic of the Compact unfurled over the world, just Alasie's love and how smart and fair she was, how he could think of no one better to base an entire system of power on. She loved him, and there was nothing that could be *wrong* in a world where that was true.

And then it was done.

"It's weird that my story started with a flash drive and ends with one," Carina said, taking the flash drive from Toren. "The whole Compact is in there?"

The little old woman who had been comparing library notes with Tania cackled in joy. "It's probably on the cloud, too." She seemed deeply amused by the entire notion. "I was certainly thinking about *system redundancy* for some reason."

Mackenzie was looking at her hands in confusion. "I don't think I have chaos magic anymore."

Kenth wrapped an arm around her shoulders. "You will always be magic," he insisted.

Drayger decided that making a joke would spoil the moment, just as Toren pretended to gag.

"Get a room, guys," the young king suggested.

Alasie finally took her hand back and Drayger felt a moment of loss as she went to do a circle of the cave, looking for more clues in the broken glass and debris.

The spirits looked as confused as the humans, and were milling about, testing their powers and flexing their fingers. "We are still mortal," a water-man snarled, drawing blood from his own arm as a test.

"We were supposed to persist," a plant-woman said, her face cool but her voice sharp.

"Persist doesn't really mean invulnerable," Raval said thoughtfully. "Perhaps the new Compact took you literally."

"We need a new name for it," Rian said. "It's not the Compact anymore, and I don't know if there will be Small Kingdoms again."

"The Pact?" Tania suggested.

"The Alliance?" Kenth proposed.

"Compact the Sequel," Tray joked.

"With even more naked, shrieking terror!" Drayger added.

"Compact Two, The Talkening…" Carina giggled hysterically. "Sorry. It's a very serious subject, I'm sure."

The fae were not amused. Some of them vanished, but several remained.

Toren stepped up to face them. "We may not *have* to be

friends, but we *can* be, by choice. We can forge an alliance that isn't based on force or manipulation. We can recognize that we are both our best when we work together."

Drayger wanted to warn him that his boyish optimism was ill-suited for this situation and was surprised when the remaining fae regarded him with interest and curiosity.

"I would welcome a treaty," the stone man said gravely, looking around at his companions. "This is our world now and we should protect it."

The plant woman was gazing around like she was seeing everything new for the first time. "I…feel," she said in wonder. "I *feel*."

Had the fae gained a new kind of compassion from the magic? Drayger had been focusing his entire being on love. Was it possible to change something that basic and fundamental with an act of enchantment?

"I…mourn her," the stone man said in awe, looking down at Angel's burnt corpse, tangled with Fask's. Someone had thrown a shawl over the two, but it did a poor job of covering the gruesome tableau. "I *grieve.*"

They shared a moment of silence over the two bodies, and finally Leinani said, "Look, the sun is coming up."

A growing beam of light was shining down the tunnel to the cave, it wasn't just that Drayger's eyes had adjusted to the dark.

By unspoken agreement, they all went out and wandered down the stone path along the lagoon towards the beach, marveling in the sunrise that was coloring the sky.

Katy was rapturous. "Look, there's an airplane! And a city! I see a city at the end of the bay! That was never there before!"

"I told you it should be there," Raval said matter of factly.

Katy didn't seem to take it as an *I told you so*, even if it technically was. She clung to Raval's arm and continued pointing out features of the beach and the lagoon that had changed.

All of them wandered out to the edge of the trees. There were a few people along the beach, clusters of nervous beachcombers and swimmers watching the sky. How much had they seen?

Leinani looked longingly at the water. "I wish I had a board," she said to Tray. "I'd teach you how to surf."

"Maybe we can stay here a while," he suggested. "I want to see the island that you love so much."

Leinani's brother kissed his mate. "I want to go tell Mother and Father what happened. They'll be worried. Wait for me here!"

He shifted as he leapt for the sky and Drayger was alarmed to find that his natural camouflage didn't do a thing to hide his form.

He was a white-gold dragon, and everyone on the beach shouted and pointed as he rose up over the trees, banked and flew towards the capital city in plain view of all of them.

"We're not hidden," Rian said, staring at his hands. "What happened to our concealment magic?"

"I always assumed it was part of a dragon's natural magic," Raval said. "But maybe it was tied to the Compact the whole time."

"We're not secret anymore," Kenth said. "Maybe we don't have to be."

The people on the beach were milling, but it didn't seem to be in universal alarm. Some of them were cheering.

"What do we do now?" Toren wanted to know. Some

of the people on the beach had caught sight of the royal party and were pointing and speculating.

Drayger wondered what kind of impression they were making. None of them looked fresh from a magazine page, but most of them were clearly wearing royal regalia from all over the world. They would not be able to mistake the company for anything other than what it was, even at this distance.

"Will they be angry that we didn't tell them the truth for so long?"

"Wouldn't you be?"

"This is a diplomatic disaster," Kenth said flatly.

"You know, all I wanted a nice quiet reign as a king in name only," Toren groused.

The dragon prince from the Falkland Islands only shrugged. "Everyone in our kingdom already knew," he said.

"Your kingdom is only five thousand people," Rian pointed out. "Citizenship came with a vow of secrecy."

Toren looked desperately from one royal to another. "I don't know what to do," he confessed.

When no one else volunteered an idea or inspirational speech, Drayger finally did. "We honor our principles," he said gravely. "We give them the truth. We offer our loyalty. We show them strength and kindness and patience."

"That sounds hard," Toren said plaintively.

The others chuckled, but Drayger smiled. "Then we must be *courageous.*"

He took Alasie's hand in his. "It's a brave new world," he said, gesturing generally towards the ocean. "We couldn't cover this up if we tried, and I'm not sure if I want to. Let's go tell them who we really are!"

They made a motley crew, some of them as dragons, some as humans, and a handful of the fae trailed with them. A few people fled in fear, but most stood their ground to greet them, and one or two of those shifted into animals and seemed relieved that it was safe to do so.

Drayger let the other royals take point, hanging back with Alasie until the others were out of earshot.

"Alasie…"

"I love you," she said, and it was no less thrilling the second time, even if it wasn't accompanied by a world-shattering magical event.

Drayger had a dozen responses at hand. He could use flowering poetry or a mutual confession. He could explain what it meant to hear it from her, or beg her to say it every day. Finally, he settled for his usual flippant reply. "It's about time you admitted it."

She punched him in the arm and then kissed him, and everything was right in the world.

CHAPTER 50

Granting Nathaniel and Pickle their freedom from prison was Alasie's first priority when they arrived home by mundane jet a day later.

"It wasn't so bad," he assured Alasie, pounding her back. "We had everything we needed and Pickle's going to miss that couch." Still, he breathed deep of the crisp spring air when they left the castle and his eyes looked suspiciously bright.

Alasie's eyes were not entirely clear either.

Fask got a state funeral a hasty week later, paired with his father's formal funeral, which was fitting because the last of his dragon had been lost with Fask's life, his body falling into a husk of ash and spent magic. Mrs. James had fussed a great deal about getting the carpet clean to hide her deep grief as the old king's passage was made official.

The royal brothers were up front about the details of their father's lengthy sleep, now that dragons and magic were a known quantity, and although Alasie had been reluctant to agree to a public ceremony, the Kingdom turned out with black and gold Alaska flags, voluntarily closed their establishments, and embraced a period of mourning. Whatever their feelings were for the exposure of magic and shifters, Alaska had loved its dragon king, and however complicated Fask's death was by his betrayal, they were willing to honor both lives.

Alasie and Fask's brothers were the pallbearers, all of them wearing black uniforms with gold stars. Their mates walked beside them during the ceremonial procession through the capital city.

Drayger had no qualms about this arrangement. "You can do the heavy lifting," he said to Alasie. "I will carry flowers and weep."

"Please don't," Alasie told him.

"Can't I at least wear a fetching black veil?" Drayger begged.

It was a lengthy and very emotional ceremony, followed by a public feast and a day of holiday.

Toren gave a speech that they all wrote together and offered public apology for any deception or falsehoods, promising to move forward in the best possible way, and announcing that there would be democratic elections to decide if Alaska still wished to consider itself a monarchy, or if they would pursue a new method of fair rule based on choice of the people.

"*You* are Alaska!" Toren finished rousingly. "*You* will decide!"

Whatever hardships he had endured, Toren had proven to be a charismatic speaker, and although he claimed that it made him sick to his stomach, he continued to step up to do it.

"You did great," Carina assured him.

"I'm going to throw up," Toren said, but he never did.

Afterwards, Alasie and Drayger slipped away from the

subdued final festivities and walked to the pedestrian bridge over the Chena River.

"You ever think about just jumping right in?" Drayger asked.

"What? No! Why would I?" Alasie looked down at the swirling water below the bridge.

"I thought polar bears loved swimming."

"I couldn't just dive in as a bear!" Alasie protested. "There are people watching us."

"Why not? It's already out in the open," Drayger reminded her. "You said yourself that we needed to normalize it in order to get people comfortable with the fact that magic lives side-by-side with the ordinary."

"I didn't mean by making a spectacle out of ourselves," Alasie protested, but she was smiling.

"Speaking of spectacles, Alasie, I've got a question for you."

"Any time that you preface a question by warning me that you have a question, I know it's a question I'm not going to want to answer."

"I hope you'll want to answer this one," Drayger said, and to Alasie's astonishment, he sank down on one knee before her.

Alasie stared down at him.

"Alasie, my heart, my soul, will you marry me?"

For a moment Alasie's heart was too full to answer him.

"You're supposed to say yes," Drayger prodded. "Not leave me kneeling at your feet like some kind of loon in front of half the city."

"Did you decide to ask me in front of everyone so I couldn't say no?" Alasie sounded much more cross than she felt.

"This is hard on my knees, Captain Luke. Will you please make up your mind?"

"It's *Alasie* to you," she told him fondly. "And yes, I'll marry you."

Drayger stood straight up to sweep her into his arms and kiss her passionately.

There was a cheer from each shore where they had become the focus of the remaining funerary crowd.

"There's no escape!" Drayger said in mock alarm, clinging dramatically to her. "They've got us trapped on this bridge with no way out!"

"Sure there is," Alasie said, shaking off his arms and pulling him up onto the bridge railing with her. "Meet you at the boat launch!"

Then she dived off into the swirling water, shifting into a silver bear as she fell. She surfaced to find a shimmering black dragon flying overhead. With the end of the original Compact, the natural camouflage of dragons had vanished. They were now, if not a familiar sight, at least not an uncommon one.

As Alasie pulled herself up on a boat launch downstream, shaking water from her thick fur, she looked up to see eight dragons making lazy spirals in the air, sunlight glinting off their wings and scales.

A few people at the boat launch stared in wonder as she emerged from the water and then shifted into her human form, but no one seemed particularly alarmed.

This was a new world, a better world, a world without such secrets, and Alasie was full of joy and relief.

# EPILOGUE

"*By a landslide!* Toren is still officially the King of Alaska! Long live the king!" Drayger raised his arms in a victory V over his head as he sauntered into the informal dining hall to mooch breakfast.

Toren put his head down in his arms and groaned. Carina patted him sympathetically.

"It was his sweet baby face," Kenth surmised. He didn't seem the slightest bit offended that as the oldest remaining brother, he had barely registered in the polls.

"It was that speech he gave at the funeral," Rian guessed.

Tray agreed. "People love that kind of feel-good rhetoric."

"I think that everyone had already gotten used to the idea, since we've been calling him the crown prince for so long," Raval suggested logically.

"It was probably his Facebook fanclub," Carina teased. "Seven hundred *thousand* members strong now!"

"Wait until your Queen Carina fanclub gets that big," Toren groused into his sleeves. "It won't be so funny then."

Alasie had a different idea. "Toren won because the people of Alaska knew what they were getting. You own the land, but you earn the people." She tipped her head towards Toren. "Your Highness stepped up, and everyone saw that."

"I didn't do it alone," Toren said plaintively. "I couldn't have."

"That's one of your best qualities," Alasie said with a kind smile. She smiled so much more easily these days. "Do you have your speech ready? The press is already gathering out front and we don't want to leave them out in the mosquitos for too long."

"Yeah, yeah," Toren said, sitting up and pulling a stack of cards from his pocket. He'd come a long way from the fumbling young man that Drayger had seen through the scope of a rifle. "Let's go wow them, love."

Carina gave him a kiss as they got to their feet. "I know you will," she said confidently.

Drayger lingered to snag some of the remaining breakfast as the rest of the family trickled out of the room to present a unified front for the press release. "Are you coming?" Alasie asked from the doorway.

"I'm just putting some pastries in my pockets," Drayger said. "I was planning to stuff them in your mouth later when you got hungry and unreasonably grouchy."

"I told you, that's not romantic." Alasie's soft, grateful eyes belied her hard words. "Toren asked me to be there; he wants to introduce me as his first chair advisor."

"I'll be right out," Drayger promised. "Don't let me hold anything up."

She flashed him a grin before she disappeared, and no matter how much she smiled now, every one of them still felt like a triumph.

Drayger wandered to the quiet throne room and

looked out of the windows down at the drive. It was clogged with journalists and a crowd of citizens, many of them holding signs. "Hail King Toren." "One of the people, FOR the people." "Our new dragon king."

Drayger was tempted for a moment to moon the audience through the window, just to see if it would be captured on film and immortalized forever as part of Toren's acceptance speech. It was probably too bright outside for it to show, but it did remind him of another question he still needed to ask Alasie.

Toren was well into his speech by the time Drayger had finished his breakfast and sauntered down to join the rest of the royal family in the sunshine and spotlight.

The new king had already gone through his primary talking points, focussing particularly on equality and fairness for both magical and un-magical people. He had some impressive lines, which might have been rhetoric from someone less sincere. "When no one is less, we are all more together," he said passionately, and the crowd cheered enthusiastically.

He introduced each of his brothers, emphasizing that he would be drawing on their strength and expertise, and each of them got rounds of applause and expressions of affection. Someone shouted at Rian to take his clothes off and everyone laughed, especially Tania, who wagged her finger at the crowd and took him jealously off the stage.

Toren brought Alasie up next. "The Captain of the Royal Guard has always been a position of trust and responsibility, and I would add to that list that the Captain has always been a friend. I am eager to have her at my side as my primary advisor. Please give a warm welcome to Counselor Alasie Luke."

Alasie exchanged a warm handshake with Toren and gave a brief, professional speech relinquishing her position as Captain of the Royal Guard in order to act as advisor to the King and focus her attention on helping the kingdom transition to the world as it was now as a representative of non-dragon shifters. She had tapped a human for her previous job, confident of his capability and invested in showing that people did not need magic to be successful and hold power. She pinned his new stars to his collar and relinquished the stage to Toren, who drew Carina forward with him.

"Counselor Luke may be my primary advisor," he said honestly, "but I will always turn first to my heart, and the keeper of my heart is Queen Carina."

Carina's speech was even shorter than Alasie's, and met with just as many cheers.

Toren took the microphone again and waited patiently until the last applause had died and the audience was quiet in anticipation.

"Thank you," he said, and outwaited the resulting cheer again. "Although I am a dragon, I am not the dragon king my father was. I am *your* king, and I will serve you well."

They went wild, and the press conference eased into a public party as refreshments were brought out, picnic style. Toren went to shake hands and meet people personally. Drayger moved through the crowd at Alasie's side doing meet-and-greet-and-flirts for a while, and, as soon as they could, they escaped back into the castle.

"Are you sorry you aren't going back to Majorca to help rebuild?" Alasie asked him. She accepted a hard roll from his pocket but wouldn't let him feed it to her.

"Mirrim and Forsch will do a fine job on the new elected democratic council," Drayger said confidently. "But Alaska is under my skin, and I'm not sure I could live anywhere else now."

"Alaska is special," Alasie agreed. "It's not an *easy* place, but when you come here, you either leave immediately, or you love it and live here forever."

"I will live here and love you forever," Drayger said, taking away her roll to kiss her up her arm.

"That's not what I said," she chuckled, snatching back her food. "But it is just as good."

~

It was a few weeks later, after Toren's public recrowning, that they took a royal retreat to Angel Hot Springs.

"Is it weird that it's named after a spirit who tried to destroy the world for her misguided goal of freedom?" Drayger asked, stepping into the steaming pool.

"It's no weirder than naming mountains after presidents like they do in America," Alasie countered.

It was a cool early morning—as cool as it got in June, and early morning meant the sun was high in the sky, as it had been most of the night. Fluffy rain clouds spotted the sky, but weren't heavy enough to threaten precipitation yet. By afternoon, the midday heat would give way to scattered thundershowers, but for now, the air was still and the surface of the mineral spring was only disrupted by the waves that they were making wading into the pool.

It was a big pool, and reserved on that day for only the royal family and their guests, so everyone had a private corner to float and soak and talk privately. Drayger pulled Alasie into his arms and kissed her until they almost drowned themselves. He didn't think that he'd ever get used to the idea that she was his, and that she *loved* him.

She didn't say it often, but when she did, it was like

fireworks and flying. It was like flying *through* fireworks. It was as good as sex, and the sex was *good*.

"The upper pool is open," Drayger noticed. "Want to ditch these boring royals and use the pool with a view?"

Dripping wet and distractingly hot in her sporty swimsuit, Alasie led him up the trail and they slipped together into the bracingly hot water.

At first, Drayger thought that the sparkles on the surface of the water were just reflections of the sun on the ripples they'd made, then they resolved into a half dozen leaping and playing little figures, ranging from a few inches to a hand-span in size.

"Hello," Alasie said in wonder.

Suddenly shy, they dove down into the water and disappeared. Only one remained, a slight figure the size of a doll with dark hair that floated in impossible directions. She stood easily on the surface of the water.

"You're the Makers of the Pact," she observed. "You are why we *procreate* instead of *persist*."

An unexpected effect of the new Pact was that the spirits, in embracing their mortality, had discovered that they could propagate. Tania suggested that perhaps it was because the human elements of the Compact were all adults this time, and several of them were pregnant.

"It's not something you can really avoid thinking about," Leinani had admitted. "I probably was."

The fae didn't manage it quite like humans did, but they had certainly come to an understanding of their own process and gotten busily to work. Little fire elementals were being found in furnaces and fireplaces everywhere, and plant spirits were wooed in by gardeners like good-luck charms. Water spirits like these haunted streams and springs, and air spirits were often spotted by people in planes. Sometimes they were friendly, sometimes shy, sometimes curious, and not uncommonly, a pain in the ass.

But their power was curtailed, with their size, and this new generation seemed content to explore the world without malice and keep their mischief low-key. Drayger honestly didn't think they had the capacity for organized revolution on the scale of Angel's uprising, but he also wasn't interested in antagonizing them.

Some of the innocence had gone out of the world.

Shifters and magic were no longer secret, for all of the complications that would result, and if it was a relief, it was also a lot of unknown. People weren't always sympathetic to things that were different, and fear could have ugly consequences.

But there was more hope now than ever. Shifters were breathing a sigh of relief that they didn't have to hide their natural abilities. Casters could openly study and find training. There was even talk of magical schools and shifter Olympics. It was a wide new world, and the Compact that defined the use of magic was based on *compassion*.

"I have just one more question," Drayger said, drawing a suggestive line along Alasie's shoulder to her bathing suit strap. Even her swimwear was completely and utterly her: a basic Alaska-blue one-piece that was molded to her figure but not that low- or high- cut.

"When you warn me that you're asking a question, I always get suspicious," Alasie said dubiously. "Last time you did that, I ended up agreeing to marry you."

Drayger had to kiss her for that reminder, and he toyed with the engagement ring that she wore before he remembered to ask the question he'd been meaning to. "What was the bet that had Rian wandering naked around the castle? If we're going to get married, you can't keep a secret that huge from me."

Alasie's eyes danced, even though her lips were as serene as ever. "That *was* the bet," she revealed.

Drayger stared at her, waiting for the sentence to make sense. When it didn't, he persisted. "What was the bet? How was that the bet? I don't get it."

"It wasn't Rian wandering the castle in the nude," Alasie said. "It was Tray. The bet was that he could mimic his twin so successfully that even if he spent a week completely stark naked he could still fool everyone."

Drayger stared. "And he *did*."

"To Rian's eternal chagrin."

Drayger gave a shout of laughter. "What did he earn for winning that bet? I mean, he didn't even get bragging rights! Those photos have been attached to Rian for the posterity of the Internet."

"He said that the win was satisfaction enough," Alasie chuckled. "Though I believe he has also collected a brag book of flattering Internet comments."

"It's brilliant," Drayger said in grudging admiration. "I should have thought of that. All the fun of public nudity, none of the pressure."

"You don't have a twin brother I don't know about, do you?"

"No, I'll have to come up with something better that will give me an excuse to wander nude and get Internet notoriety."

"Please don't," Alasie begged, but she was giggling.

"You're right," Drayger said, pulling her closer. "I should save all of my nakedness for you alone, now that we're getting married."

"Please do," Alasie said, letting him kiss her.

"This is a very private pool," Drayger pointed out suggestively.

"Not that private," Toren said, splashing down beside him.

Drayger pretended to be cross as he gathered Alasie up against himself and they edged aside for the rest of the royal party.

"I can put my feet in!" Katy was insisting to Raval. "I know the rules, you can stop worrying!"

Leinani joined her on the ledge with her legs dangling in, as the rest of the family crowded into the pool.

They chatted for a while, about the food in the restaurant, the trip out, the weather, and the upcoming weddings, until a moment of conversational silence crept up on all of them at once.

"It's different," Toren finally said, into the morning stillness. "The whole world is different."

"Isn't it better?" Carina suggested, nudging him with her shoulder. "It's still magic."

There was a general murmur of agreement.

And the most magical of all was Alasie at Drayger's side, her ringed hand in his under the steaming surface of the water. She was his and he was hers, and everything was exactly as it should be, even if nothing was as it had been.

# A NOTE FROM ELVA BIRCH

After three years, it is so bittersweet to bring this saga to its big finish and I thank you so much for joining me on this journey!

I will confess that my original excuse to write this whole series was that I wanted to paint northern lights dragons for the cover. And if I was going to write about Alaskan dragons, I might as well go all the way and make them *royal* Alaskan dragons and throw in some magic!

From there, I was off to the races, and I have absolutely loved bringing this alternate Alaska and all these amazing characters to life. The books took on a life of their own, and some of my best-laid plans took off in unexpected directions, with time-travel and magic cars, the kidnapping of magical children, suddenly dragons, and the intricate Compact that was controlling it all. I had a blast doing all the detailed world building and figuring out how to fit all the moving parts to a cohesive finish. Some of the elements I'd planned from the beginning and a few occurred to me in the eleventh hours of writing. I fell a little in love with every one of my characters, and with Luke and Drayger most of all. ("Sex on the Compact!")

I hope that you enjoyed this magical romantic adventure as much as I enjoyed putting it together. A giant thank you to my amazing editors, beta readers, early reviewers, and most of all to my enthusiastic readers, because without you, I could not write.

This series has been dear to my heart and while I am sad to see it end, I am excited for the tales to come.

Your reviews are very, very much appreciated! I would love to know what you thought of this book...and this entire series! Please feel free to email me any time at elva herself@elvabirch.com.

To find out about my new releases, you can follow me on Amazon, subscribe to my newsletter, or like me on Facebook. Join my Reader's Retreat on Facebook for sneak previews and cut scenes. Find all the links at my webpage: elvabirch.com

I also write under other pen names—keep reading for information about my other available titles...

# WRITING AS ELVA BIRCH

**A Day Care for Shifters**: A hot new full-length series about adorable shifter kids and their struggling single parents in a town full of mystery and surprise. Start the series with Wolf's Instinct, when Addison comes to Nickel City to take a job at a very special day care and finds a family to belong to. Funny and full of feeling, this is a gentle ice-cream-straight-from-the-container escape. Sweet and sizzling!

∽

**The Royal Dragons of Alaska**: A fascinating alternate world where Alaska is ruled by secret dragon shifters. Adventure, romance, and humor! Reluctant royalty, relentless enemies… dogs, camping, and magic! Start with The Dragon Prince of Alaska.

∽

**Suddenly Shifters**: A hilarious series of novellas, serials, and shorts set in the small town of Anders Canyon, where something (in the water?) is making ordinary citizens turn into shifters. Start with Something in the Water! Also available in audio!

∽

**Lawn Ornament Shifters:** The series that was only supposed to be a joke, this is a collection of short, ridiculous romances featuring unusual shifters, myths, and magic. Cross-your-legs funny and full of heart! Start with The Flamingo's Fated Mate!

∼

**Birch Hearts**: An enchanting collection of short stories and novellas. Unconstrained by theme or setting, each short read has romance, magic, and heart, with a satisfying conclusion. And always, the impossible and irresistible. Start with a sampler plate in Prompted 2 for fourteen pieces of sweet-to-sizzling flash fiction, or the novella, Better Half. Breakup is a free story!

# WRITING AS ZOE CHANT

*Zoe Chant is a group of friends that includes Elva Birch writing similar shifter books under a single name.*

**Shifting Sands Resort**: A complete ten-book series - plus two collections of shorts. This is a thrilling shifter romance set at a tropical island resort. Each book stands alone but connects into a great mystery with a thrilling conclusion. Start with Tropical Tiger Spy or dive in to the Omnibus edition, with all of the novels, short stories, and novellas in my preferred reading order! This series crosses over with Shifter Kingdom and Fire and Rescue Shifters.

~

**Fae Shifter Knights**: A complete four-book fantasy portal romp, with cute pets and swoon-worthy knights stuck in a world of wonders like refrigerators and ham sandwiches. Start with Dragon of Glass!

~

**Green Valley Shifters**: A sweet, small town series with single dads, secret shifters, sweet kids, and spinsters. Low-peril and steamy! Standalone books where you can revisit your favorite characters - this series is also complete! Start with Dancing Barefoot!

∼

Also by Zoe Chant (but not Elva Birch): **Virtue Shifters**: Sexy and funny, each book set in the little town of Virtue promises a heartwarming story, a touch of fate, and a little bit of adventure. Virtue Shifters and Green Valley Shifters share a world! Start with Timber Wolf!

# BEHIND THE SCENES

What is Patreon?

*Patreon is a site where readers and fans can support creators with monthly subscriptions.*

At my Patreon, I have tiers with early rough drafts of my books, flash fiction, coloring pages, signed and sketched paperbacks, exclusive swag, original artwork, photographs…and so much more! Every month is a little different, and there is a price for every budget. Patreon allows me to do projects that aren't very commercial and makes my income stream a little less unpredictable. It also gives me a place to connect with my fans!

Come find out what's going on behind the scenes and keep me creating at Patreon! patreon.com/ellenmillion

# A PREVIEW OF TROPICAL TIGER SPY

*When Amber booked her vacation at Shifting Sands Resort, she was expecting a lazy tropical vacation at a luxury escape for shifters…she wasn't expecting to meet a sexy under-cover tiger shifter spy who set her blood on fire, or to become a part of his investigation into why shifters are disappearing from the resort! An excerpt of* Tropical Tiger Spy.

Amber walked meekly with the guards, trying not to be too obvious about looking around. The dog-catcher was lying unexpectedly loose at her shoulders, and when she glanced at the man holding the pole, he glared back and fingered a button on the handle. The other guard, walking behind her with the gun trained on her, cleared his throat, and Amber put her head down and continued to shamble with them. She was short, so it was easy to walk slowly and look like she was using a normal pace.

The looseness of the noose around her neck got her brain spinning.

They were expecting a mountain cat—an American mountain cat. A *big* mountain cat. If she shifted, the dog-catcher would be tight around the neck of a big cat. But around her small Andean mountain cat form...

As quickly as the idea occurred to her, Amber put it in motion, shifting as she pretended to stumble.

Her clothing fell away from her cat form even as she jumped—straight through the noose—and scrambled for the wall of the mesh enclosure they were walking past. She heard the crackle of the dog-catcher rather than feeling it through her thick fur, and realized belatedly that it must be electrified. She wasn't sure if she would have made this attempt if she'd known that, but it was far too late now, and her coat, meant for cold mountain winters, had protected her from the worst of it.

She climbed in a panic, the agility of her cat form driving her, and as the guard behind her fired and missed, and missed again as she switched directions up the enclosure and reached the roof.

She heard the zoo erupt into roars and animal cries of encouragement. A human voice even cried out, "Go, kitty cat!"

"Shit!" the guards said in unison.

More wild shots followed her. Needles hissed by as Amber made it up to the roof of the enclosure. She ran and leaped to the next. She was already two cages away while the guards were still peering up onto the first. Then she switched directions entirely and leaped across the path to a new row of cages.

Her night sight let her see better than she had as a human, and her height gave her a clear view. Lights all along the wall had come on, showing her that she had no real chance of getting over them—though she could probably squeeze between the barbed wire with little damage thanks to her coat, she was too small to make it to the top of the wall to try; nothing was built up close to it. She noticed the cameras, too, now swiveling back into the enclosure to try to find her, and had a glimpse of a helicopter on one of the low roofs towards the back.

"Goddamn it, do you see it?" one guard called to the other.

"Beehag said it was a mountain cat, not a goddamn *little* cat!" the other complained.

Their voices were clear to Amber's excellent hearing.

Instead of immediate escape, Amber looked for hiding spaces, and found one in a pile of construction materials towards the end of the zoo. While the cameras were still re-positioning to try to follow her, she dashed out of sight down the side of one of the enclosures and flattened herself to fit in a tiny space on top of a pile of rocks, under dimension lumber and roof tiles. From here, she could see a dozen more hiding places that she'd be able to make it to in short order, and she had a good vantage for seeing oncoming intruders.

She could see that the entire zoo was actually much more suited for containing big animals. She'd be able to get out, she felt, with her first taste of confidence as the adrenaline began to release its hold on her. She just had to lie low, and she'd be able to sneak out of the front gates when the timing was right.

"Call it in!" one of the guards was saying.

"Fuck no, you call it in," the other protested.

Eventually, they worked out who was making the call, and the little two-way radio crackled in return as they explained their mistake.

"Escaped?" Even over the poor quality radio from a distance, Amber recognized Alistair's voice, and it made the hackles on her neck rise.

The guards fell over each other to justify their actions,

and Amber gave a little cat smile to hear them describe her as basically supernatural.

There was a moment of silence in response, and then Alistair's crisp accent. "She won't get far. We've got her *mate* here."

Mate?

Amber knew without a doubt that they meant Tony, and it was everything she could do not to bolt from her hiding hole right then to find and defend him. But what did they mean by 'mate?' She could all but hear the emphasis that Alistair was putting on it.

The waiter at the resort had used the same word.

Whatever they meant by it, she knew that Alistair was right—knowing that they had Tony—that they might *hurt* Tony to get her, meant that Alistair had Amber as surely as if that noose *had* been tight around her neck.

Read the rest in *Tropical Tiger Spy* by Zoe Chant or dive right in with the four-volume *Shifting Sands Resort Omnibus*, which includes the short stories and novellas!

Printed in Dunstable, United Kingdom